The Vineyard

IDWAL JONES

The
Vineyard

FOREWORD BY
Robert Mondavi

UNIVERSITY OF CALIFORNIA PRESS
Berkeley · Los Angeles · London

University of California Press
Berkeley and Los Angeles, California

University of California Press, Ltd.
London, England

First California Paperback Printing 1997

Library of Congress Cataloging-in-Publication Data
Jones, Idwal, 1890–1964.
 The vineyard / Idwal Jones.
  p.   cm. (California fiction)
 ISBN 0-520-21090-5 (alk. paper)
  1. Wine and wine making—California—Napa Valley—Fiction.
 2. Napa Valley (Calif.)—History—Fiction.   I. Title
PS3519.043V5   1997
813'.52—dc21   96-38103
                                                 CIP

Printed in the United States of America

1 2 3 4 5 6 7 8 9

The paper used in this publication meets the minimum requirements of
American National Standard for Information Sciences—Permanence
of Paper for Printed Library Materials, ANSI Z39.48-1984. ∞

As the vintages of earth
Taste of the sun that riped their birth,
We know what never cadent Sun
Thy lampèd clusters throbbed upon,
What plumèd feet the winepress trod;
Thy wine is flavorous of God.

—Francis Thompson

CONTENTS

FOREWORD

This new edition of Idwal Jones' *The Vineyard* is being published at quite an appropriate time in the history of wine in the United States, and in California and Napa Valley specifically. The book takes place in the years prior to the onset of Prohibition in 1919, but it also foreshadows many of the positive developments that began occurring soon after its publication in 1942.

In the generation after Jones wrote the book, Prohibition was still quite present in the minds of the vintners who began the post-World War II renaissance in Napa Valley. I was fortunate to be involved in that movement, with the inheritors of the traditions of Charles Krug, Gustave Niebaum, Jacob Schram and especially Henry Crabb—all mentioned in *The Vineyard*.

I always knew we had the soils, the climate and the grape varieties to produce wines here which would be on a par with the finest in the world. Prohibition had forced the growers and vintners to plant grapes which were suitable only for shipping, home winemaking and table consumption. Now we have found the most appropriate microclimates for the noble grape varieties which are flourishing in the valley.

The sense of disbelief among those early growers and

vintners when the Prohibition movement began is clearly portrayed in the book. The past few decades have seen another group of people—Neoprohibitionists—who wish to end the production of wine, and of course all beverages containing alcohol. Fortunately the health aspect of the Prohibition argument has been researched by independent health professionals and research institutions, who are proving that for most people the moderate consumption of wine has a positive health outcome.

The role of wine in American culture is also much better understood now than in the early 1900s. I and others in the industry continue to work—often as hard as we worked as vintners—to educate Americans about that positive role as well.

But Idwal Jones also saw into the heart of the fascination that winegrowing has for us in the wine business. The book offers a positive view of many of the values of this endeavor. The place of the family down through generations, the importance of honoring the prime vineyards where the best grapes grow, the importance of understanding the special needs of each variety, and the crucial place of research are all here.

One vineyard mentioned by Jones is a perfect example: the To-Kalon vineyard owned by Henry Crabb and now part of the Robert Mondavi Winery in Oakville at the center of the Napa Valley. When I started my winegrowing career in Napa Valley in 1937—Jones had probably started writing *The Vineyard* at that time—my father had searched throughout California for the best grapes and wine to sell throughout this country; much of it to immigrant Italian families like his own.

He soon recognized that Napa Valley was the home of the best; To-Kalon means "the highest" or "best" in

Greek. When we purchased the Charles Krug winery in 1943 we began serious examination of the best Napa vineyards, and when I began the Robert Mondavi Winery in 1966 I was successful in bringing To-Kalon which was considered California's finest vineyard into our operation. Since that time it has proved to be one of the best Sauvignon Blanc vineyards in the country and is the source of our Napa Valley Fumé Blanc.

The hit-or-miss approach practiced by the heroic family in *The Vineyard*—evaluating the fruit from each parcel after the harvest and then waiting often years for the wines to taste the final test—has changed dramatically over time, although tasting is always the true judgment. Work with rudimentary sugar testers has now been replaced by highly sophisticated laboratory equipment; our winery was often called the "test-tube winery" when we began because of our commitment to research.

But many of the problems have remained the same. The family fought Phylloxera and Pierce's Disease, just as we are doing now. To give a contemporary example: we are working with NASA on a project whereby satellite overflights can photograph our vineyards and pick up early keys to those diseases.

One interesting bridge from the book's past to our present is in the concept of natural winegrowing. Like most other vintners, we experimented with many artificial approaches to vineyard and winery operations. But about twenty years ago we adopted a natural winegrowing philosophy more in keeping with that of *The Vineyard*. The approach puts foremost the wellbeing of our growers, environmental protection, improved grape quality, and above all the effort to assure that the land will be appropriate for fine wine grapes for the forseeable future.

Idwal Jones captured one of the most important values in winegrowing, in my opinion. This is a commitment to do your best—to excel. The "Regolberg" wine of the book was a beacon to the family, just as the top varieties have been to ours, and the best is achieved by unwillingness to accept second best. A theme of the book, "Thy wine is flavorous of God," makes clear the devotion that's needed to bring out the best from the grapegrowing and winemaking process.

The financial struggles of the families in *The Vineyard* are of course not unfamiliar to today's winegrowers. In fact the renaissance of Napa Valley's wine industry is due in large part to the financial institutions which participated in this new chapter. Grapegrowing has always followed the traditional ups and downs of agricultural economics, and it is interesting that Jones' family was able to survive through other traditional farm crops.

But it is not profit that motivates most of us in the wine business, and Jones makes that clear in the book. The families that succeed will be those that "honor the vineyard" and make the best wines they can without putting profit first. To-Kalon is a prime example of this. We believe that chemical-free farming, as I mentioned above, combined with advanced viticultural practices, will lead to greatly enhanced grape quality in the coming years. By implementing natural winegrowing techniques, we are not only protecting our Napa Valley environment and the people who work and live in Napa Valley; but we are growing fruit that more fully expresses our outstanding climate and soil. This fruit will have greater concentration of flavors, aromas and color, and will also have more distinct varietal character.

While we have done a great amount of research with

the vineyards lovingly described in the book, I predict that we will make more progress in the next five years than we have made in the past twenty. We'll be making wines then which are more gentle to drink, yet will have greater depth and complexity.

Reading *The Vineyard* is a lovely experience for everyone interested in wine. While it brings back the early history in the valley, it also points the way to much that we have done and are doing so that we can continue to produce fine wines more consistently than any other place in the world.

I grew up with wine at the table, with wine as an integral part of each family meal. Good food, good wine, family and friends have always been the best things in my life, the things that make life worth living. Idwal Jones' *The Vineyard* reflects and supports this view, and its pages truly bring honor to the vineyard.

Robert Mondavi
February, 1997
Napa Valley

The Plowing

1.

THE hooded cart rolled hub-deep through muck and gravel, the ponies plunging ahead now, with earnestness, as if they were suddenly aware that so weary a road must end with rest and a stable. It was pitchy dark; the drizzle had turned to a plumping rain. The girl flung slack on the reins and resigned herself to the guidance of the animals, cunning in all the wagon-tracks on this wooded slope of Napa Valley.

They were close now to the foot of St. John's Peak, in a jumble of gullies, cleared pockets, torrents and stands of fir and madrone. Montino was at the end of this road. She had come close to it once when she was a child and her father, with bundles of vine cuttings to sell, had taken her along for company. But that was long ago, on a midsummer day, and she remembered only the smells, the dust, the reek of tarweed and whiffs of pomace from the wineries. And this was winter's end: the dank air pungent with odors of eucalyptus, sodden earth and leaves.

At the crossroads the ponies took the left fork. The steep banks, glistening in the rain and the glow from the lantern hung on the shaft, had streaks of black and white, and a painted look. Soon the wagon tires were crunching

3

over lava. The girl listened curiously. Her father had never a fair word for the men that lived at Montino, but for the fields they tilled, his praise was unbounded.

"It's fine and honest earth, girl. Full-handed to the grape and the trees that keep off wind and sunburn. Too good to be merely rich. There never was a Regola that deserved that farm."

The animals pulled up at a wooden barrier. The girl got out, in sou'wester and thigh boots, held up the lantern and examined the gate. It was heavy and large, secured by a rusty chain; and above it was an arch upheld by two pillars of masonry lost under creepers. The legend on the sign board was hardly legible: Villa Montino. G. Regola, Propr.

The grandeur of the entrance impressed her. It was only the great wine estates in this part of California that had both a gate and a name. She tied the animals to a post, climbed with the lantern and sat a moment on the top rail, looking into the darkness before her.

"You wait here a piece, Old-timer," she said, speaking towards the cart. "I'm going in to enquire. Maybe they'll let us stay, maybe not. But it won't be the first time we've camped out."

She whistled through her teeth, fastened the strap of her sou'wester, and jumped down. The gleam of her lantern had carried far, and as she trudged up the path under the dripping firs, a dog came charging at her. Eyes burning, he contested every foot of her progress, recoiling on his haunches at each throat-splitting outburst of frenzy. Being half mastiff and half coyote, he had both muscle and lungs. In one swoop she caught his paw. Alda Pendle had the vine-dresser's strength of grip, a well-gloved hand, and a way of her own with dogs. Caught in that paralyzing

4

squeeze, the dog, unable to bark or snap, suffered the indignity of a rub and pulled ears.

"Now will you be quiet, huh? You going to be good? You trot along now and show me the way."

Another hard squeeze, and the dog surrendered, faced about, and with sidelong glances walked before his conqueror through the trees to the villa. She could discern it as a blacker bulk in darkness, with a silhouette of peaked gables against the torn sky. Her father, who had visited the Villa Montino when it was new, and had sold some of his best vines to the Senator, told her it had iron deer on the lawn, and statues and palms in the hallway. The estate had begun to run down when she was a child, long after the Senator had sold much of it and given the rest to his son. But it was still the Villa Montino, and the eminence of it bore upon her and weighted her spirits. The dog led her to the back. She could not see much in the lashing rain: only shadows, more trees, and a pump, from which duckboards were laid to the rear porch. The dog crouched there, on the porch, fangs white in the gleam from the window, and grinned amiably.

It was perhaps the only welcome she would get at Montino. The fatigue of a long day's journeying through the valley, for she had been looking for work at every farm this side of Rutherford, the steadiness of the downpour, and the gloom of the house had combined to oppress her. If Mr. Regola turned out to be unhospitable, she could hardly ask shelter of him, not even at the barn. It would mean sleeping at the gate, then going over the ridge in the morning, into Sonoma county and its vineyards.

"You can come in with me, if you like," Alda said under her breath to the dog. "Nobody else I'm likely to know here. Not by the looks of it, my lad."

5

She wiped her rain-dashed face, and knocked on the door.

It opened, not widely, only a crack. A surly, grizzled man stood looking at her through the screen. Beyond him, sitting by a coal-oil lamp on the table at the far end of the kitchen, sat another man, reading.

"What is it you want?" asked the man, grunting round his pipe. "You lost the road?"

"Can I put up here for the night? It's kind of late to go over the ridge. Been looking for work. Pruning. I figure on going over to Sonoma in the morning."

"This ain't no time of year to go looking for jobs."

"They're scarce. I know that. Could I have a shake-down in the barn? I've got blankets."

The puffs of smoke were non-committal. The grizzled man—he had the look of retainer, or coachman—held the door still tightly, not widening the crack so much as an inch.

"You got blankets?"

"In the wagon. My team's out there by the gate."

He pondered a moment this guarantee of respectability, seemed about to relent, and the glint through his spectacles was less frosty. Then the door flung wide open, and Hector Regola, twice his size, obliterated him, and pushed open the screen door.

"Come in. You got lost, you say?"

"Not quite that. This was the nearest place to come into."

"I see. Well, you can warm up. Port, you fix her up something."

"You are Mr. Regola?" she asked, as she unbuttoned her oilskins.

6

"I'm Regola, yes. Port, you got that coffee warming up?"

"Coming now," grumbled Port, poking at the fire. "And I'll hot up some frijoles while I'm about it."

He was hardly gracious, but he was not chary in serving, for he soon put before her a heaped-up plate, a cup and a smoked coffee pot so full that it bubbled at the spout. The kitchen was so warm that Alda had to fight off drowsiness.

"I'm turning in now." Port hauled out a silver watch and consulted it with mouth tightened in disfavor. "Late. Durn near midnight. Got to be down on that job by sun-up."

"Good-night, Port."

Port gave a nod that was more like a negative head-shake, left the room, and the girl could hear his boots clumping up the stairs. Hector stood on the hearth before a very large grate where a log was smouldering. It was a spacious kitchen, larger than the one Alda had seen at the hotel in Calistoga, and it was not the kind of kitchen she had expected to see in the villa at all. It had a foreign look. Then she remembered that the Regolas were Swiss-Italian. That Hector was a bachelor, and lived alone with his surly retainer, accounted for the disorder of the place. Though comfortable, it might have been an annex to the stable. Flasks and boxes of horse medicine cluttered the window-sill; under the sink were bootjacks, wickered flagons, and kindling wood. It was bachelors' hall, but very much this side of squalor. Alda perceived signs that did not betoken neglect. A pair of shirts on a line were as white as if they had been given a last rinse with blueing; the bright-work on the stove was polished; the floor, for all the stray bones and spent cartridges, was more than reasonably clean. It was clear to her that someone came at intervals to scrub up and put things rigorously in order.

The girl set down her cup abruptly, and listened.

"Thought I heard something," she said, lifting the cup again. "Down the road."

"Port," he said. "Upstairs. Turning in early for him. He's got a chore over to Schram's place in the morning."

It occurred to her that she had seen the retainer before, at some of the vineyards or at the Greystone winery.

"Ayton—Port Ayton, isn't he?" she asked. "He does coopering."

Hector looked at her a minute, then gave a short laugh.

"You knew me. You knew Port. I dare say you knew the dog, too. How came he to let you through that gate?"

"I climbed over it," said Alda, wiping her plate with a crust. "He didn't bother me any. He was friendly."

"Lobo?" His throat clicked. "Lobo's as friendly as a sore timber wolf. He did yap his head off tonight. We thought there was somebody gone astray again. Always somebody looking for the road over the mountain, and getting lost. But nobody comes here. If they did," he laughed gently, as he filled his pipe, "they might find Montino. It's been lost a long time."

His ironic smile vanished, and he looked at her indirectly from under his heavy brows. He had a quieter, a stranger manner than any of the Swiss-Italian vintners she had ever known. Old Giorgio's son was a solitary. He had the habit of slipping away for days, hunting in the wilderness that stretched from St. John's Peak to the crags and underbrush on the slope of Mount St. Helena.

8

He cut his own trails, blazing them with a hatchet: a huntsman alone, without even a dog at his heels.

"A wrong one," her father used to say. Himself a saintly man, rooted in his nursery, he saw only evil in anyone who neglected his vines to go hunting, like Hector, or frequented races and prize fights like Giorgio, the most benighted of that tribe. "Depend on it, when a man prowls alone like that, there's something wrong with him. A sorry place, that farm now. Down to half its size. Where there's great evil, there's small prospering."

Hector looked at her steadily. "What brought you here to Montino? This time of night. You were not lost."

"No," she said. "I couldn't get lost, not in this valley. I was born here. Over at Mayacamas."

He looked at her hands. They were strong, tanned, and graceful, though heavy at the wrist, the fingers scarred by the grafting knife, the cuts stained with bluestone. She was a little ashamed of her hands, and folded them in her lap, to hide the fingers. After her father's last stroke she had done all the work at the nursery. The half-acre of Pinots she tended herself, and in vintage time made the wine. Her back and her arms were strong. The autumn before, she stowed the Burgundy, five barrels of it, into the cart, and driving to the far towns of Vallejo and Port Costa sold it from door to door, at grocery shops and tamale parlors.

Hector plucked a splint from a block of Chinese matches, and struck it. He waited for the fumes to drift off.

"Mayacamas?" His eyes narrowed. "Turn your head."

She did so, lifting it. He took in her sensible, well-blocked jaw, the line curving finely from it to the small ear under her ropes of golden hair. These were, like her assurance of manner, more than the externals of breeding. Old Giorgio, with his dead-sure eye for quality and his insight into character, would have called her *simpatica*. She was a farm girl, of no more schooling than himself, he could see that, but she was not a peasant.

"Oxhill Farm?"

"That's right. Abel Pendle was my father."

"So I thought." Hector pocketed his briar and sat down. "What brought you here? You were heading out for Sonoma?"

"I was heading for any place where I could find work."

"Things are quiet now, mighty quiet. Nobody's doing any hiring until spring."

The girl laughed easily.

"I'm hiring out now."

He scratched his cheek in reflection, still frowning, still watching her. It was queer that with a hundred wine farms tucked about in these hills, old Pendle's girl should have chosen Montino, of all places. He looked at the window, the raindrops sliding down the black panes, listened to the clamor in the trees, and groped in his slow mind for some clue to her intention. He could find none.

"It's early, too early. Ground's too wet even to plow. You should have waited until vintage time."

"It isn't only in vintage time there's a lot to be done, Mr. Regola," she said, straightening up. "No farm's any good that runs itself. I found that out, running our place."

He nodded, listening to the rain dropping in sheets. He worked prodigiously himself. But that was his secret. Indifferent to what anyone said of him, he was glad to be thought indolent. The dispraise fostered his reputation for eccentricity, and people left him alone. That gave him time to indulge in his passion for shooting, and for a still greater passion for labor. His love for Montino was un-bounded. He lavished all his affection upon it, and re-turned from his shooting trips with vision cleared, seeing its beauty with fresh eyes, welcoming its demands as would a returned lover the exactions of his mistress.

His physical strength was so great that he seldom knew fatigue, and really believed he was lazy. Still, there wasn't much he could do now, or as long as the rains kept up. As soon as the ground was workable, he would plow and harrow it, turning over the cover-crop of legumes. There were still boulders to drag out and sled to the walls that encircled each field. Montino was an old vineyard, but it yet had rocks. (Giorgio used to say that whenever a toad-stool grew in Montino it pushed up two boulders.) He made his own wines, and stored them in the limestone cave he had dug into the hillside, with small help from anyone.

He did his own vine-dressing, and there was the coop-erage to be kept up, though Port did most of the work on that. Then there was a new field, the old Boal tract, he wanted to set out to Zinfandel. For cuttings, he would probably have to drive over into Sonoma, perhaps as far up as Asti. He had a full year ahead of him.

"You been figuring on setting out some new vines?" the girl asked. "I saw Bascomb a week ago. The Viticul-ture man. He told me about it."

"That's so. It'll be a job. Breaking that field."

He nodded to himself, looking at her. The staunchness of her body was noticeable; she was built with the loose grace of a foal. No nonsense about her, either; all the time he had been listening to her talk: she was as level-headed as she was strong.

"You can work here, if you like. I do everything myself, pretty near. If there's too much to do, I get me some China help. But this year they won't be along until vintage. We have to go easy. Wine is too cheap. You've got blankets?"

"Down by the gate, in the wagon." She rose. "I'll bring it up."

"There's some rooms upstairs, a string of them. The stable's over by the winery, but there's another small one in the yard you can put the team in."

Hector went out into the downpour and led the cart to the porch. It was piled up, like an immigrant wagon, with furniture, tools, hampers and barrels bulging under tarpaulin. Alda handed out a carpet-bag and a roll of blankets. He carried them into the kitchen, lighted a candle, and went upstairs with the load.

"You come along this way," he called down, quietly. "Far end of the corridor."

At that end was the largest spare room, cobwebby after years of disuse, but sound and dry, with a brass bedstead and space for all her effects. He flung the blankets upon the mattress. A window was open, the candle flickered in the draught, and his shadow danced on the sloped wall. He closed the window, after prying out a nail. The girl was entering as he turned. A boy was in her arms. A sou'wester hung from his neck. He was about five, pinkish, with hair like a tousle of flax.

Hector exploded with mirth. He laughed wholeheartedly, then leaned against the wall, thumbs in belt, chuckling. What a night! He had been sitting before the fire with his pipe, with not a thought for the world outside, then this materialization. Pendle's girl and a small boy. It was like a conjuring act, but more amusing. He grinned, pipe wagging in his teeth.

"A boy! *Prodigioso!* What's his name?"

"Cleve," said Alda, untying the hat of the prodigy, and throwing a blanket over him. "That's his name. Never had no other."

"Not your boy?"

"He's mine now."

"He must have some milk," said Hector, pointing at the white head. "I'll tell Wing to bring in some milk. He tends the cow for Miss Lane."

"He was brought up on claret, mostly. Wasn't any cows over at Mayacamas."

"Then he'll be a vine-dresser before he gets teeth. But it ain't too late for him to taste milk. I'll tell the Chinaman tomorrow. Good-night."

He creaked off on tiptoes.

Upon the floor was another mattress; she sat upon it, and drew off her boots. So here they were, under a roof, and she had counted on no more than refuge in the barn. Their luck, when things had been most disquieting, and their wheels had turned in every corner of the valley, had faced about. They had gone as far as Vallejo, and she had for a day worked at a hotel, scouring pots and pans. She could have stayed on, but since she would have had to live in, the boy was disapproved of. Then they tracked back into the valley, intending to enquire at St. Helena, perhaps visit Montino, then go over the pass into Sonoma and the vineyards at Asti and Healdsburg. The Swiss colonists would remember the Malbec strain that Pendle had developed for them, and "Oxhill Farm" on the cart would be her passport.

Montino she had reserved as her last venture before leaving the valley forever. Of the old Senator, whose renown had sprung from the fabulous Regolberg, made

13

of the White Pendle grape, her father had never spoken without asperity, had never forgiven him for destroying the one great hybrid born at Oxhill. Some of his feeling had been communicated to her. At the gate she had hesitated. Tails up at the throw of a penny, and she and the child might have gone on. But in her the feeling was dispassionate, an energy that she might have explained as a mysterious and powerful impulse. Montino attracted her more than it repelled her. It was a tie between herself and her father who was gone. She thought also of Cleve, asleep under the wet canvas, and then she climbed over the gate.

She was glad she had come, but if she was not in hostile territory, she was at least out of bounds, and it was probable their stay would be brief. Hector Regola seemed amiable; ordinary, perhaps, and no more prosperous than the remnants of Montino itself, which he owned and worked, so it was said, half-heartedly, and under the thumb of the old Senator who came to it for the summer, sometimes with his daughter, but usually alone, for he was jealous of his seclusion.

The son was perhaps more a hunter than a grower. She knew many such solitary men—mercureros, content to work a small cinnabar claim and distill a flask or two of quicksilver a month; and vignerons, quite as independent and prideful of craft, content to grow six or ten sound casks of wine a year, and the rest of the time living with rod and gun in the wilderness beyond the upper reach of the valley, above Silverado or towards the lakes. She might be able to care for the vineyard in his absences, even stay until the end of the vintage. She might. He knew the Pendle name. And the boy had amused him.

These Swiss-Italians liked children; their own were dark, mostly, and Cleve's hair was a funny, silvery tumble.

To Mayacamas Ridge she could not return again, not ever. Oxhill Farm had been struck hard, to die of wounds and a thirst she could not assuage. Its slope, the two acres at the back, which she and Abel, with help from Cherokee, who lived with them, had cleared of madrones, briar, and rocks, and planted, rose before her like a nightmare. The thought of the long travail upon it made her limbs ache.

"I was thinking, girl," Abel said to her one day, "I'd like to leave you a bit of good vineyard. The Pinots are all very well, but they won't make you a great lady. The nursery's a man's job—work from morning until night, and no wages to speak of."

He tapped a pile of cuttings with his knife.

"You'll try cross-breeding, too. You can't help dreaming when you're alone. I got something once, but only after trying a thousand times. I should have kept that for you, girl."

That was the Riparia White Pendle X, which he sold forthright—knowing little of patents and law—to Giorgio Regola of Montino, who made from its grapes the Regolberg. Later, Giorgio tore up the vine to plant money crops, though the Regolberg had made his name immortal in California. Not even a shred of that vine had been saved, so completely had Regola controlled it.

"I'm going to make you a bit of vineyard, girl. On that slope. I should have begun it before this."

The slope was a moraine of gravelly earth, kept moist by the drainage of an old quicksilver mine a mile and a half away. Water from the channel above seeped into the declivity, keeping it green always with deep-rooted mallow and flowering brake, even in midsummer. It was nearly ten degrees cooler than the flat where the Pinots grew.

"Sand and earth, all mixty-maxty. You know what I'll plant for you? Johannisberg. Won't be any Riesling to touch it in Mayacamas, nor in all the valley. It'll grow shy, but it should run you maybe four tons to the acre. It'll be something that nobody else grows around here."

"That would be wonderful, Father!"

"I'd develop you a new hybrid if I could, and put your name on it. But my time's running out. The great gifts are possible only to those who can receive them. But I'll grow you a Johannisberg you'll be proud of."

"Where'll you find the cuttings?"

"Leave that to me, girl!"

There was no holding him once he had made up his mind on anything. He was in his mid-seventies, and the winter had been severe on his chest. Alda knitted him a new muffler against the fog. Cherokee greased the axles of the buckboard, and shod Chess and Ring. Abel drove off fast, exalted at the notion of planting a vineyard of the true Riesling.

Where he found the cuttings, no one knew. It was late in the season, the vines had all been pruned, the brush burned. None were at the To Kalon, nor at the Degouy place, nor at the vineyards of the "three Jacobs"— Schram, Beringer, and Grimm, all named Jacob. They heard later that he had been seen in San Benito County, and far up on Russian River. That was probably true. He was a noticeable man, and the vignerons had all heard of Abel Pendle, the viticulturist who had gone to Europe with Colonel Haraszthy, and who had managed his wine farm in Sonoma. Abel Pendle, who had grafted European scions on the native St. George roots, and made them proof against the blight of the phylloxera.

It was Cherokee who heard reports of these wanderings. Cherokee—nobody called him by his real name, Thomas Garth—was a quiet man who stayed with the Pendles when he was not touring with his wagon up and down the state, selling Old Cherokee Medicine Oil. His wife, a Calistoga girl devoted to Alda, her schoolmate, had succumbed on the road, leaving him and their small Cleve to trail back to Oxhill, which they called home. Cleve stayed on at the vineyard, ruling Oxhill and the Pendles. Cherokee, grown taciturn, came more and more rarely.

He stayed for the plowing, though, and helped plant the Johannisberg. Abel had come back with a hundred wired bundles of cuttings. Alda chopped out stakes. The plants rose blooming from the foot of the slope to the ridge-top, a flock set out to pasture on the magical thin air of the heights. The earth was lambent with green flame. On the pomegranate limbs the blossoms were large and vivid. Abel, with Cleve hanging to his coat-tail, peered at them over his glasses. They were too large, too red, almost trumpery, like rosettes cut out of paper. He looked at them daily for a week, shook his head and said nothing.

It was a lovely spring, Alda often remembered its loveliness, and also that there was an urgency in it, an impressment, as if some instinct were pushing it to premature fruition. The winter had been quite dry, with no glacial tang from the Cascades, and Mount St. Helena had not once drawn on a white cap. The air was heartening, but at times she wondered if it were not ever so slightly arid and electrical, and there was not a need for a rousing storm. Abel went about preoccupied. The atmosphere was not quite what it should be. At times he was nervous, and appeared to be listening as if to some obscure message rapped out by static.

Mayacamas, that upper end of the valley, might have been a kind of retort in which some gaseous omens were taking shape, but no eyes could discern them clearly. The season continued warm and merged into a summer of disquieting heat.

Bascomb, the viticulture man, drove to every farm, looked at the rain-gauge readings. He told Abel he felt uneasy at the look of things. The dryness, of course, had no relation to a number of queer things that happened that year. The celestial department in charge of rains had nothing to do, for example, with the fire. It broke out in Calistoga, razed the hotel and the warehouse next door, where Abel had stored his reserve of wine. That was a blow, and he crumpled under it. Then, Cherokee did not come back. Something had gone out of him, and he no longer barked and snapped on his banjo under the naphtha torch when he sold his medicine oil. He was gone for three months. Then a cashier's check for a hundred dollars came to Alda from somewhere in Mexico. There was no covering note with it. She knew they would never hear from him again.

Jules, one of Schram's workmen, who had often done odd jobs at Oxhill, came to stay for a month. He did the harrowing. Alda trimmed the Riesling to heel and spur. Abel no longer mounted painfully up the slope. He kept to his nursery, or worked about the Pinots on the flat, Cleve always at his side.

"Them vines up there, Abel," remarked Jules one day, sticking his head through the lath-house window, "I dunno—but I was thinkin' they don't look so good."

"They're young," said Abel quietly. "They're thriving."

A week later, Jules looked from one to the other at table, took a long time over his soup, then downed his claret in a gulp. It was dusk, the evening was cool, but he wiped his brow as if he were perspiring, and finally opened his mouth to speak.

"I didn't want to say nothin'—but I went up and seen them vines."

The old nurseryman had finished his meal, and was reading the Bible under a lamp. Alda was teaching Cleve to hold a fork in his left hand.

"I seen them vines," Jules insisted, as if arguing with himself. "This afternoon. An' I go up the slope again."

"Yes?" said Alda. Jules was no farmer at all, only a handyman, good at plowing and at heavy work in the winery. "What did you see?"

"Them vines was yellowin'. From the foot of the slope up."

"Sunburn," Alda remarked. "Where there's shade they're greener."

"Yellowin' off," Jules said doggedly. "I seen them."

She was perturbed, nevertheless. After she had washed the supper things she started up to the ridge. The yellow tint was indeed noticeable. Could it be the leaf measles? A spraying of arsenite would control that easily, but she had never known the malady to affect plants so young. She climbed higher, and now could see the weeds that lined the channel. They were powdery and withered, for the channel was stone dry. It must have been dry for a long time. A dread chilled her heart and spread over her limbs, and she knew fear.

It would not do to alarm Abel. She did not call out, but she waved and waved, like a semaphore, caught the attention of Jules, and he came hurrying. He did not catch up with her for a mile, and they walked on together as far as the mine. It was very silent. No life could they see about the workings. The bunkhouse was empty, the bedding gone; lizards sunned on the derailed ore trucks. Alda looked into the mine-head, barred with planks, and threw in a rock. It plashed far below into water. On the door of the office was nailed a paper, already faded. It informed them under a date that the Montezuma mine was to be closed down. A snake vibrated its rattle in a mesquite bush near the door, but Alda leaned against the wall and closed her eyes.

"It will open up again?" she asked.

Jules trod thoughtfully up and down in the cinnabar dust, then he stopped and pointed at briar-covered scars in the hills above them.

"All mines. They didn't open up again. Montezuma, she's dead. They let her drown. Worked out, I guess."

"Listen, Jules!" She stared at him. "We can't let nobody kill that Johannisberg. It must have water! We got to bring water up to that ridge!"

Jules stood rooted in the sunlight, looking at her dully.

"How? Oxhill can buy pumps and run up a water-line? And let water run down at twenty, thirty cent maybe a gallon? For three, four year until we get a little wine and pay back the loan Oxhill borrow?"

He only echoed the thought that had already gone through her head. The gravel under the Johannisberg overlaid deep hardpan, and the tract was steep, far too steep to hold rainfall. The vines would run to wiry cane, and work on their care would be lost. If only they had been planted on the flat. She and Jules walked home silently. Abel was working at his bench in the nursery, Cleve at his side, when she came in to tell him.

"Girl, I'll find you another hill. I'll plant you a good vineyard—for you and Cleve. Cherokee will plow, you can make stakes, and I'll find you the cuttings—"

He was like an old general, fighting over once more a lost battle. He smiled gently and folded up his knife. Then he looked very small and empty, as if something had gone out of him, and his head dropped on the bench. She and Jules carried him out of the nursery.

Before the rains he was gone from Oxhill.

Alda and Cleve stayed on at Mayacamas until after the farm and its effects were auctioned off. The ponies were hers, also the cart, into which she put her own belongings. Nothing else was left, not a coin. Nothing except the Pendle heritage in her head and fingers; and Cleve, the bond with the vine upon him, laid on by Abel's hand.

The wick smouldered, and she blew it out. She crawled under her blankets, listened to the bark of a drenched coyote on the hillside, and before the watchdog of Montino uttered its answering growl, she was asleep.

2.

ALDA opened her window to the gray breath of the morning. Her rest had been brief, but she was refreshed, for all the thinness of her mattress. Had it been plucked from under her in the course of the night, she would have slept on undisturbed, for she was immune to discomfort. She could, indeed, have slept just as soundly in a wheelbarrow. Howsoever late she retired, she woke up punctually at six. At Oxhill they had all been early risers.

It was hardly more than six now. Port was leaving; she heard his footsteps on the walk. Cleve, fortified with a handful of crackers, had gone out exploring. As she stood there, lacing her boots and peering through the mist on the vineyard, in which she could discern only the tops of olive trees, she heard barks running the gamut between joy and craven submission.

From the other window, looking into the back, she had a glimpse of the yard, a block of mist hemmed in by blue-gums, their foliage wet and emerald. There was her cart under the shelter, a splotch of yellow. Cherokee had given it a coat the hue of his own medicine wagon, using up, a week before his departure, all the paint he had left. The flash of very bright silver disappearing behind the further wall of trees was probably Cleve's head. The dog knew a path or two worth following to anyone with a taste for adventure.

It led to the Lane place. Alda knew where it was, just uphill, and those trees, and the whitewashed picket fence, separated it from Montino. She had never been there, but she knew the location of all the farms at this end of the valley, for Abel had a chart map of it on the wall of his nursery.

She went downstairs. The kitchen looked squalid in the gray light. The water was outside, at the yard pump, which had a housing and a bench for the wash-basin. The luxury of it, for Oxhill had merely a rope and bucket at a well, pleased her. She washed and toweled herself with vigor, a Spartan young person in high boots, re-wound her coils of hair, and strolled through the lifting mist to a sort of pergola that, on a high terrace, overlooked the entire vineyard. It was a habit of hers to go walking through fields as soon as she got up, and when nobody was around: it gave her the illusion that all she saw was her own. Her feeling for possession was strong. Her father, wherever he had worked, had always owned a piece of earth, if only large enough for a cabin and a tree to give it shade. Oxhill she had lost, but here were the same ranks of vines and olive trees, tall pines murmuring with aves; same smell of earth, and home was about her suddenly, the warmth of it in her heart.

She turned back into the yard, the enclosure of huge eucalyptus trees, their columns streaky from whitewash that had been laid on in days of a more zealous steward-ship. It was more like an outdoor hall with its chairs and long tables ranged before a stone barbecue, whose irons had fallen to rust. In summer it should be cool and inviting. In a week or two, when she had the hang of things, she would rake it out and burn all the untidy litter of bark and leaves.

Hector was up; she heard him open his window shutters. She went into the kitchen, put water on to boil, and spread out the tableware. The larder had a slab of smoked pork, bread and some eggs—strange-looking eggs, quite large. With these, and coffee, she contrived a meal.

"Good-morning," said Hector. He slouched in, his hair wetted down, easy-mannered, wearing corduroys. "You've been to a lot of trouble."

"I'm used to that."

They took their places. She was used, also, to breakfasting with strange vintagers; twenty at a time, as often as not. Through her mind drifted the thought that what she was doing now she would continue to do at Montino for ages to come.

"Ground's not so bad," he said. "Rained so hard there was a run-off. The creek's near half full. Not anything I like to see. There's a chance the trouts'll get washed out."

"You're going to plow today?"

"Too heavy."

Hector drank a tumblerful of claret, then a finger of black coffee, opened the table-drawer and took out a deck of worn cards.

"You're going fishing, maybe?"

He smiled, teeth clinching on his pipe, and pushing cup and plate aside began to play. His hands were large and gnarled, and half closed as if they were gripping a mattock. She remarked again his quietness and slow movement, and again it surprised her. He seemed less the owner of Montino and heir to the prestige of Giorgio Regola

24

than a workman so long familiar to the place that he had become a part of it. He was slow also in speech, but he had a quick glance that lightened the heaviness of his face.

"I'm going over to Yountville. Reckoned I ought to get me a pair of dogs. Coursers. You've been over to Yountville?"

"A few times."

"That's a lot for ridge folk." He adjusted a card, thought a while, and remarked, "They don't never travel about much. Some of them never go anywhere but down to Calistoga."

She laughed.

"My father used to say, 'Why should we go anywhere? We're already in Mayacamas.'"

After a moment he chuckled at that. Mayacamas folk were proud of their grapes and their dry wine. They held themselves a grade above those who farmed in the valley bottom. None of them were newcomers; they had been in the region longer than anybody else, and had staked out the best parcels of land on the hillside. They were small farmers. And perhaps from the psychological influence of living at a height, they were inclined to be aloof and distrustful, and their women were said to be shyer than most.

"They had some good roots over at Oxhill. What came of them?"

"The roots went with the farm."

"What did they go for?"

"For the mortgage. My father took mostly notes for his cuttings and stock. He gave away more than he took out of Oxhill. After forty years of it he found he had lost."

Hector looked at the cards in doubt, then sank back

in his chair, pipe glowing red in his fist, and eyed her.

"It wasn't a farm he ran for money," she explained.

Hard-headed men he had known all his life, and Montino for long was governed by the cleverest. At times Hector wondered if hard-headedness were not sanity itself. Giorgio and some of his contemporaries had thought for nothing but to grow a drinkable wine, and turn out as much as the market could stand. They had no crotchet. They came down to brass tacks. And if these others had any dream at all, it was to match the fortune of Giorgio Regola, who made the Comet champagne.

The Comet had fizzed out, in other hands. Giorgio had the knack of riding any boom, and getting out before it broke at the crest. Other champagnes had come and gone: Dusky Hill, which everyone drank at the Cliff House; and the younger Haraszthy's Eclipse. But none had been so profitable as the Comet, drunk even at the Poodle Dog, and the restaurants on Commercial Street where the mercury barons and the Comstock plungers dined. To outsell everyone else was the game played in by the Coast growers and warehousemen and their rivals the French syndicates. The game was won by Giorgio Regola, who played alone. It was the Comet, the worst and the flashiest of all the champagnes, that went down the throat of a populace that at the time had an easily filled purse. Weeks before a strike of jewelry ore was announced at the Comstock, Giorgio's winery began to work at night, and drays, loaded down with full casks from the outer world, came pulling into it in darkness. Wise men sold their Chollar and Potosi shares as soon as they heard Giorgio had sold his Comet.

It was forgotten now, the Comet. But Giorgio was still remembered as the grower of the Regolberg. There was little of it left, no more than ten dozen bottles in the world. Those who had known the wine remembered it to the end of their days, as they would a vision of beauty in youth. The charm of the Regolberg, with its elfin sprightliness denied to hierarchy of the ceremonial red wines, forever haunted the heir of Montino. It was a divine accident that had acquainted him with grace. The recollection of it was like an upsurge of heart-gnawing music on a horn, filling him with mingled rapture and regret. Hector had been born with taste, as his father had been born with a blind spot. He never spoke of the Regolberg, as some men speak not of their religion. The theologians are eloquent; the deep worshippers are often silent. He was content to be a workman in the field where it had grown.

Giorgio, so that no one else might grow the Regolberg, had torn up the vines, destroying them to the last root and twig. Having done well by the creature—after all, immortality was a quite satisfactory return on his investment—he planted the field to the gross Mataro, which hatched for him the spectacular iniquity of his champagne.

"There was one thing your father couldn't lose," said Hector, slowly pawing the cards back into the drawer. "That was being Pendle of Mayacamas. Wasn't anybody, not even De Turk or Charles Wetmore, that knew so much about vines. And hybrids. Nor anybody who gave away so much."

"Mostly," said Alda, "it was the right vineyards that got them. Crabb's. To Kalon. Captain Niebaum's. Inglenook Farm."

He nodded in acceptance of a just reproof. Then tumult broke out in the yard and Cleve burst into the

27

kitchen with a yell, lifting a furry and limp object, Lobo capering and bowing about him in a circle.

"Look what I got! A rabbit! A Chinaman gave it to me. There's a Chinaman up the hill. He's got a pet turkey, too."

Cleve pulled up short. He had not seen Hector before, and stood lowering at him, without curiosity.

"This is Mr. Regola," said Alda. "He lives here. Montino's his place."

The boy let the rabbit fall into the wood-box by the stove, which was where rabbits wound up at Oxhill, and with bare feet wide apart, looked at him.

"Can you set traps like the Chinaman?"

"I don't go much for traps. I like to give things a chance. Any rabbit that's smart, he can run away from me. They're safe here. Lobo chases 'em. But he's a four-flusher. He can't run worth a cuss."

"Lobo's a good hunter," said Cleve. "Wing said so."

"He did?" said Hector, respectfully. "Well, then, Lobo must be good. But there's some dogs that can run faster. Greyhounds. We call 'em rabbit-dogs around here. I was thinking we could buy Montino a pair. They can run with Lobo for a month, and learn something. And once they get on to catching rabbits, greyhounds don't ever stop."

"We've got b'ars over to Oxhill. I saw two big ones and a cub on the slope one morning. You've got b'ars here?"

"Well," said Hector, "there's a b'ar-skin rug for every room in the house. On Montino when I was small, b'ars were as thick as fleas. But they got sort of thinned out."

He pulled on a coat, and brushed off a hat with his sleeve.

28

"You'd like to come along with me to Yountville and look at those pups?"

The boy turned to Lobo, and the dog looked up at him, heart in his face, eyes and tail pleading.

"Oh, he's coming. He's just saying you come along with him," said Hector. "He knows what Yountville means. It means the butcher's and a dime's worth of raw bones. The butcher's a friend of mine, and he's got the pups."

"What time'll you be back?" asked Alda.

"Kind of late. Don't you do too much, Miss Alda. You just look around the place and get the feel of the ropes. If Wing comes over, you tell him to bring some milk regular."

She walked over with them to the stable. He took out the buckboard, harnessed a stout, gray cob, and she watched them drive down the wagon road to the highway. Cleve, bolt upright, hair flying in the breeze; Hector in corduroys and a high-crowned hat raked over an eye, giving him a gypsy-like or foreign look, and Lobo curled up under the seat.

The day had set in bright and windy. She went again to the pergola, her skirt flapping in the gale, and looked over the vineyard. It astonished her to perceive what an air of thrift it presented. She had expected to see negligence. The trellis wires were taut, sounding in the wind like guitar strings. At the end of each avenue was a pile of cobbles that had been raked up in the harrowing. The vines were cut back, severely, all of a height, like rows and rows of black dwarfs. She admired the hollow pruning of the olive trees. It was not her idea of the best pruning, but once begun it was easy to keep up.

"Oh, he's a farmer all right, but not pernickety," she

had heard Bascomb tell her father. "If he's got something to do, he does it so it stays done. That finds him time to go shooting."

The girl went down into the field, which was drying in the wind, and stood on the redwood bridge that spanned the creek. Hawks swooped from the firs to the basin upstream, dipped wing, and sailed hovering over the gully that divided the farm in two. Not many farms on this slope were so blessed with flowing water. Two or three farmers whom she knew had rued their creeks, for sudden and heavy freshets, even cloudbursts, had sent floods, with trees and boulders, hurtling through their vineyards. Alda cupped her eyes and looked upward at the firs. Santa Lucia firs, they were—incense trees, brought in from the Monterey canyons. Her father, the first nurseryman to come to the valley, had planted them when Giorgio Regola was laying out Montino. A priest in St. Helena, Father Clare Lecombe, came often with a basket to pick a little incense gum, but Father Clare was now at Los Gatos, and few people now remembered these lost Incensios, murmuring in the gully at Montino.

She had a good sweep of the farm from this bridge. Giorgio—the older dwellers always called him by that name—had plotted it out himself when the slope was a wilderness. He had plotted boldly, taking advantage of the contours, dips, rises and slopes so that all the vines, strung along on high forks or trellises, could lift their foliage to the sun.

How boisterous the wind was! From the blowing, Alda knew that frost was not an infrequent visitor during the rains. But these were European vines, and accustomed to a shiver in the winter. Some of the eucalyptus trees before the pergola had suffered, their tops had been cut off, and crowned with oaken tubs, like urns, from which lippia flower poured out, like froth on wine.

Alda walked back to the villa. In the kitchen she set things to rights, more or less. It wouldn't do to turn the place upside down the first day. Then she explored the corridor to the end, to the parlor and the entrance hall. The doors of the rooms opening into the corridor stood open. Even so, the rooms were fusty, with odors of horse-hair and camphor. The large one off the corridor was probably Giorgio's. It had a parquet floor, a grand piano, a table laid with pen-and-ink, stacks of *The California Farmer*, and an abalone shell full of matches and dusty, black cigars. Alda sat to the piano, jammed the pedals down and went through the andante religioso from *Zampa*. Then she remembered the *Bird Suite* that she used to thump out when very young with Cherokee's wife, and she played that.

She played sitting on a high-backed chair. The keyboard was notched with cigar-burns. What would Abel have thought of her playing on the piano of his old enemy?

"It can't be helped now, old dear," she thought. "We've got to live somewhere, Cleve and me. We haven't a vineyard of our own, but that's nobody's fault. And besides, Giorgio isn't around. He may not be coming to Montino again, by the look of things. It's quite run down, the house part of it. And I don't think you'd have minded Hector, or not very much. He does plow, he does prune, and he seems good-natured."

She could see Abel's frosty eyes crackle at that plea, and hear his rasping, "That's another of them! I know that tribe!"

He had a rough tongue and fine-edged Aroostook mind. Bleakness was in him, and also a fanaticism that had, in youth, got shifted to plants and entomology. Only plants and bugs interested him, not men. Fanaticism was his driving force, and he had great need of it. He had need of it as head gardener for the mild General Vallejo, who saw no reason to grow other than Mission grapes; and he had need of it as nurseryman for Colonel Agasthon Haraszthy, who bred European vines at Sonoma yards, and fought to promulgate them in every nook of California. And as adviser for the State Board of Viticulturists, exhorting farmers from the Oregon border to San Diego, Pendle of Oxhill, freezing at night, roasting by day, living as hard as any friar, was Fanaticism in the saddle.

Alda, playing steadily, looked about the room. It was hung with photographs that limned a familiar text. Photographs of Giorgio as a young man before the Matoche. Bank, already a partner, for he had married Miss Matoche, who divorced him, but not before the union had begotten him a fortune and a son; and of Giorgio in their pergola at Montino with his friends; on the deck of the Napa River boat; on the steps of his Nob Hill mansion, where his handsome second wife ruled until her inevitable divorce, and left him a daughter—Hector's half-sister—and another fortune, for clever as she was, Giorgio was still cleverer. The firm of G. Regola, Incorporated, was erupting wine depots from the Bay to San Diego, and grew and battened on its own funds.

Hector grew vines on the remnant left after his father had sold off all he did not want to keep of Montino. Of the two children, it was Carola who had dash and the Regola charm. Giorgio was immensely proud of Carola, who had married into the shipbuilding family of the

Baynes: a marriage of equality, also, for the Regolas were landed people, owners of Montino, whose prestige in the history of the wine trade was inviolable.

Alda turned, giving a last flourish on the keyboard. In the doorway stood a Chinaman.

"Where boy f'om?" he asked brusquely.

"We came here from Oxhill," said Alda.

"Pendle place?"

"Yes."

"How old boy? What he called?"

"Cleve is going on six."

"I bling him milk. Ev'ly mo'ning. I wo'k in Montino."

He went, was gone for a brief while, then returned with a pitcher of milk.

"Miss Lane, she come bimeby."

Wing attacked the kitchen, sluiced water over the tile floor, mopped, cleaned up the stove and washed out more shirts. As he was about to hang them over the stove, she said, "We'll put that wash in the yard. The posts are up. You go find a clothesline."

He blinked. The order was something unheard of. He rebelled. After all, he was the majordomo of the villa.

"You bring rope, too. We'll make a swing for Cleve."

"Can do."

He poked into a tool-house near the shelter, and came back with armfuls of line. She helped him string it from post to post, and they had the wash flapping in the breeze. She went up a ladder and made a loop for the swing.

"Find some rakes, and we'll clean up the yard."

They raked up the leaves, and those not from the gum trees, he spaded deeply into a corner where clumps of New Zealand flax were blooming. She plucked a flax leaf.

"Here," she said, giving it to him. "You can twist that?"

33

He rolled it in his palms, making it a string. He was an old vine worker, used to tying cane with flax instead of wire or cord. She could remember when all field work was done by the Chinese. They cleared wilderness, planted vines, and gathered and pressed the grapes. When prices fell low, to twenty cents a gallon, and grapes were left to dry on the vine, they trailed back to the city; all but a few who, becoming attached to a vineyard, or its owner, stayed on.

"I wo'k fo' Oxhill," he explained.

That had been a password for Chinese foremen in the valley. Many of them had worked a while at Oxhill, turn and turn about on the small farm, and learned tricks of grafting and pruning. After they left, they bossed vine-yard gangs, and their superior knowledge earned them five dollars more a week.

"Abel was my father," she said. "Cleve is Abel's god-son."

"I make him kite."

Two hours of steady work, and the yard looked tidy. Alda set fire to a heap of bark and rubbish. It burned fairly well after some coaxing, and released a world of smoke, pungent of eucalyptus, with pine-nuts crackling in the heart of it. As she turned to wipe her eyes, a woman approached from the gate behind the trees. She knew it was Miss Lane. It was possibly the older of the two sisters, Elva and Miss Marthe. Elva was a widow living in Oakland with her child. Miss Marthe maintained the old home. Their father had bought up half of Montino; he had always been rich, and even when wine fell into its dolorous state, suffered no decline in his fortunes.

"How d'ye do? Did Wing bring you over some milk?"

"It came. Thank you. Will you come in?"

34

"I just came over for a minute." She looked about the yard, and she glanced at the wash on the line. "Are you— staying here?"

Miss Lane remained standing by the chair at the rustic table. She was not making a call on the social basis. She was in a black dress with a frilled apron, a fichu, and a brooch. Spare, rather tall, with the easy, dignified smile of one accustomed to deference from all persons in the valley, she was also handsome in a taut and notable way. Miss Lane was at least fifteen years older than Alda. Her handsomeness was so manifest that she had to give it no more concern than if it were a familiar and always-worn cameo brooch.

"I'm working here now. Helping with the vines."

"Oh, I see."

She showed no surprise at Hector Regola taking on a helper considerably ahead of the season. Only, her smile was a shade tauter. When the Regolas came over to Montino for a week's stay, Hector usually hired an Indian woman to help Wing who then managed the house. "You are from the neighborhood?"

"Upper end of the valley."

That would mean nothing to Miss Lane. She was of a family distinguished in the region, but took no part in the communal affairs of the valley, unless it were a concert, an Admission Day ball at White Sulphur Springs, or a Ladies' Aid social at St. Helena or Calistoga, which would be helped by her assistance.

"Is Mr. Regola about?"

"He went over to Yountville, to see about some dogs. He took the boy along. They'll be back towards evening."

"Wing looks after Mr. Giorgio's quarters," said Miss

35

Lane. "So you don't have to trouble about those rooms."

"If I could make some arrangement with him about the milk," Alda began, giving the fire another poke with the rake, "I should be very glad—"

"You may have all you wish. We have more than enough when my niece is not here visiting with me."

Miss Lane stood there, a little irresolutely. She would have preferred more candor, more openness, but the young woman, with the quite unexplained child, had not come forth with more details about herself, had spoken only in response to questions, and Miss Lane never cared to show curiosity about the doings of vineyard workers.

"It's very kind of you," Alda said.

Having been thanked, Miss Lane went. Alda, leaning on the rake, her mouth touched with a smile, listened to the departing steps and the click of the gate. She had not wholly been approved of, she suspected that. Her reticence must have been taken for stupidity, and why she was really here at all, ahead of the season—an abandoned mother, to all seeming—she had chosen to keep to herself. Thereby she had the advantage in this encounter. But the meeting had, on the whole, amused her, and she was glad about Cleve's milk.

The Planting

The Planting

3.

BEYOND the olive trees the dogs were in cry. The young greyhounds, under the fang and tutelage of Lobo, left the turkeys alone now and had transferred their attention to rabbits. For every rabbit skin Cleve brought home, he was the richer by a penny. The dogs brought down the prey, Wing skinned it, and Montino paid over the staggering bounty, which ran to four or five pennies a week. The tumult neared, and a rabbit tore urgently across the wet Mission field.

"Shoosh!" roared Hector. "You get that one, Cleve!"

The dogs sped past, the master of the pack after them, a furlong behind.

"Pups are firming up," Hector flung to Alda. "Still kind of floppy. They keep old Lobo on the move, all right. I bet he'd like to hole in somewhere and catch up with some sleep."

It was early dusk. Alda had been in the field since daybreak, planting and tying up the rootlings, kneeling before them in the ooze. She had strings of raffia between her teeth; her hands were still going briskly.

"We'll finish up in the morning," he said, from atop the tray cart. "An hour or two more, and we're done."

"Now we're here, we might as well go through with it," she replied, straightening her back. "I've got this bundle more, and there's just that half row."

He nodded and resumed his task, pounding in stakes with a sledgehammer. The echoes thudded back from the dim blue hillside. Alda worked on with her dibble, put in a cutting, and packed down the earth. It was a month after her coming, but the rains were still heavy, though sporadic, and she wanted to have the entire field done before the showers started afresh.

Good earth it was in this Mission field, dark, rich, and spongy. Perhaps too rich, she thought. The cuttings she had to cut back heavily, lopping off the four top buds, so they wouldn't run to cane. The cover-crop, too, had been chick-peas, which brought in more nitrogen. Later on, the field should have a dressing of potassium, to prevent the wine clouding. It had amused Hector at first, the way she took over the planting of this field. It was the oldest field on Montino; not the best, perhaps, but the traditional field of the estate, and Giorgio had always grown Mission grapes upon it. Hector had dug up the poorer roots, plowed the tract, and had decided to plant Malvoisie.

"But why?" she asked. "there's a lot of iron here. It's just the soil for Zinfandel."

They were standing on the veranda, just before the window of Giorgio's den, looking through the rain at the field which sloped down to the creek. He shook his head. He had made up his mind what to do. Malvoisie was the vine for that field, and when he was at Yount-ville, looking at those greyhound pups, he had bespoken a wagon-load of cuttings a year old.

"Zinfandel won't do," he said.

40

"I'd like to know why. It's cool up here, and there's a run on dry wine. You'll get something near fine."

He was silent, but she persisted, returning again to that last phrase. "You had always wanted a full dry red."

She could have said, recklessly, "It's your field, isn't it? So why don't you do what you please? You are so afraid of him that you don't plant Zinfandel? Just because he'll never give in about that vine?"

Giorgio, she knew, was adamant in his opposition to the Zinfandel, merely because Haraszthy, with whom he had quarreled, had fostered it. The Hungarian had brought that vine, with thousands more, from Europe, where he had been sent on a commission by the Governor. On returning home, he had footed the bills himself, for a clique in the State Legislature had refused to approve them. Giorgio, then the Senator from Napa, had been the most obdurate. He cherished his dislikes. Had it not been for the Colonel, he, Senator Giorgio Regola of Montino, could have gone as Commissioner himself on that spectacular tour, and not have had to wait until he made the Regolberg to achieve honor. Abel Pendle had gone with the Colonel, as the horticulturist in the group. Giorgio, since he had done well by a Pendle hybrid, had been fairly lenient to Abel. Haraszthy, exploring in a Nicaraguan jungle, had fallen into a stream and drowned. That was not the end of his strain, either. His son Arpad made Eclipse, a champagne that ran Giorgio's Comet brand damnably close in the time when the Comstock Lode was cracked wide open, and everybody in San Francisco and Nevada was drinking champagne. Giorgio had to trumpet in the East and work up a demand for Comet before he could sell out at a profit. The Hungarians had trod on his toes twice. He would have none of their truck in his vineyard. Zinfandel—so named, though it was an unknown waif that the Colonel had found without tag in a bundle of his imported cuttings —he would not touch with a ten-foot pole.

"We've got along without it here," Hector said. "I'll tell you why some day. It goes back to the beginning."

"You don't like it?"

"It isn't that."

"It'll do well for you here. Better'n what you've got in mind. The farm is yours. You don't have to let anyone tell you how to run it."

He turned and looked at her with a glower. She knew something, this girl from Mayacamas. Almost everyone knew of the old trouble on this farm. And she probably knew more about it than he did. Knew other things, too; like what was going on in his head. She was gazing into the field, her strong hands flat on the veranda rail, and he might not have been there, so disregardful of him she was, so intent with her own thought.

"My father thought he owned a vineyard. But it belonged to me, because I worked in it and helped it do the best it could. It doesn't really matter who owns the field, so long as you can belong to it, and live for it."

"I never wanted anything on Montino but quiet," said Hector.

"Quiet? And where do you find it? You have to drop everything and go away into the mountains. You are paying too high for it. No, it's Montino that has to pay. By growing miserable vines that somebody else tells you to put down. I wouldn't plant them—not if the field could grow better. I'd fight to let it have what it should." She smiled stubbornly. The stubbornness of

42

women could be terrible. "I think sometimes you don't belong to Montino at all."

"Don't say that," he said quietly. "I won't have you say that."

"Are you going to plant down that truck?"

He trudged to the end of the veranda, and heavily trudged back.

"It's late," he said. "Too late now. You can't root cuttings overnight. And I've got to plant that field."

"Would you plant Zinfandel?"

"If we had enough," he hesitated.

"I'll find the stock tomorrow."

"Find it," he said.

Alda brought it in the next day. Zinfandel rootings, a year old. They had taken much finding, and as soon as there was a crack of dry weather to go out in, he began on the fields.

He pounded in the last stake, and there Alda planted the last cutting.

She rose, slapping mud from her burlap apron, and they flung the tools into the cart. Chess and Ring, who had grown over-plump, were doing the hauling these days.

A coppery moon was shouldering out from the hill, and against it stood the winery.

With its pointed window and high Gothic roof, the winery, mantled to the eaves with creeper, and so remote from the busyness of the highway, had the aspect of some convent in Tuscany. It was the oldest in the valley, and the most imposing. Travelers, looking up at its embrasured windows through the poplars, remembered the glory of the Regolberg.

It had cellars cut into the limestone of the hillside, a dungeon full of cobwebbed vats, a bottling-room, now thick with dust, baking chambers for Madeira, and a floor where the estate now made its small parcels of wine.

At the end of its pomace yard were the coach-house and stables. Hector turned the ponies loose, flung them an armful of hay, and went on to the house with Alda. She walked in her loose, coltish gait, singing her endless song,

> Clairette, Clairette, come on,
> The hardest work is done.

Cleve trailed up to the porch at the same time, the dogs, sag-headed, behind him.

"You got some rabbits?" Hector called to him. "I'm hungry tonight. I could eat ten rabbits, per Bacco!"

Alda slid a pot over the fire and heated up a stew. She spread out plates, three-pronged forks and tumblers, and they dined on oilcloth by the glow of a lamp like a red cannon-ball. Usually Port dined with them, but he was late tonight. Hector speared another lump of meat from the pot. It was turkey. About fifty turkeys led a wild life on Montino, battening on grapes, pomace, and pine-nuts on the hillside. They hatched eggs, and roosted in the hay-loft of the old stable, which was a sort of self-replenishing meat larder.

"What we got to have," said Hector, "is more rabbit. Seems like we get nothing but turkey. Cleve, did you catch that rabbit?"

"He ran too fast. Faster'n the pups. I want to have a gun."

44

"Wait till you're ten," said Alda. "Give you a shotgun now, and there wouldn't be a dog or anybody alive on the place."

"Hector had a gun when he was five," said Cleve. "Wing told me."

"It was an air rifle," Hector said, elbows on table, paring an apple. "Only good for rats. They used to go to the winery to keep warm. The room where we baked Madeira in winter was crackety hot. Sometimes the rats got smothered."

"There was a gun in the Bee Hive window," Cleve persisted. "Wing and I went there to buy a bell to tie on Mike's neck. To scare off coyotes. I'm going to buy that gun with the rabbit-skin money."

"You'll be ten all right when you get enough saved up," said Hector. "The way you catch rabbits now."

He set himself a game of solitaire, and Alda, the dishes cleared, took up her knitting.

"Those old St. George roots, were the Madeira canes grafted on them?" she asked. "I had almost forgotten they ever made Madeira here."

"Those were the roots," he said, after a long pause, and she looked up. Hector was absorbed in his game, with the mild, intent frown he reserved for solitaire. She expected more about the Madeira, but he was silent.

Perhaps she should not have referred to those vines, she thought, and returned to her knitting. There had been some scandal, even talk of a murder, involving that Madeira field.

It was only Hector who recalled now most of the details of the affair. His father and Gaspar Bual, the foreman, were often at cross-purposes. As a child he had

45

often heard them wrangling behind closed doors; Giorgio obdurate, and Bual, a very grave man with delicate hands, equally firm, never giving in.

The cause of the quarrel was a mystery to the boy. He did know that the Madeira venture had not been profitable in its early stage. Giorgio, impatient, wanted the field cleared of the Portuguese canes and replanted to Mission grapes. Bual, who had invested in the enterprise, and had designed and built the estufa, the baking room with its coils of heating pipes, declined to abandon it.

Giorgio raged and threatened. Even the workmen took sides. For Bual, who had taught him to shoot, bought him an air rifle, and now and then took him to visit with friends, pigeon-growers in the Portuguese settlement of San Leandro, Hector had an affection. After a more violent row than usual between the partners, which Hector heard from his room upstairs, Bual left. No one saw him for two days. He had not even told anyone he would be going anywhere.

Wing looked after the estufa, and continued Bual's task of setting out poisoned wheat, three or four grains, at the foot of each vine, for the squirrels were a pest that summer. It was a hot afternoon, and Hector was playing on the shaded front veranda. He became aware that Giorgio, sitting in his den, feet on the window-sill, was looking at one densely green spot in the field.

He looked through a binocular. The boy could see nothing more unusual than birds fluttering about the crown of a thick vine.

"Blue jays," said his father. "Past nesting time, and they're acting plain loco. Tell Wing to go and find what's the trouble. Must be a rattler."

46

Hector found Wing, who armed himself with a hoe and marched ahead, followed by the dogs. It was Bual they saw, huddled quite small under his sombrero, and quite dead. A mishap rare among the older workmen had befallen him. The blade of his pruning knife had sunk into his thigh, severing the femoral artery, and unaware of it as he sat under the shade of the vine, he had bled white. Hector remembered how the birds chattered at him, and how Wing, rising from his knees, scuttled as fast as he could to the villa.

The people in the valley were sorry at Bual's passing. Of the two partners, he was far the better liked. The funeral was quite large, and Abel Pendle came to attend it. Giorgio privately thought Bual's end a favor of Providence. After the last batch of Madeira was sent out, no more was made on the estate.

Hector gave a little whistle. Then he slapped down the last card.

"Got it this time," he said, and gathered up the pack. "Yes, those were St. George roots. Scions were Mantuo."

"Mantuo?" asked Alda, plying her needles. "What's it look like?"

"Jointy wood, kind of gray. Loose clusters, and long, with a shoulder to them. Pretty, the Mantuo. I've never known anyone else that grew them."

Cleve went to bed with a roll of paper and crayons. It was just as warm in his room, for the stovepipe came up through it to the ceiling. From the drawer Hector took a grimy little notebook, that advertised a patent medicine, and with his pipe gurgling, he worked out abtruse calculations; so many hours' work, so much for stakes and raffia, so much wire for trellis. It was, perhaps, not

47

oftener than once a month that a sense of order urged him to undergo the affliction of bookkeeping.

"Lime," he said, jotting it down. "They got some down to Ashmead, and I can make a deal. Port's working there, and he can haul it up." He looked at the clock. "Eleven. If he was here I'd ask him."

"He's gone to a wrestling match," Alda said.

Port had been thawing the last week or so. He still disapproved of women about the house, but he was muttering somewhat less. This one had come in from nowhere one night, moved right in, and in all probability would stay. His hostility to her had been self-respecting. If he had been watching the place while Hector was off shooting, he would have safeguarded Montino by letting her stay only for that night, and at the barn, which had a bunkroom.

Pruner, indeed! he had thought. It was all right for women to prune vines, but only on their own farms. And this woman had come along at midnight, with a cart-load of furniture, and came to Montino as if she had it all planned.

Marthe Lane had spoken to him that same week, calling out to him from her dog-cart as he was going down the sidewalk in St. Helena. Quite cordially, too. He was surprised at that, for if there was anyone he distrusted on the slope it was Miss Lane. He had always been polite to her, for the Lanes, after all, had been wine people, and old "Wildcat" Lane had bought a chunk of Montino land when Giorgio was whittling it down before he settled the rest of it on Hector. That had been a rough deal for Hector, and Port, being unable to feel resentful towards Giorgio, whom he admired, blamed Carola for it, and Miss Lane—the two had always been quite thick.

He believed Giorgio had been drawn into it by Carola, who had planned on Miss Lane marrying Hector.

It was women that had about wrecked Montino. Seemed there was no keeping them off Montino.

Miss Lane questioned him, lightly, as he stood by her rig. But he wasn't going to let her know too much.

"Pendle—that's her name? Widow is she, or what? I had Wing take some milk down to the child."

Port was brief in his responses. Miss Lane was Carola Bayne's eye and ear on the slope, and she was pumping him.

"Don't know she was ever married to anyone. The boy's all right. An orphan. Mother was a Watson girl in Calistoga that run off with a carnival actor. Somebody's got to look after him."

"Rather early for Montino to hire vine-dressers, isn't it? Is she staying long?"

"Mayacamas folk don't move around much. They just stick. You've got to say that for them. They're great stickers."

And that was all Miss Lane got from him, and she drove off with a nod. If she wanted to learn anything more, she would have to find out for herself, and it wouldn't be easy. After the death of her one-sided romance with Hector, whom she met now very seldom, she never came into the villa unless the Baynes were there.

The Pendle girl was not one for asking questions. She just worked in the fields and tidied up the house. Only the other morning Port had taken her through the winery and showed her the vats. She praised the ovals that had come knocked-down from Portugal, and which he had put together. Those were the best ovals on Montino.

49

Few women knew the fine points of cooperage. He rather felt he would get along with her.

"Wrestling match?" said Hector. "Didn't know there was one this week."

"Over in Napa City, Port said. He's putting five dollars on it."

Out on the veranda Lobo growled, and the pups flopped down the steps. Hector lifted his head.

"Must be Wing coming," Alda said, giving her yarn a tug. "I told him to get me some needles at the Busy Bee Notions. He was going there to buy a bell."

"I guess Mike's been tight again."

Mike had been a hatchling turkey like any other until Miss Lane's cow poached a hoof on him. Wing stitched him up. The other hatchlings plucked out the threads. As often as he was re-sewed, they undid the surgery. He was belled. All turkeys fearing him—unless he invaded their stable—he grew up large, pompous, and truculent, kinging it about Wing's shack. He was fond of bread soaked in wine dregs, and when forcing himself between fence stakes, when tipsy, he often tore off his bell.

Wing came in with the needles. "I go post office. Giorgio he come."

When the post office was open, he brought up the mail, if there was any. When it was closed, he would peer through the front of the letter box. He knew the handwriting of the Baynes and Giorgio.

"You better tell Concha to come up," said Hector.

"She be here in mo'ning," Wing said, going out.

"When they come in the spring they come in a bunch," said Hector. "And Vic, too. Vic's Cleve's age. Maybe they can play around."

Alda felt disquieted. All the family together, and she

50

the one outsider. What should she do? Stay with the boy in the town until the visitors were gone? But how could she suggest that to Hector? Pride forbade her letting him see she was perturbed. Perhaps he was himself uncomfortable now. There was no close bond between him and his half-sister. It was not so much the Senator she minded as Mrs. Bayne. And she was quite unwilling for Hector to be forced to combat on her behalf.

"I wonder," she said, "if—perhaps they won't like my working here? Being, you see, from Oxhill."

"No!" He put out a protesting hand. "It don't make any difference to me—and it needn't to them."

"Perhaps Mrs. Bayne—"

"She's got nothing to say here, Carola hasn't. It's mostly Giorgio. But don't you let that bother you. You just act as if there wasn't anybody around. Everybody gets along with him, if he isn't crossed too much."

"Very well."

He smoothed out a crease in the oilcloth. "If they left yesterday, they should be here about noon."

"We'll have to get their rooms fixed up," said Alda, putting aside her knitting.

Hector took up the lamp, they went down the corridor, then to a wing closed off by a large folding door. Carola had a double room in the shaded part of the house, on the ground floor.

"This," said Hector, entering a room like a dark cave. "It's the fanciest, and the stuffiest."

Glass prisms on a chandelier reflected the lamp. They jangled as she opened the window and let in the night air, moist with a snuff of balsam and ivy.

"Ought to be some linen in that press," he said.

Alda took out sheets and covers, made up the great

bed and a couch behind a curtain in the alcove. She had never seen furniture so bulky. She wondered how the dresser and the oaken bed with its fringed canopy had ever been squeezed through the doorway.

"It's her own room," Hector said, "even if she doesn't sleep in it more than twice a year. Bed's older than anything in California. It belonged to three Popes, they say, and then to some banker who hung too long onto the Comstock. Father didn't. He hung to the Comet, and bought the bed."

"How did they get it in?"

"Built around it, I guess. And it was too heavy for Carola to pack off to Nob Hill."

Hector, leaning against the door jamb, looked about the room.

"All fixed up now. Giorgio stays in his den, mostly. If he isn't there, he's in the winery with Port. They scrap like hell over old times. If there's a big fight anywhere around, or a wrestling match, they both go to it. Wouldn't surprise me if they're both in Napa City."

"I hope Concha will show up."

"She'll be here at sun-up. Wing, too. It's late." They went down the shadowy corridor. "You better turn in. Good-night."

She went upstairs, and sat in the chair by the half-open window. Against the stars the madrone, its twigs brushing the sill, was swaying in the wind. The air was full of night sounds—wind blowing through foliage and trellis wires. She was never alone when she heard the night speaking. Along the pike she could hear the drumming of hoofs. That would be the last stage, rolling on to Calistoga, then up the escarpment of Mount St. Helena to the forest of dark larches above the clouds. How clear was the sound. It was as if the air, set in fluid motion by the voices of night, were full of waves, and a sound had but to leap upon one and be carried far.

She had not travelled far, herself. But last autumn she had driven to Vallejo, with grapes to sell, and went as far as the dock, from which a boat, filled with passengers, was ready to steam out in the dusk. It was the "*Zinfandel*." It had the name of a wine, it smelled of wine. Above the wheel house, where the Captain stood in a laced cap, hung an immense and gilded cluster of wine grapes.

"Look, Cleve!" she said. "That's a steamboat. It's going to San Francisco. Wave goodbye to it!"

The light was dim, nobody saw them, and they watched it go out, under a convoy of wheeling gulls, into the mist of the Carquinez Straits.

She had sold all the grapes, and they started back, going over the marsh road. Cleve fell asleep. Chess and Ring plodded on. Home was far beyond in the darkness. An unutterable loneliness seized her; it was cool, and she half drowsed when they reached the warmer air inland. Sharp cries, and she awoke with a start. Lanterns thrust into her face, and into the cart, where hands turned over the boxes and sacking.

"You've had grapes! Where are they? Where did you come from? You're from the South—from Anaheim!"

"No. I've never been out of the country."

They were riders, posted at this ingress to the valley, pouncing on every grape, leaf and shred of vine that came over the Straits. Voices shot at her, in French, in German, and she shook her head. The southern vineyards were under a blight. One of the riders smiled at her.

"Seen you around Calistoga, haven't I? Sure enough. You're a long ways from home, ma'am. Pass on!"

53

She was relieved to be home the next day. She hoped never to set foot out of the valley. But she and Cleve would have indeed been out of it if they had not come to Montino.

As she got up to close the window she saw a flurry of sparks in the yard. Hector was walking about. The unwelcome travelers were coming in the morning. He was probably disturbed at the thought. Then it occurred to her that if he intended to leave for the hills, he would be cleaning his gun and oiling his boots. She would not be left in Montino alone. She closed the window gently and groped in the dark to her mattress.

4.

IN THE brilliance of a spring morning they went into
the field to bestow the last pre-growing touches on the
vines. Concha was polishing the silver in the kitchen.
Wing, who had already tidied up the parlor and den,
and aired the dining room, set out for the shops with
baskets slung on a baying pole, Cleve and Lobo with
him. The belled Mike, outraged at being left behind,
was taking it out on the pups. They fed in snatches at
their plates, recoiling in fear whenever he bore down on
them, gobbling and portentous, like a choleric police-
man.

Alda found more strings to tie, wires to tauten. To the
high, upright stakes Hector had bolted arms on a slant,
to support the trellis wires, which were glistening in the
dew, and stretched over with cobwebs.

The lowest row in the gully was almost a fulfillment.
Here Madeira roots, planted before it was the custom
to spring European vines from native stock, proof against
phylloxera, had lived a hard and obscure life, like gods
in exile. Alda had pulled them into the clear after hacking off bramble, weeds, and cartloads of unpromising
growth. In gaps—since she had no more Zinfandel cuttings—she bent down and buried canes from the parent

stock, so they would strike root, like banyans, to be severed next year and grow separately.

Engrossed in her work, she was unaware the morning was almost gone. Hector stood behind her; his eyes dwelt on the hair tendrils that softened her tanned neck.

"Pretty's anything I've seen," he remarked.

"They're deep and solid," she said. "A miracle they lived here so long without help. Father used to say if it weren't for the phloxy, Mantuos would last two hundred years. That's almost forever. A pity they had to be killed—we'll take care of these. It's all there is to show for the long work Bual put on this field."

"I'll run a furrow topside of them. It'll hold water better'n anything. We ought to be having a couple more good rains. There, the trellis is all done. When I was a boy we never had trellis here. Just rows and rows of forked branches stuck into the ground." He looked at the sun. "Must be close to noon. They ought to be here any time now. I'll pack my tools in. If you want to spruce up, you better go."

He lumbered to the barn, whistling. The tools he carried lightly, as if they were no more than straws. Alda, half sitting on the ground before a vine, watched him depart, and was struck again by his hugeness and the broad yoke of muscle across his shoulders. It pleased her, too, his thrush-like whistling and the lightness with which his head turned as he glanced from one row of vines to another. She heard a call. Over at the barn was Port, hands in pockets, waiting for him with all the details of last night's match.

Alda went on to the house and dressed. Wing was back. On the buffet, with its cruets, rows of Venetian

56

tumblers, a large painting of dead birds hanging over it, he had arranged a salad and a platter of cold turkey. Between were bottles and a blackened opium bowl heaped up with pomegranates, walnuts, and pippins. Fat ginger jars held sprays of red pelargonium and New Zealand flax. He was a magisterial hand at contriving effects with almost nothing.

After laying out silver, Alda went to the kitchen and ironed out an apron and her best hair ribbon. The ribbon was her one piece of finery. She dipped it in sugared water, then pressed it out, steaming. When it dried it was stiff and glossy.

The visit was important. Hector ought to be pleased with the look of the dining room. Carola was fastidious and stylish. Alda had seen her just once, at the annual dinner of the wine farmers about Calistoga. Behind a mound of roses at the head of the table, Carola Bayne, in lace and white gloves, read a paper in her crisp, distinguished voice. She approved of women in the vineyard. It offered them a more healthful means of gaining a livelihood than work amid the din and impure air of factories and close sewing rooms. They lived at their own homes; they neither gambled nor fought; they were more reliable, and, glad of the opportunity of being useful, they were less exacting in the matter of wages.

The other speakers talked about the refugees from Anaheim, who had lost their vineyards through destruction by malady, and had settled on a tract on the opposite hillside. Their struggles had given the farmers concern. Bascomb told of plans to give them aid—tools, stock, loans of horses, and so forth. But it was Carola Bayne, of the Montino family, who was the most notable person there, and the best speaker. Everyone admired her speech. It was a speech that she read at all the growers' dinners in Napa Valley.

"Cleve," shouted Alda, "you scrubbing up? Put on a clean shirt. It's on the bed upstairs."

Hector lounged in, following Cleve.

"Is Port coming to lunch?" she asked.

"Concha will take his lunch out to him. He's sore. Lost a ten-dollar bet on the wrestling. And he says he'll be damned if he'd slick up for anybody."

"I never knew any coopers that weren't ornery. They must breathe a lot of charcoal fumes that go to their heads. There's the dogs now, all barking. Must be the wagonette's come."

Hector went round to the front. Wing was already there, in a clean tunic. Baggage was slid onto the front veranda. There was commotion, and a slamming of doors. Alda went down the corridor, and the visitors were in the hallway.

"Miss Pendle," said Hector, "this is my father. And this is my sister, Mrs. Bayne. And here's Vic, my nephew."

She shook hands with them all, and shortly they all trooped into the kitchen, then into the yard, which was warm and leafy. Cleve was there, with the greyhounds; his hair roached and wet, his clean shirt wrongly buttoned.

"Your boy?" asked Carola. "What is he called?"

Carola lit a consciously maternal smile for him, but he came no closer; indeed, he surveyed them all from under a glowering brow, still wet from the pump, and then fixed his gaze on Vic. With a poker face he turned slowly, glanced elsewhere, and lifting a new whip, a gift of Wing's who had bought it at the Bee Hive Notions, gave it a resounding crack. It sounded like a pistol shot. He executed three more cracks, but they were not quite up to the mark. But the first had established him; the dogs gave tongue, and fawned about him, like so many quelled lions.

"That's Cleve," said Alda.

Carola, beaming still, looked at her sidelong. Both girl and child were blue-eyed and with the same flaxen hair bleached by the sun. It was a resemblance, assuredly; Marthe Lane had not erred in describing it.

"Cleve," said she, "this is Vic. He hasn't been here in a long time, and you can show him around."

"We got a turkey that wears a bell," said Cleve to nobody in particular.

"How very interesting!"

Vic moved forward, in neat black suit, and patted the now unresponsive dogs. The boys went through the yard, like automatons, a formal distance apart, the dogs behind them in single file, heads down. Wing announced that luncheon was ready, and the adults went to the dining room.

"They will get along very well, I'm sure," said Carola. "From what I've been hearing of the boy."

She was large, tight-corseted, and agreeable in a masterful, smiling way: as fair as Hector was dark, with a strong, well-rounded face, and her skin had the groomed, expensive sheen of the pearls clipped to her earlobes.

"You've been here some time, haven't you, Miss—Miss Pendle?" she asked, helping herself from the platter. "You find Montino interesting?"

59

"I'm used to vineyard work," Alda said. "Interesting" was hardly the word, she thought. "We came here from Mayacamas, the ridge."

Carola was not unacquainted with that wilderness. It was where squatters grew vines and corn in the stumpy clearings they had hacked out for themselves, and lived primitively in huts. She had heard of Oxhill, of course, and the Pendles. That this girl was presentable lessened not at all her annoyance that Hector should have gone there to recruit a housekeeper for Montino. She had complained sharply to Giorgio about it. Hector, who had altogether too free a hand, needed to be pulled in sharply.

"I see. The ridge."

She smiled, for after all the girl was at table with her, but from behind the smile she looked at Alda with resentment and a cold wonder. The girl had looks of a sort. The boy, too, had an angelic head. When her eyes first lit on that seraph with his flaxen mop of curls, his scowl and sturdiness as he faced them among his dogs, she had to fight an impulse to snatch him into her arms. He would probably have given her a cut with his whip. He appeared to belong in Montino.

The luncheon was going along well. Giorgio was enjoying himself hugely. He lounged in his armchair; a bony, dominant old giant in broadcloth, a cheroot sliding in his mouth; garrulous, full of quips, and bubbles of chuckle. He was deep in his home again, familiar and easeful, larding his talk with scraps of patois that Hector and Carola had spoken here in childhood.

"Good dogs you've found, Hector," he said. "Got 'em in Yountville, eh? I thought so. Lobo's good for a while yet. His grandmother was old Fan, the best hound we ever had in the valley."

60

He turned his satyr head at Alda, his forked beard pointing straight at her, eyes half closed, smoke rolling luxuriously from his nostrils.

"Yes, we had mighty fine dogs here in the old days. The Napa Hunt came here for a barbecue every fall. Port was the whipper-in. Tally-ho, red coats and bugle! We made wine here, too!"

Mirth clucked in his throat. "Carola, I think we'll leave Vic in Montino to hoe and get some country air."

"When he's older. He's got his music, and there's college ahead of him. Later on, of course—"

"Pshaw, pshaw! No winegrower's any good unless he's caught as a pup. If he's more than six, it's too late. You're pampering him, Carola. Fiddle music and books! What he wants is some dog races and prizefights and three years with the hoe. I've known many farmers spoiled by books."

It was his humor, sly and belligerent, and it quivered him to the tips of his forked beard.

"I'm not sure school did much harm to Hector," said Alda.

"It didn't? Then why isn't Montino bigger? Why isn't it five times as big, like when I had it, eh?"

Hector's face twitched painfully. His father's goadings were beginning to exasperate him.

"Because," Hector said, "there's no more Comstock. And when trade pays for champagne, it's champagne it wants, not soda pop—not Comet!"

"That decanter on the buffet, Wing," Alda said. She dreaded a flare-up, and she pointed elaborately. "And you bring over those glasses. The little glasses with the gold band."

Wing served out a dessert wine. It was an old golden Muscatel that Hector had found behind some planks in the vat room, and part of a batch made before that end of it was partitioned off.

"*È poco!*" With eye hooded, and head aslant, Giorgio sipped it again. Alda watched him. It was syrupy, full-bodied and aromatic, she knew, but he tasted it wryly. "Not quite up to the mark."

"'No," rejoined Hector, doggedly. "You made it here, a long while ago."

"Didn't improve and mellow with age, like me," chuckled the tyrant.

"Went mousy," said Hector. "The barrel should have been sulphured."

"It was good when young. Nothing wrong with the blending, either. Time of its best, Doctor Beers was here for luncheon with McEachran and a Scotch friend, a Mr. Louis Stevenson, who was a writer, McEachran said, and had a cabin up Silverado way.

"We were in the cave, smoking over this bottle and that, and the wine was almost as good as the talk. Mr. Stevenson said when he was a lad he went over to shop for a roll of tobacco. He found the old grocer emptying his shelves of all quarter-bottles and fingers of Hock, Marsala, Claret, everything else, into a tub and stirring it up. The lad had to ask him what he expected to get.

"'I have the con-veection,' said the old grocer, 'that with care it will turr'n out to be a two-shilling Port.'"

Even Hector smiled faintly at that, and refilled Giorgio's glass. His father quipped his way through the fruit and coffee. He actually did seem to mellow. His tongue crackled with jests, his cheroot sparked like a fuse. Politics and smoke filled the air. It was getting to be a family party, even if Hector's eyes strayed to the window and the foliage beckoning in the sunlit air.

62

Alda excused herself and went to the kitchen. The luncheon had been an ordeal. Giorgio's jests were withering, and Carola had been intent on watching her every move; judging hardly, she was sure, her roughened hands, her hair ribbon, the way she lifted her fork. Still, the meal had gone off reasonably well. Concha brought in and washed the dishes, and Alda dried the silver. That done, she went round by the front door, to go up to her room for a rest. As she came to the stairway, the Regolas were entering the corridor. There was no escape.

"Come along with us, Alda?" said Hector. "We're going for a look at the buildings."

She came down with her corduroy jacket, her father's black hat, and since Carola had gone to change her shoes, she waited about in the corridor. Giorgio went into his den, pawed over the music, and crashed into an aria, with fingers of brass, his teeth nipped on a cheroot. It was something from *Fidelio*, and the charm of it survived the jangling of the strings. The tone was ghastly, but volume and loudness overlaid that as the old man hammered out form from chaos, the piano trembling under the assault, a center of energy that set the whole house in vibration.

Alda leaned against the doorway, listening. She had heard nothing like it in her mother's parlor, where she and Cherokee's wife had decorously played their four-hand pieces.

"A pile of junk!" Giorgio said, still pounding. "I'll have it tuned. Bet some eucalyptus roots have got into this barrel organ." He thumped out a final and lingering chord.

"How was that?"

Alda's head still rested against the door jamb. The tumult, if cataclysmic, had been orderly, and the last note of the chord was dying like a remote echo.

"Quite well, I think."

"But," said Giorgio, fixing a gimlet eye upon her, "with not much feeling, eh? *Non simpatico!*"

"Not very much, no. It may, of course, have been the piano. It hasn't been tuned in ages."

He turned his back upon her, looking out into the vineyard and its sombre quietness, his head wreathed in smoke.

"You play on it?"

"A little. Like everyone else, I played more once. We used to have a piano at home."

"I'll have it tuned for you."

Carola appeared, in boots and a black straw hat. "We're going now."

They went out, Hector and his sister going ahead to the winery. Giorgio walked with Alda, and they went through the pergola, which was like a belvedere, its pillars encircled with brown cables of vines. At the end of it, by the steps heading the path that led down to the winery, was a little croquet house, octagonal, with a spire and tinted windows.

"Mr. Hector thinks of planting a few table grapes here. Rose of Peru, Rish Baba, or other lady-fingers."

"Pretty yes," snapped Giorgio, sauntering on, flicking with his cane. He was energetic and sharp. A bit contemptuous, she felt, but perhaps the fault was hers, mentioning "lady-fingers."

"Over there," he said, pointing, "we had Alicantes running from the road to that crag. And up to those trees near the Lane house. It was all Montino then. Five hundred acres. We rolled out a lot of grapes."

Twenty-five acres of Montino were now in tillage; as much again had reverted to chaparral and scrub. From here the whole domain was visible; the six fields in sun-

64

shine, the files of olive trees, and the service buildings. Below these was the tract of Pinot grapes, the backlog of Montino.

They walked down to the Pinots. "Not bad here," he said, his shoes deep in the loose, rich tilth. "Not half bad."

Weeds were absent; not a vine showed a scar, the least scratch of a tool. Gang help on this canted field would have done butchery with harrow and even a single-plow. Around these vines Hector worked with the hoe, piously, entrusting the work to no one else.

"The gentlemen of the vineyard," said Giorgio. "They pay the tax money. Rains have been good?"

"Two inches this month. Maybe an inch more to come. The furrows checked the run-off, and the water sank deep."

Giorgio listened. The girl had a quiet voice. She spoke as if she were sensible. These were prime grapes, and it took old hands to care for them. They were in good tending certainly. The girl had uppance, knew what she was talking about. Young, strong, born for the field. If he had found her in some hotel in Calistoga or St. Helena, he would have engaged her at once for his kitchen. Only one way to get sensible wenches, go into the country for them. He had always had luck with his help. Bettina, his cook, was pettish and aged, and he was keeping her on just to make his pet dishes, his fish, salads, and gnocchi. He was renowned for his dinners. The trouble with girls once they got the hang of proper cooking was that they expected the wages of a prima donna, like any Chinaman, and quit for jobs in some restaurant.

"That boy of yours going to school?"

"Not yet. I'm teaching him."

"You're married?"

"No. I've adopted Cleve."

She was unattached. That would make it easier. There was plenty of room in his house, and perhaps a school near-by; Bettina would enquire about that.

"What are you doing here? Field work's rough for a woman. I'll offer you a job, at my house. You can bring the boy along."

"Thank you," she said, as they walked on. "But I won't ever leave the valley. I'm not a servant. I'm a grower."

"Hrrumph!"

They had come to the field she and Hector had just planted. Giorgio stopped short.

"What's been going on here?" He looked at the trellis vines. He froze, then slowly touched a rootling with his cane. "What's this?"

"Zinfandel."

"What!" He shouted in anger, eyes blazing, his thin mouth atwitch, one eyebrow up in a straight line. "Zinfandel! Why didn't he plant what I told him? He could have put down Grenache here, or Mission, and got twice as much for the yield. Zinfandel!"

He wheeled about, blowing hard, his cane vibrant. He looked at the winery. No trace of Hector and Carola, and the girl was thankful.

"Why not Grenache?"

"Everybody plants Grenache," she said. "Mission grows coarse, and ranky. It would be a pity to waste this good field on it." She looked at him defiantly, her smile set hard. "He put down Zinfandel because he wanted something very good, almost fine, and a good run of it. It'll do very well on this iron. And down there, we found some sound old stock to graft on." She came out with it. "Mantuos. Bual's Mantuos."

Giorgio's head went back with a jolt. It was an artistic head, under a velour hat. It reminded her of a faun's head she had seen in a book at school. His eyes still glared. His mouth went slack, and his hand beat helplessly on the knob of his cane.

"Where is he?" he shouted. "Where is Hector? By God, this place is certainly going to hell!"

He champed his jaw and fixed her with the gaze of a basilisk. "Some of your work, I guess! You been telling him what to do?"

She couldn't help but admire that splendid, fiery old head. He loathed her. But she had a way of looking upon rage as something impersonal, like lightning, or a hailstorm. It could never last. His eyes trailed from her to stare down the slope.

"I thought the last of those damned Mantuos were plowed up long ago. They should have been burnt up, every bloody one of them!"

"They were sound," Alda said. "It wouldn't have been saving to waste them. We had some on our farm, older ones, and the black-rot never touched them."

"What farm?"

"Oxhill. I'm Abel Pendle's daughter. I never worked anywhere else until I came here."

His jaw slid.

"And so," he intoned with dry sarcasm, "you've had to come to Montino and Hector Regola to work—is that it?"

She could have cried with vexation. She was near choking, her chest heaved, and she breathed deeply in a tense effort to control herself. Waves of homesickness swept over her. Her eyes filmed. This was her father's enemy, and she had not her father to lean against. He

67

would have defended her, conquering him. This was his old fighting ground; he had come to the valley before the Regolas. She looked away. She had a sense of nearness to home. She saw the winding highway, the crown of Mount St. Helena, the steam, like ostrich plumes, above the Calistoga geysers. All this her father had seen and known and loved before his enemy ever came upon the slope.

"What if I had?" she asked. "Montino's a better vineyard than when you had it. What do you know about vines except to kill them if they don't make you richer? You killed the Mantuos. You killed the White Pendle—after you had put your own name on it—and you stamped it out forever! A murder of Herod's! You murdered it to plant cheap trash in its place. To make a miserable champagne that brought shame to the farm that grew the Regolberg!

"You're still killing. You are still trying to kill Montino, and you're strangling your son who strives to do his utmost because he is proud of his vineyard—and what its name once meant! Go ahead and finish your killing! Try and uproot the Zinfandel, if you dare! I made him plant them. But I'll fight for the vineyard if nobody else will!"

Alda turned to leave. She heard a deep intake of breath; then another one.

"You stay right here!"

The command snapped at her. She faced about. Giorgio looked suddenly old, old and tired. He moved to a wheelbarrow near the vines and sat down. He removed his hat, and stared at the ground. He took out his cigar case, his eyebrows drooped in fatigue, chose a twisted, black spike of a Toscano, and fitting it carefully to his mouth, lit it. He smoked deliberately, looked at the

68

ash after a long-drawn puff, then pointed to an upturned keg near the wheelbarrow.

"Sit down a while."

She obeyed. The sun was warm upon them. Save for the butterflies that flitted in the light vapor, order was the only beauty on the tract still dormant on the edge of spring. The upright stakes, the cane-bearing trellis wires, taut from post to post, the gnarled roots, like arms lifted to the sun, wheeled to pattern from this knoll. Beyond were the patches of Cabernet, Herbemont, Gamay, Refosco and Pinot, on their undulating fields. On that jumble of crests and dips the sun could not be impartial. It would linger an hour there, pass over lightly here; with the sky shifting to a different mood in a brief traversal. Even at night subtle influences moved about them, some twin vine awakening at a breath of mist, or the light of a strange star, to sleep again unaware of its interior change, that it was set apart from its twin, and in a sense they were twins no longer.

"Your hands," he said.

Alda showed them. She had kept her roughened, nicked hands closed at table, so that Carola, who had beautiful hands, would not see them.

"You tend those vines." He cleared his throat. "You've got the right hands, and you've got the right head. You think what you damn please, too. And that's all right. I've been wrong about a few things. I was wrong about the Zinfandel."

Elation swept through her, she was glad for Hector's sake. Then she was full of pity.

"I hope, Mr. Regola—I hope you won't think that I wanted to—"

"I do!"

69

With cigar raked skyward, his head wagging, his eyes gleamed with an unholy joy. He looked at her with something akin to pride.

"I do! You wanted to fight Giorgio Regola—and you did!" He chuckled. "You gave me the axe a couple of times, and you gave it fast!"

He waved his stick over Montino. "I always had good fights here. I fought to keep the place alive. We didn't make wines for love in those days. We were out for all the tin there was in it. All of us, except fellows like Crabb, Haraszthy, and Abel Pendle.

"I fought Bual, too, my partner, when he kept on growing those vines of his. I tore 'em up. And I tore up the Regolberg. I let nothing stand in my way, I didn't.

"They fought, too. They were all damn good fighters, never gave in. They knew better than to give in. They were all in cahoots with something beyond me. I don't say I understood them. I'm not sure I understand Hector either, at times."

Alda interposed for him. "He only wants to be left alone in his own vineyard."

"He doesn't want that badly enough to fight for it."

"He fights in his own way."

"Well, it isn't my way! I've always fought for Montino because I like the old place. I often got near licked, too," he chuckled, "but since nobody knew that but me, I won out. Except this time. And all over a parcel of twigs not yet sprouting!"

The grim humor of it struck him, and he laughed harshly.

"Those Zinfandels whipsawed me—after forty years. Pendle of Oxhill's girl swung that trick. Oh, well, I had a good time fighting. I don't say that if I started all over

70

again I'd be different. I haven't changed any. But when a man's eighty, nobody fights him any more. They give in to him, as if he were a sage, even when he's mulish wrong.

"I'd think more of them if they'd just knock him down!"

Giorgio tossed the end of his cigar into a furrow. He laughed, then looked at her quizzically.

"Tell me one thing. What brought you here?"

"Well, I've got a boy, and—"

He nodded. The wheelbarrow was already in cool shade, for the afternoon was far advanced. Sometimes it was Alda who talked; more often it was Giorgio, who had gone back to the beginning of things.

gave it back. "And I haven't a thing on, and so what when I
need a dinner jacket or when I'm a bit more—they give it
to him, as it by way of a fee, even when I'm whisked to my
— I think more of them. If they'd just knock him
down."

Jack turned away or did he shrug into a furnace. He
began then, then looked at her once again.

"Tell you something. When I'm at, but you know."

"Well it was a shrug and—"

I nodded. The bowl barrels. We already in said
indicator, the invisible area far advanced. Something
wiser said who stood some of what was Chicago who
had got back to the beginning of things.

The Ripening

The Ripening

5.

IN A week of rain and drizzle, white fogs from the sea and conquering black fogs from the tule marshes pushed into the valley. They sought egress, rose to the crown of the slope and the shoulder of Mount St. Helena, found a ceiling of high winds, then surrendered to lie densely on the soggy, black fields. A furlong of the highway was under water, and the road from the forks to the Montino gate was a swamp, hubdeep, but the villa was not marooned. Visitors came and went, or they stayed. They came to pay their respects to Giorgio, and their wives to Carola. Hector hid out in his refuge off the vat room.

Here he smoked and read while society packed the drawing room in the villa. His laboratory, he called it, and it was to be entered by a low door under some scaffolding and ladders. The walls were plastered with colored posters advertising horse medicine, plug tobacco, gum boots, and Green River Whiskey. Also chromos of monks jovial in wine cellars, framed awards for the Regolberg and Montino Burgundy, and photographs of Golden Gate Park and Cliff House. On a shelf were a retort, scales, a set of hydrometers, and textbooks held between a pair of bricks.

Alda entered.

"Marthe's at the villa. She's brought her niece to live with her—except when she's in school in the city. Marthe came back this morning."

"I didn't even know she'd been away," Hector said.

He was deep in a wrecked but comfortable armchair, and he put his spectacles into Grant's *Memoirs* to mark the page, and laid it on the bench.

"What's the niece come to live here for? About Cleve's age, isn't she?"

"Same age. Her mother's gone East, Ohio or somewhere, to marry again, I hear."

"I never heard of such a family. Must be the third time."

"They're all in the kitchen now. Concha's giving them frijoles and milk. We're turning them loose in ponchos to go hog-wild with the pups and Mike. They can go anywhere—except to the basin in the gully, so long as Giorgio's here."

Hector, according to legend, had once been almost drowned in that basin, and the belief among the young was that it was to be visited only at the cost of a thrashing.

"Cleve goes, but that's all right," he said. "He doesn't let anyone see him; and he can swim, anyway. What's Carola doing today?"

"She's going with Marthe and Giorgio to Calistoga. The new Ladies' Aid shop is opening."

"Raining still. They'd better take the phaeton. It's leak-proof. And if they take the wagonette, it'll get all muddy."

"The phaeton'll do, I guess," Alda said. "You'd better hitch the gray. He's got the best-looking harness. It's near two o'clock now."

Hector struggled into oilskins. "I'll take Chess out to

76

the Gamays with the single-plow. They're on clay. Plowing will drain it. Gamays never did like wet feet."

"You'd better wait. It may be fine tomorrow."

"That's what I figure it'll be," he said, yanking down his sou'wester. "If it's clear tomorrow I may go for a bit of shooting. Haven't been up to St. John's Peak in a couple of months. Port says there's some bucks running loose."

"The growers will be here next day," she demurred. "Father Clare, too, from Los Gatos. Houseful of people, and you the host."

"Well, then, after tomorrow," said Hector, ducking through the low doorway.

Affairs had been running smoothly this visit. So far there had been no explosion over the Mission field. Alda had taken Giorgio through it, but he must have taken the change as a matter of course, whatever he thought of it privately.

She had told no one of her row with Giorgio in the field. It was a matter that concerned only themselves. Like her father, she understood plants; but unlike him, she understood men who had all their lives cherished their fanatical beliefs. Abel could not live away from his vines. Giorgio flourished only in a climate of strife. She loved perfection, and the old Senator was perfect of his kind. Having won in her encounter with him, she was finding herself taken with his gusto, his deviltry, his pagan head.

"You might go into the den this morning," Hector told her at breakfast, when they were both up early. "He's got the piano tuned. He wants you to try it."

"More likely he wants to argue," she said. "Or have a scrap over vines. I don't mind, with him."

"You're getting to be a favorite of his."

Hector shook his head wonderingly. For himself, he

kept clean out of the villa, finding jobs to do in the field. This was the slack season now. Ordinarily, he would have camped in the pergola with his pipe, or gone visiting with Bascomb at his rendezvous, Flores' tamale parlor, where most of the small growers hung out; or gone fishing, not going near the vines until they began to drop their blossoms in June. But he was now finding himself many unsuspected little tasks. He gave the stable a coat of whitewash, and hacked away with chisel in the storage cave in the hillside.

After hitching up the gray, he parked the phaeton on the terrace, ready for Carola, then went back to run a furrow among the Gamays. Alda was at the nursery, looking over the Rish Babas she had planted against its eastern side. They were her mother's preference, and the only vines she had brought from Oxhill. Two years old, field-grown, they were already in leaf.

"You'll have fruit this summer," he remarked, pulling up Chess.

"They'll do here. I'll girdle them, soon's the berries are set. The Fair is giving a prize this year for table grapes. We ought to try for it. There's nobody but us growing Babas."

"You ought to have a field of them."

"Some day. Got to have plenty of cuttings first. But I'd like to see Montino win the big-cluster prize."

"I'd like to see Montino win something," he said, going on.

Gulls squalled through the fog. Blackbirds whirled like leaves in a gale, and dropped to hunt in the wake of the plow. It was a long row, and back in the grayness he had a glimpse of an elf, a poncho slapping about its raw legs, as it darted among the birds.

78

"Bait," thought Hector. His bones ached at memory of an old agony. Cleve would be gathering bait. The pool had not been forbidden him, though Vic and Jule had been warned to keep away from it, and he experienced a joy in visiting it secretly.

Faster than the birds Cleve gathered worms, a tinful, then left the field. The wind blew his poncho straight out, and he groped from post to post, tacking to the stable where he kept his rod. It was behind a barrel under the eaves; rain plumped on him, and drenched his head. He tacked on, and caught in another gale, hid under the dry side of a madrone, like a toad under a leaf. The gale plunged and roared through the madrones, wheeled and plunged again, capsizing the gulls that were swept on, uttering their bleak, hopeless cry. In a lull he slipped out, and only Hector, lurching behind the ponies through the muck, saw him vanish through the fog to the pool.

Hector thought back to the days when another boy lived on Montino, and the same Wing gave him fish hooks to catch trout in the gully. Wing did until Giorgio, despotic even in his middle years, forbade him under pain of expulsion. Hector was forbidden to go anywhere near the pool, for fear he might tumble in and drown. He could not swim. He had never been allowed to play near deep water.

One August day his mother had sent him to the post office, and he returned by a shortcut through the Mission field. The basin of water in the gully, shaded by tall firs, was cool and enticing. Wing had planted lily roots far beneath in tubs, and on the surface, nibbled at by carp and trout, floated the pads and white blossoms. Hector lay flat and hung his face over the brim; with a switch he tickled the sides of the fat carp. All things moved in that

79

deep water; the stick might have been a weed swaying in the current. The red-waisted goldfish came up his fingers, shaking out their tails that were like swatches of silk. In the spear of sunlight that came through the foliage, their beauty was almost unbearable. But it was the carp that fascinated him: the fat, indolent carp, their gills working, like so many pompous aldermen blowing out their cheeks, their eyes glazed, as if sated after a banquet. A group of them hovered behind a mossy rock, just out of his reach. He hooked his foot on a root, stretched himself out and poked down the stick. The root was firm, the water below him, ten feet deep, looked as solid as glass. He kept perfectly still, oblivious to the world about him, looking into that abyss.

Even more still, like one paralyzed, lay his father, watching him. Giorgio, awakening from a doze in his fever, saw him from a bed in the villa. He called out, but his shout was too feeble to penetrate the wall. No one was upstairs, and he was supposed to be fast asleep. He stared helplessly at the child hanging above the pool, face to the water, his foot precariously held by a root. Horror froze him. Then his hand moved, he managed to reach his cane, lifted it to the fowling piece above the book case, and pulled it towards him. Somehow, he contrived to point the gun over the footboard of the bed.

The blast rocked the villa. The women came running, found the room smoke-filled, the window blown out, and Giorgio waiting.

"The boy is at the pool. Bring him here."

Hector, stiff with fear, was brought in. "Women leave the room," said Giorgio. "Out! *Fuori!*" Rage enabled him to crack his fingers. "Lock that door now, boy."

Giorgio drew himself up on the pillows. "Come here!" The child drew nearer, hands lifted, whimpering.

The first Mrs. Regola, a rebel for once, beat at the door with her small hands, and screamed. But nothing could interrupt what Giorgio had to say in the room, no pleading could unlock that door and release her child before the end of that hour in which something in his breast was forever broken.

For weeks after that, the child rose crying in the night; by day he had the eyes of a frightened spaniel, and hid whenever Giorgio came into the house or the vineyard.

The storm had quieted, and Hector, turning Chess about, drove back through the Gamays. At the end of this tract was a rail fence, which separated Montino from a field that once had been part of it, but which Giorgio had sold to the Lanes. Here the Regolberg had grown. It was now leased to a cattleman; a pasture with here and there jungly thickets of cane, twenty to thirty feet long, that never bore fruit. Elsewhere the livestock had eaten the green shoots as soon as they appeared, and the vines had died out. There was small likelihood of it being planted again. Hector sometimes dreamed of buying it, but the land he tilled hardly more than kept Montino going. And the Lanes set an inordinate value on their holdings.

Hector turned Chess into the corral. The ground had been heavy, and they were tired. Little remained to be done in the vineyard. Drip from trees was still flurrying in the wind, but holes had been torn in the fog. Tomorrow might be fine, and he thought of the bucks. Up he went past the winery, then into the black entrance of the cave in the hillside.

81

The laboratory was one of his private haunts, the cave was another. It had been started when he was small—the Chinese help, between seasons, hacking out the limestone —and he himself had carried further the excavating. The Montino wines had always been hauled to the city for storing in one of the great warehouses, a reservoir that the trade tapped at need. The cave had room for fifty barrels; it now held twenty, and when the next vintage came in, space would be lacking. So Hector worked away in his tunnel. It had always troubled him that his reserve should be sent away for storage. To Giorgio, wine was something that could be regarded in the abstract, like drafts or bills of sale, and could be disposed of with no involving of sentiment. Those twenty barrels of Malbec he would have sold at a price made acceptable by its sprightliness, its bright youth. But Hector had been aware in it of a fine note, a determination, a finish to come with age. Malbec vines were temperamental; they had quirks, they were tricksy, they sulked if they were not pruned one way this spring, and quite another way next spring. They were often ungrateful enough to die before their fruits could be gathered.

But last summer had been cloudless, with heat reflecting from the ground, and Hector had coddled the vines slavishly. He packed the wines into the tunnel, not even Giorgio knowing of them, and here they were mellowing, within reach of him. He had the small vigneron's dislike of relinquishing grasp on his wealth in hand.

Lighting a pair of tallow candles, he spiked them on the rough wall, turned up his sleeves, and began to cut into the rock. It was limestone, easy to work, hardening on exposure to air. The tunnel was already a hundred feet long; on this slope only the Schram place had a larger cave, and like the Regola's, its temperature varied no more than five degrees in the cycle of the year. Hector worked massively, with hammer and chisel, but through the cave doors not a sound of the mining carried on to the villa.

The guests had come back from tea at Calistoga, and a fire burned in the parlor, where Carola and Miss Lane sat over their embroidery, and Vic played lotto with Jule. Giorgio was in his den, smoking a cheroot, his quill moving rapidly. The tasks of posting books, writing letters and despatching them he compressed all in one particular day, as was the custom of the older merchants in San Francisco; and this was steamer day, a survival of the time when the packet sailed out of Meiggs' Wharf for the East. The smoke was asphyxiating, the room stuffy and just right, like his office in the old Montgomery Building; he wrote off a dozen letters, and was in excellent, crisp form. On the whole, this had been a good day. In Calistoga he had been recognized, he had liked the tea, rewarded the Ladies' Aid by purchasing a cake and a jar of spiced peaches. Also, he had heard a pleasing comment as he walked by the veranda of the Calistoga Hotel, where some villagers sat lounging in chairs.

"That's him! That's Mr. Regola of Montino. He made the Comet, and the Regolberg."

Giorgio had marched on finely with his stick, between Carola and Miss Marthe Lane, old Wildcat Lane's daughter. Oblivion had swallowed up most of his contempories, but he was still remembered. He had made a big smash in his day, set off a lot of fireworks, and necks still craned as he passed by.

He stamped the letters, then went into the kitchen. Alda was pressing out a shirt for Cleve.

"Where's Hector? I want these taken to the post office."

"He must be in the field somewhere."

"In the wet! Well, then, I'll have the Chinaman take them in. Oh, by the way—" He frowned. "That boy of yours, he's been down in the gully. Fishing! I saw him come up with a rod and a fish as we were coming through the gate. We don't stand for that in Montino. Never did!"

Alda, trying the iron at her cheek, looked at him thoughtfully. "You just can't keep your hands off other folks' business, can you?" she wanted to say.

"You must forbid it at once!" he said peremptorily, with the aspect of an indignant schoolmaster, the ribbon of his pince-nez tangled in his beard that was vibrant like antennae. "He will drown there!"

"He's swum in deeper water than that since he was five," she smiled, clumping with the iron. "Cleve just took to water like an eel."

"Hrrumph!" Giorgio paraded up and down the floor, then gave another snort. "Well, this isn't getting my letters posted. Hector not around, nor Port. Nobody around!"

"There won't be any mail going out tonight, but Wing'll take the letters down in the morning."

"Steamer day, and they ought to be off now."

The sky had cleared a little, and the damp air was sharp, full of oxygen. A stroll would do him good. Anything was better than hanging about the house, with all these women getting on his nerves. He had a notion of calling Vic, but Vic would have to change his clothes first, and there he was, sitting before the fire playing games, pampered like a girl. Boys of that age, when not at their books, should be kept outside.

"I'm going up to the shack."

Giorgio turned up his coat collar as he walked through the yard, picking up Lobo, who went up before him in a shambling trot. The air was velvety, but indeed cool, and he was glad he had on his heavy suit of broadcloth, his Sunday best. He climbed the hill, ducked under some wet alders, and rapped at the door. At a shout from within, he entered. The shack was as hot as blazes from a stove on which pots were steaming. There was a Chinesey smell, laundryish, something like camphor, but without the smell of camphor; and overlaid with a reek of feathers and sour wine. Mike was snuggled in the wood-box; before him was a pan of bread soaked in wine dregs. He looked drunk; in fact, he was drunk. The shack, otherwise, was orderly and clean.

"You have chair," said Wing, and Giorgio seated himself.

Wing and Cleve were at the table, playing a game that must have been going a long while; it was also very intricate and solemn. The Chinaman, with eyelids drawn down, as if he had relinquished the external world, sat like an antique statue in ivory, holding a long pipe to his lips. The greyhounds fixed their gaze on the turkey. Cleve played with gravity and a detachment from surroundings rather like that of the dogs. Giorgio edged his chair closer. Cleve dealt. His hands were small and grubby, but dexterous.

They played for markers, which were ch'iens, coins of unrivalled fine casting, aquamarine blue, very thin and old. When cast into the pot they rang with a wan, dulcet music.

"You want to get in, Giorgio?"

"What are you at? Spit-in-the-ocean?"

Cleve dealt him a hand, and kept the pack face down. "Shasta Sam."

Wing, tapping his pipe, spoke also with brevity. "Ten points. High, low, and the jack."

They played round after round; Giorgio, a cheroot in his teeth, elbows flat on the table, playing with the animateness of a terrier. Both he and Wing puffed cheroots. The pot rang with dollars and silver.

"Gobble-gobble-gobble!"

Mike, rising majestically from the wood-box, addressed the dogs that were under Cleve's chair. They were aggrieved, they rolled their eyes and backed off with yelps of fear. The din was hideous, befitting a barnyard more than a house.

"Here, you!" chided Cleve, fetching Mike a smack on the feathers with his bare foot. "Quiet!"

Mike made an onslaught, and the dogs tripled their protests. Giorgio peered over his glasses. "That turkey looks crazy to me."

"He's just tanked," said Cleve.

"I don't like to be near any turkey, drunk or sober."

"I'll put him in the woodshed," said Cleve, opening the door. The greyhounds scuttled out. With the broom he pushed Mike towards the lean-to, but this time the bird, gobbling in an apoplectic rage, his barred tail feathers spread out, was not to be imprisoned. The dogs, dismayed, but resolved to fight back, were inside it; and Mike was not accustomed to roost this early. He turned and sped downhill. Cleve yelled frantically.

"He's gone to the old stable! He's gone home!"

Wing, his slippers flying, hurled his corpulence out of the shack. Then he pelted down after Cleve. There was no help for it. Mike faced death, or worse. He would be unstitched—his scornful kin would pull all the stitches out of him, and drive him out, an outcast from the society of all right-minded turkeys. Cleve got to the old stable first, and headed off Mike, who vaulted to the fence.

The corral was mud under a film of green slime. It had islands of rocks. He bumped from one island to another, as wary as a condor, but wobbly on his pins. Wing led the chase, holding up his trouser legs; he had again lost his slippers, this time in the mud. He howled execrations. A steady drizzle was closing the afternoon, and pelting on his face.

"There he goes!" yelled Giorgio. "Corner him now!"

Strategy was futile. Mike sailed over their heads to the next rock or stump. It was like a game of battledore, the shuttlecock a drunken, twenty-pound turkey in erratic flight. The dogs came in, and the pursuers splashed about, breathless and mud-soaked. Mike perched on a log in the furthest corner, a redoubt in deep slime. He was an adversary terrible in splendor, tail fanning, chest bursting with rage and defiance, his red wattles swinging like a metronome. The dogs wilted, their eyes going limpid with fear. Even Wing hesitated. Giorgio clung to the fence, helpless from excess of mirth.

There was a truce. Cleve took deep breaths. Wing recoiled his pigtail, clapped it atop his head in a bun, and skewered it with a pencil. Giorgio, his shoes plopping out of the mud like corks, crawled along the fence into ambush.

"If that wino sobers up, we're lost. Rush him in that corner."

At the right moment Cleve made a leap and a snatch

at Mike's tail, and plopped face down in muck. A cry of triumph broke out as he struggled upright. Giorgio had collared the bird with the cane handle.

"Got him! I've got the hellion!"

"Hold him now!" yelled Cleve, pulling off his suspender. "He's slipping!"

He tied the suspender about Mike's neck, and urged him, with Wing's help, through the bars of the corral. All trooped up the hill, Cleve, hair plastered over his face, miserably holding up his pants. Giorgio, weak from mirth, tottered helplessly on his cane, gasping for breath. Mike's rage was unquenched; he clamored, pinions going like an electric fan, and was pushed into the woodshed. Wing, cursing hard, fastened the door with wire. Whether it was strong enough to hold in such desperate villainy was doubtful. He reinforced the door by propping logs against it. Giorgio exploded again, groped into the shack, and moaned feebly as he shook out a handkerchief and dropped into a chair.

Behind the woodshed were a barrel and dipper. Cleve washed himself blue and clean, drew the poncho over his head, and went in. The poncho stuck to him, he was worm-naked under it, and his teeth chattered. Wing, who had made a pot of tea, gave him a hot cup. They all had cups, all talked at once, and the elders lighted cheroots.

"Never saw such a hunt in my life," said Giorgio. "It was like catching an eagle." He guffawed again. "An eagle with tail feathers riveted on." He emptied his cup. "Now for that game. We've got to finish that game. It was your play, Wing."

It was finished on the edge of dusk, just as a voice floated up from the villa. It was Concha's voice. Giorgio, eyebrows wagging, the Toscano cheroot rolling in his teeth, totted up the winnings.

"You're four-bits to the good, Wing." He slid over the money, then a dime to Cleve. "Yours. Me, I got skunked."

They left, Wing staying to change his slippers. On the step was a dripping handful of pants and shirt, which Giorgio speared with his cane.

"I'll pack 'em along."

Cleve had the dime locked in his fist. Thoughts of a fish hook set at the Busy Bee—twelve hooks for a dime—tantalized him. It was either fish hooks or one of those marvellous camel's-hair brushes, good for watercolors, that Lum Yat sold in his shop. Wing caught up with them. Giorgio handed him a packet of letters.

"Don't bother with them now," he said. "Tomorrow will do."

"Tomollow," said Wing impersonally, "not steamuh day. I go post office tonight."

Alda, in white bibbed apron, met them on the veranda. Her forehead rose in amused query. Giorgio's suit was rumpled and moss-stained, his shoes pulpy, the blacking washed out of them.

"Been chasing that damned turkey," he said. "I'll have to scrub."

If Carola and Marthe, to say nothing of the guests, saw him in the hallway, he would be in for a twitting. He looked like something fished up out of the creek. Alda held open the screen door.

"There's nobody this end of the house. You can slip up the back stairs. Wing will take you up a hot claret, and bring your suit down to press. And after dinner he can post your letters."

89

So she remembered the letters, too. He nodded and obeyed; went through the kitchen gratefully, and upstairs. She had saved him, and done it quietly, without fussing like a hen and making a to-do. If only he had someone to look after him like that at home. That notion had come to Carola likewise.

"She'd be so much better off in the city, Father. Room, board, a little wages. Those country girls would be grateful for just that. And with Bettina growing so old—"

If she had brought it up once, she had brought it up twice. Prodding him about it, too. He couldn't for the life of him see her transplanted to the city, any more than if she were a deer. She was no ordinary, strapping country wench, the kind needed to scrub in the kitchen and put up with the imbecilities and pettish exactions of Signora Bettina. Even Carola could see that, unless Carola were stupider than her brother—which she wasn't. Let her fight it out for herself if she wanted to get the girl away from Montino—she'd soon learn how far that would get her. Giorgio, hauling off his boots, was grinning diabolically at the thought as the door opened and Wing entered with the hot claret.

6.

IN THE let-up of rain Hector was gone. Alda heard him leave the house before dusk, before anyone else was awake, and drive out in the buckboard with the gray. No one appeared to be aware of his absence. He had always come and gone as he pleased. The vines had given him a holiday, and it was being marred by the stream of visitors in and out of the villa. Port came up, and Alda told him. He had hoped to go along with Hector and try out a retriever pup.

He gave a wry chuckle. "I should have known." Then went on to find Giorgio.

Port, though he dined at the villa once a week or so, no longer slept there. Alda he liked, but even one woman was too many to have about, and he had, moreover, snug quarters of his own in his shop behind Flores' tamale parlor.

"Oh, aye, she'll do," he said to Giorgio. "She knows growing. More'n anybody here. Quiet, too."

"Yuh, yuh," assented Giorgio. "A professor. Without the book."

He was sitting in a rattan chair at the entrance to the cave, on the broad step, with ferns and ivy dangling overhead from the arch. His eyes, as he leaned back, in immaculate dark suit, stiff shirt, and hard cuffs encircling his wrists, with a long cigar in his teeth, reflected the periwinkle blue of the sky. His satyr head was framed by the limestone blocks of the portal, cracked and weather-stained. From within came antique odors of barrels, moss and wet stone. This was his favorite sunning place in spring. He had a feeling for antiquity, and he had also a lively sense of the present.

"What d'you hear in the valley?"

"Peter Jackson's training over to Edge Hill. Runs ten miles soon's he gets up," said Port, sitting on the step, exhaling much smoke. Of vineyard gossip he was chary. Discretion was as much part of his stock-in-trade as oak staves. "That retriever pup of mine goes to the dog show next month. Ain't much more happened around here. Bourn and Wise winery won't take Mission grapes for a gift. I heard tell that Tiburcio Parrott has got a Margaux, but he's not selling any. And Dr. Hiram Beers, over to Trinity Rectory, is running his Sauvignon on a few long canes without cut-back."

In the pasture the children were playing croquet. The grass was dampish, but Carola, ever since Cleve had become a hero, for Giorgio had related the tale of Mike's capture with perhaps an excess of gusto, had relaxed her strictness. Cleve hadn't caught cold, or even a sniffle. So Vic could play anywhere he liked, except at the pool.

"That him?" asked Port, nodding towards the field. "All fixed up in velvet?"

"That's Vic," Giorgio said. "He ought to be here all the time. Growing up, too. Kind of a dark strain coming out in him. My grandmother, I guess."

"Other one's smart, too. Cleve. I'm going to take him along to Edge Hill on that coopering job. We'll see Peter

Jackson." Then, with a grunt, "I got to roll up a stake for the Hayes-Kanski scrap. I'm betting on Kanski."

Giorgio rocked in his chair thoughtfully. "You better make it Hayes. And there's no hurry, either. Every time they get set, the old women and the Sheriff chase 'em right out of the county. The scrap'll have to be pulled off in a slough, somewhere, the boys on stilts."

"How'm I going to know, if it's sub rosa?"

"I'll have them wire you from the Olympic."

Port looked impressed.

"I'll be obliged." He rose. "Don't know if I'll come to your growers' meeting Thursday. Won't do me any good. They can make any wine they damn please so long as I can make the vats."

"You come," Giorgio said. "There's that business of the Anaheim colonists. They ought to be helped out. What have they got the most of?"

"Alicante," said Port. "Old vines, and heavy-bearing."

"They could make a sherry of it. Trade wants a cheap sherry. If they had a baking room, like that Madeira lay-out of ours, they could work up a big parcel. Or some winery around here would make it up for them."

"And use my vats?" said Port, turning. "Well, they think a lot of my vats."

The day after Hector returned, rain and mist came back. Water poured from the roof in sheets; the fields were again a morass. But that late afternoon Montino was lively. Wagons and carriages came drawing up the muddy road to the villa; the growers, before scattering for their homes, were to be guests of Giorgio Regola. Money dropped into the pockets of Vic and Cleve. As soon as they heard barking down the road—they had

93

chained Lobo and the pups at the gate, one chain with three heads, like Cerberus—they donned ponchos on the veranda, dashed out and held the horses while the guests descended.

Horrocks of La Belta, the grower of Refosco grapes, drove up. The boys swooped down upon him. They might have been Indian brats hired to park the carriages.

"Keep my seat dry now, or I'll wring your necks!" On the veranda he turned, laid a dollar on his palm, gave it a thump, and it rose in a parabola to drop into the mud, where Vic hurled himself upon it.

"That's mine!" shouted Cleve. "I grabbed the team first. Give me that!"

"I wont!"

"You will!"

"It's mine, and Montino's mine, and your mother's only working here."

They fought, striking out blows from under their ponchos, but Vic kept his cartwheel. Their gains, on the whole, had been equal. The idea of turning footmen was Vic's. To keep the dogs tied up at the gate, like buzzers, was Cleve's inspiration.

"Looks as if everybody's come," he said, after they had counted their coins on the veranda. "Shall we go in?"

"We'd have to be quiet. You go in first," said Vic.

In the parlor and drawing room were the women. Alda and Concha moved about, seeing to the refreshments. Here was buzzing enough. In Giorgio's suite—the two rooms had been thrown into one—and the corridor were the cellar-masters and growers, the personages, the immortals of the valley. Cleve had been hearing of them all his life. Here they were, all about him, afoot or on chairs, listening to the debates. The den, in the light from the

94

tinted windows, was churchly, and sitting near Giorgio, listening to Professor Hussmand and Charles Krug, the first wine-maker in the region, were Bishop Lyman of Old Mill Farm, Dr. Beers of Trinity, and aficionados of the vine like Mr. Wedge, the schoolmaster. Father Clare of the Los Gatos Novitiate, and Carl Wente, who bred Gray Riesling on gravel in Livermore, had come back for a visit.

An eternity of talk, and this half of the meeting was over. Wing, his pigtail lustrous, pushed in a serving table on wheels. He sliced turkey, ham and smoked venison, with a knife like a cavalry sword. At the sideboard Flores served rice cakes, olives, and wine. The men sipped wine with bird-like lifts of the head. The talk of grapes, the colonists, prices and the weather gave way to jests and politics. Giorgio's voice crashed through the smoke.

"Bryan, gentlemen! To Bryan and silver! To silver and the Comstock! Nevada rivers all flow over the California border to us. May silver profit by their example, and do us good!"

Father Clare smiled in the doorway.

"I trust, Senator," he breathed, "that won't portend another Comet."

Giorgio laughed. More debates rose over silver—and Bryan, Bryan. Cleve thought Bryan was a vineyardist who lived too far away to come to Montino, but was a famous grower nevertheless. Cleve and Vic, and half of the guests, wore big silvered discs, as large as a soup plate, with a "16 to One" on it, pinned on their coats.

Mr. Wente lifted a glass in the corridor.

"Here's to the growers just beyond the rims—down in San Benito and in Los Gatos. Father," he tossed to the priest, "I hear the Novitiate's brandy is like a sunset, and as strong as the Reverend Abbott's faith. A health to him!"

Carola came smiling through the corridor and uplifted a monitory finger. "Victor's playing."

Clamor arose on strings. They formed after a moment a melody. Cleve crept to the parlor and peered in. Vic was in his velveteen suit, his long black hair combed back and glistening, playing on a violin. He looked handsome, dreamy, with his eyes closed, and he played gracefully, with something of the courtly air of the dancing master in St. Helena.

The ladies, sitting under the chandelier and amid the statuary, holding teacups in their hands, with fingers apart like tendrils on a vine, sat like beings held in an entrancement. The piece ended. They broke into cries of delight. Vic bowed, straight from the waist, hand on his belt. To Cleve it was an incredible and humbling sight. Vic, with whom only an hour ago he had been fighting in the mud over a dollar, was henceforth a creature apart. The ladies made much over him as he sat on a long hassock, next to Jule, eating a huge piece of Lady Baltimore cake with a fork. Homage flushed him, made him almost beautiful.

"I don't really think Vic should go," said Marthe. "Can't he stay on here? If only for another month, like Jule."

"It'll do him no good to fall back in school," said Carola. "He has trouble enough with fractions, and bounding states. And there's his music to keep up."

The party dulled for Cleve. Vic and Jule sitting in the parlor. In the dining room were more dishes to raid; he went in and got a handful of olives and fried acacia blossoms. He was nibbling these when he saw at the window, absorbed in a book, his lips moving as he read, a figure in a plum-colored gown and a pigtail.

96

It was Duke Liu, the visible head of a community in Sonoma, the Brotherhood of the Utopian Life. It had grown rich, but its head still worked in the vineyard, where labor had hardened his muscles and made his speech terse. He made its wines, and his taste in wines (he blended a dry Madeira that had won three medals at expositions) was known to be exquisite. He was the only Sino-Scot in the world. He spoke yet with the burr of Aberdeen, where he had been brought up on kippers and oatmeal in his un-Ducal and penurious exile as a university student. His study, where he slept, was half filled with books from the library of Swedenborg; he read hardly anything but the works of that philosopher; Saint Mechtild of Magdeburg's *The Flowing Light of the Godhead*, and the Agricultural Report. His spiritual doctrines he had absorbed in the fogs of London.

A few of the Utopians, who had come with him to Council Bluffs, Iowa, where they had laid out a vineyard, had abjured them and drifted into the world of darkness. Duke Liu plaited his own pigtail, made very good dry wines, sang Swedenborgian hymns with Auld Licht fervor, treadling at the harmonium before his breakfast of porridge and tea, and hoed in the vineyard. His earthly fealty was to the Brotherhood, the vine, and the friends of the vine.

Alda entered and talked with him. He had often visited her home at Mayacamas.

"I'd like you to know my boy, Cleve. Cleve, this is the Duke."

Cleve shook hands with him.

"An honored name," said the Duke. "Oxhill developed a strain for me. You remember it, Miss Pendle?"

"Yes, Duke. Father called it the Chasselas BF."

97

"Exactly! It has flourished well. We are devoted to it."

Hector came in, with young Mr. Bioletti, who was Professor Hilgard's assistant.

"Duke, they're calling for you in the den. You're to read a paper."

"Of course! I shall be in."

They followed him. It was a very important paper, a monograph, and he read it in a burry sing-song, like a clergyman. The smoke was pretty thick. Few were so enchained by science that they let their cigars go out. Alda kept refilling the glasses. The paper was about the Pierce disease, which after eating up vineyards in the south, especially near the sea, was leaping northward, over this area and that, unseen, like a flying ghost.

There was a pause. Chairs slid back. There was a stretching, then the buzz of resumed talk.

"That trouble," asked Hector, "is it as dangerous as the phylloxera?"

"Fully. Kills the vine just as dead." The Duke turned to young Bioletti. "There is no control, I believe?"

"None. I cannot foresee any."

"It'll be coming here, you think?" persisted Hector.

"I hope not. There are poor folk that fled it once— from Anaheim and San Bernardino—and came here. It would be a pity if they were harassed again. We can only be watchful. Mizpah! The Lord set a watch between our vineyards and us when we are absent one from another!"

Giorgio pulled a cork from a flagon on his desk. The bottle was dusty from its bed of sawdust in the bottom drawer of the press, a bed which, ordinarily, might have bred insects, but the cork had been armored with green sealing wax.

98

"Cleve, will you get those cups down? They're on the top shelf."

Cleve mounted on a chair and lowered them. They were of gold, hammered paper-thin, and tumbler shape.

Giorgio poured into the cups. "It's a sherry we made here of Alicante. Eighteen eighty-six. That's the year I was elected Senator again. And the year they unveiled the Statue of Liberty in New York—and I went to see that, too, by the way."

The guests sipped after a health. The Duke sipped again, and his eyes travelled to Hector, who was holding his translucent gold cup to the light. The wine showed a faint red, like blood through tanned skin. Giorgio re-filled more cups. Cleve, in the function of Ganymede, carried them on.

"*Gwin o aur!*" said Mr. Bioletti, relapsing into his mother tongue. He was really Welsh. "Wine from gold! How pagan!"

Giorgio clicked his tongue, with eye set hard, as if aiming a rifle at the tiniest of birds, then smacked his lips.

"Not bad, really. Hector and I are going to make plenty of it soon. The Anaheimers have got rafts and rafts of Alicante. It was there when they came." He chuckled. "Gold cups are all right. But I've drunk from odder cups.

"I ran into Joullin, the painter, at the Bohemian Club the other week, and we went down to his studio on Montgomery Street, quite late, for a spaghetti dinner. A lot of guests showed up, more than he had expected. That's always the way at these studio affairs. So he got some boards, put them across trestles, boiled up some more paste, and thinned the bucket of sauce. We had quite a jolly time! It was rather a squeeze at the table, and Joullin ran out of glasses. We were shy five glasses when Mr. George Sterling, the poet, came in with Peter Jackson, the scrapper, and some pals, all pretty high.

"Joullin took off the shelf a half dozen cups, glazed earthenware, queer Egypt-looking things that should have been in a museum. With big handles to them. He soused them under the tap and filled them up. That gave the Dago red the ceremonial touch. We drank out of them.

"I wanted those cups. They would have set off any wine. But Joullin said No. And I couldn't budge him.

"'I'd like to oblige you,' he said. 'But they're Doctor Bisceglia's. He's the archaeologist who dug them in Pompeii. They're his tear-jars.'"

Hector stared, unhearing, into his cup. Then he glanced at the Duke and at Bascomb, the vine-farm sharp. They had averted their gaze. The look of the sherry was wrong. Too red, by far. And the taste was off. It was a planky and drab wine, with no secondary flavor, and too brief a spell of nuttiness. Three months of baking could not have pulled it up, for the grapes were short of the mark. What did Giorgio mean by saying they'd be turning out plenty more? Anger made Hector's hand tremble.

"That's what we can do with Alicante," he said, shifting his cheroot. "We tried port once, but the color broke. Won't do to tamper with color, put in cherry juice or aniline—we've never done that in this valley.

"But I think, with a two months' baking, we can run a sherry out of it for the colonists. They've got a lot of Alicante. I think we'll buy all they've got and work it up. First batch, five thousand gallons—a sample for the trade—and the tamale parlors—except the one Flores runs. Low-price goods, handsomely packaged. Chateau

Anaheim—or Schloss Anaheim." He swirled his glass. "A fair article—at four-bits the bottle?"

Hector despised the Alicante. Inwardly he raged. So that was what Giorgio had up his sleeve. The colonists might be helped, but at the cost of Montino—the Montino that Giorgio no longer owned, and that he, Hector, had begun replanting over to superior vines, and who would be injured unless the plan were nipped. He was sorry for the colonists, of course. Everyone in the valley had been helpful to them, sending over carts, plows, stock and lumber—and Montino itself had not been laggard in help.

"What d'you say, Blanqui?" asked Giorgio, his cigar raked, his eyes fixed benevolently on a Swiss farmer. "What d'you say?"

Blanqui, plainly dressed, his face stamped with furrows of rectitude, was the center of attention. He had never left the valley since his father brought him to it as a child. After laboring most of his life in the wineries he had acquired a whispered fame for the grapes he raised on a distant, rocky slope above the town.

"For the tamale trade," he said, "it's good, maybe. I wouldn't grow it. Not on my farm."

The Swiss was highly regarded. Port gave an inaudible whistle. The Utopian's turn was next. His gaze moved delicately about the room, saw the figures in the doorway and the watchful expression of Hector, who saw only the flash of his spectacles in the lamplight and stared at them as on a divining-crystal. He held his breath and waited. Giorgio shook out a match and wagged a questioning eyebrow at the Utopian.

"Signor Duke?"

Alda stood in the doorway. More faces were behind her intent; all voices hushed in the corridor. The Utopian, looking again at the son of Montino, that dull exterior with a glow behind it, tapped the ash off his cigar.

"Mr. Regola, it's far below the mark for the region. I'm of the opee-nion it would hurt Montino badly."

Giorgio's mouth twitched sardonically, he even chuckled. He was mettlesome, pig-stubborn, and to be opposed only heartened him. Hector knew that chuckle. Giorgio's decision was cut in adamant. There was one more play, and Hector took it. He pointed to the paper on the table, the thesis on the Pierce disease of vines, which the Duke had just read.

"You think, Mr. Liu, it would hurt Montino as bad as—that?"

"Infinitely worse, my friend."

Giorgio struck the table, then abruptly rose. The séance was over; it was like a séance that had ended with a murder. Alda hurried Cleve away; Giorgio strode out, thunder on his brow, and soon the house began to empty. Cleve wandered off with the dogs, went down the fields, and watched the carriages disappear up the road. He came back at dark, and Alda carried up a dinner for him to his room.

"It's a bit quieter here," she said, and then she read to him for an hour.

"Now you can go to bed. They're all going to bed. Everybody's tired."

The queer thing to Cleve was that everybody was staying up late. Doors slammed all through the house. He heard voices in the kitchen, a quarrel, and lifting the tin that covered the stovepipe hole in the floor, he peered down. Hector was at the table, having a late supper; Alda was sitting on the wood-box, stroking her lip, as was her manner when in thought.

"You tried to make a fool of me, eh?" shouted Giorgio in the doorway. "And right under the noses of those fellows! Well, you'll make that wine, I tell you. And save your hide, and save your farm. If you don't, you'll be glad to return some day with a blanket on your back and pick grapes with a gang."

Carola swept in, took his arm without trying to quiet him, and spoke peremptorily to Alda.

"I must ask you to leave for your room, Miss Pendle. We have family affairs to discuss."

Hector banged down his tumbler. "Alda Pendle stays right where she is. You can't order her about in my house."

"If you'll only listen to advice," said Carola, sharply, "we could—"

"Montino," said Hector, "happens to be mine. I am running it. Nobody can tell me how to run it, or what wine to make."

"If you're not altogether a fool," said Carola, "you'll listen to him and to me." The jet ornaments on her bosom quivered, she emanated outraged dignity. "You owe it to yourself, and you owe it to Montino."

Hector got up. "I owe it to Montino to do the best I can for it. I am growing grapes—and not for swill, neither. When I go into the pig business—which isn't yet—I will call upon you for advice."

A sound rattled in Giorgio's throat. Carola's hand rose slowly, her bosom heaving, and she plucked at her jet beads.

"Come, Father. It's late."

They left, a door slammed in the corridor. Hector filled his tumbler, revolved it on wet circles a moment, then laughed. On the wood-box Alda unfolded her arms, rubbed the back of her head, exchanged a glance with

Hector, and her teeth shone. Outside, the greyhounds were agitated. Cleve sprang up, threw open the window, and peered out. Something was afoot. He swung down by the branches of a madrone, and found the dogs with their muzzles under the fence. It was a toad. He groped, found a twig, and scratched its back. If scratched properly, he had been told, a toad would swell like a balloon, or a puff-ball, and float off on the breeze. The dogs sat back, respectfully; it was the most extraordinary event in their green young lives. This toad blew itself up, twice its size, but instead of floating, it lobbed into some grass, and though Cleve and the dogs hunted for quite a long time, by matchlight, it was lost.

Cleve slept late, awoke to find the house quiet, and the morning, on the whole, was the most unpleasant he had ever lived through. Vic, hands in pockets, stayed out on the terrace, stared at him, and turned away, whistling. Hector, as soon as breakfast was over in the kitchen, left and kept remote in the winery. At the other end of the house was bustle. Carola was directing the packing, and took no notice of him, but since Cleve had never cared for her, it was not mortifying.

Towards noon Hector hitched Chess and Ring, their coats shining after a rub with a cloth dipped in kerosene, which gave them a very fine appearance, and brought the team around to the terrace. It was a quiet drive down to the station, no one saying anything until they came to the farewells on the platform. Carola saw to the tickets, and kept Vic with her. Hector waited on the seat of the wagonette.

Cleve walked up and down with Giorgio. "You come and see me, Cleve," he said, "and don't wait too long. If you bump into that guy named Port, you tell him something for me, eh? You tell him, 'Giorgio says he'll not forget to tip you off about the big mill.' Do that, eh?"

"I'll tell him."

Then Giorgio gave him two cartwheel dollars. "One for each pocket. Ballast. You'll earn some for yourself some day. Won't do you much good until then. You've got to start from scratch, like everybody else."

The train came, the Regolas piled in, and he shouted a goodbye. With a hissing of steam the train moved, gathered velocity, then slammed round the curve. It diminished, but he could see Giorgio, gripping to the brass of the car platform, waving until he was whisked out of sight. Cleve's own arm was fatigued from waving, and he wondered how long it would be before he could visit the city.

"Well, they're gone?" asked Hector, as Cleve came to the wagonette. "Climb up, we'll go for a ride."

They drove into town, to the stores. "You stay here a while," Hector said. "I won't be long."

He got down, sauntered ahead in his best suit, paused before the window of a jewelry shop, then entered. It took him a while to find a ring that he knew she would like—a solid and plain gold band. He emerged, after looking up and down the street, and returned to the wagonette. They went on towards Montino. The spring air was diamond-clear, the sky over St. Helena Range was green, the chaparral and madrones still greener. The hillside vineyards, even the largest, were like patches of clearing in a wild and dense forest. Hector hummed a scrap of old song:

> *"Ti darò l'anello*
> *Del mio primo a-mor."*

An uprush of spirits, engendered by the loveliness of the day, must have gone to his head. He drove with feet on the dashboard, his hat slanted over his eyes. Pot-hunters were out on the slope, far up and invisible. Cleve could hear the whacketing of guns, the "pa-tup" of echoes, and saw the tiny whorls of smoke; but Hector saw nothing, and kept on humming his tune.

"Easy there, Chess," he said, hauling on the lines. "No hurry, old Chess. There's nobody working today."

They drove up by the near road, which was full of bumps, and led directly up to the winery. There he tied the ponies to a post, listened a moment to the thumping of a mallet, then went in. Cleve followed him into the shadows, through rows of vats and storage ovals. At the end was Port tightening iron buckles. The cooperage was dry and sprung from long disuse.

"Been here since noon," said Port, aggrieved, "and nobody around." He was wet, and standing amid coils of dripping hose. "I had a time finding the damn ladders. Where's Giorgio? Told him I'd be around at noon sharp."

"We just saw him go on the train," said Cleve. "And I've got a message for you. Giorgio says he'll tip you off about the mill."

"He did? He say anything more?"

"No, only that. You going to a flour mill?"

"Fighting mill," said Port. "Dunno where or when. But I'm going."

"Can I go with you, Port?"

"Guess so. Way it looks now, you'll be old enough."

Port fetched the container a sound rap with his mallet. The ovals were like two rows of elephants, engirded with bands locked by screw-buckles. It was cooperage that had

106

come knocked-down from Spain, and Port, as head cooper for Montino, had put it together in the days when the farm was making Comet.

"A week's soaking, and they'll be as tight as tight. Then we'll give 'em a lick of spar varnish."

"Port," said Hector, "you can give them vats another rest. We're not going to make that sherry."

Port gave him a long squint, with one eye shut. "We ain't?" He grunted, and not with disfavor. "You gave yourself a break for once," he said, throwing down his mallet. "I won't say I didn't see it coming."

They strolled out into the sunlight where they talked. Port gave Hector a clump on the shoulder, and they shook hands.

"I'll take him. I've got to see Rupe over to Soda Springs, anyway, for another look at that mare he bought. They sold Rupe a plug, all right! You come along, Cleve, and we'll see that mare. Might as well start now if we're going to the Springs."

Port and Cleve got into the sulky.

"Don't let him take no wooden nickels, Cleve," said Hector, as the horse bolted off.

It was a sight to watch the pacer taking those bumps down the back road, at an electric pace, feet going over them at a slant, like a mosquito's. Behind his shop near Flores' tamale parlor, he had a stable and kennel of his own. He knew animals, and would knock off work any day to appraise anything that purported to be a dog or a horse worth looking at. Usually on these trips he took Cleve along, and together they covered a lot of territory, often going over to Livermore, or down to the racing stables at Pleasanton. It was good for a lad to be in with somebody like Port. Dogs and horses first; then vines. You get the feel for breeding in creatures, and you can't miss your way in plants.

Hector dragged out the wagonette, brushed it out, polished it with a chamois, and folded a rug on the seat. He hitched up the gray, drove on to the villa, then went into the kitchen. Alda was ironing a waist. He sat down by the open window, elbow on the sill, watching her hands, her lithe movements, the easy, outdoor grace she had brought into the house from the fields. Montino was quiet. The dogs were asleep. In the yard the belled Mike was gobbling.

"It's mighty peaceful now. Cleve went on to Soda Springs with Port. Nobody around but us."

"Wing's gone, too," she said. "He had to visit a cousin, and he'll be back in two days. He wanted Cleve to keep an eye on Mike."

"He did? I never knew a turkey that couldn't look after itself pretty well for two days. Wing had a carpet bag and an umbrella?"

"Yes."

"Then he'll be home dead-broke in two weeks. He was due for a spell of fan-tan in the city. Wanted a rest, too. Company was too much for him, I guess."

"Your folks, they caught the train all right?"

"They went," he said briefly.

"You're not grieving too much about your father, are you?" she asked, pressing out her hair ribbon.

"I wasn't thinking of anything but our holiday. Our wedding. I've got it all planned. Ring and everything. After we leave the Rectory we'll drive on to the Geysers, and then come back in time for dinner at Flores'. If it was summer we'd go to the dance at Hunt's Grove. But it isn't summer, it's spring. And maybe"—he grinned, with pipe in his teeth—"maybe Flores will be fixing up a dance for us."

"For us!" She looked at him proudly as she untied her apron. "A dance! Now, isn't that a big surprise!"

She gave him a hug, then ran upstairs with her fresh waist and ribbon. In half an hour they were driving down to the Rectory.

All day the house was silent, with the dogs over at the gate, whining. When Port and Cleve came to the turn in the highway long after dusk had fallen, they saw that Montino was dark.

"Just nobody around," said Port. "Nobody. It's been a while since anything like that happened here. We'll go straight on to the house."

A leaf of copy paper was pinned on the back door. Port, donning his spectacles, held up the lantern, and read aloud.

"You come down to the tamale parlor. We're having a wedding dinner and a dance. Port, come as you are."

"A wedding?" asked Cleve. "Who's getting married?"

"Him." Port looked again at the note, dazed. He plucked it down and turned it over. "Him—and—Alda. Yes, sir! They went and got themselves married."

"What did they get married for?" asked Cleve.

"Oh, everybody does—some time or other." Port looked down ruefully at his clothes. "Don't know how I can go like this. Looking rough." He ding-donged under his breath. "No, I'm going to dress up. Couldn't go to a Montino folks' wedding like this. We better be going right now."

The greyhounds yelped and fawned about Cleve.

"Can we take them along?"

"Sure! They've never been to the town yet. And there's

some fellows," Port said, lifting the pups into the ring, "would like to have a look at them. But that killer—he stays to home."

Lobo sat up, paws lifted, expression melting. He sat like an angel mourning in a cloud. Cleve looked back twice to watch him at the gate, his garnet-red eyes burning through the mist. But in the town Cleve made a triumphal parade from one haunt to another. At Lum Yat's grocery, where he got a pocketful of lichi nuts, the three livery stables, the Europa Hotel, and Banks harness shop, the pups were appraised as wonders. Port knew all the connoisseurs, all the right places to visit. Apart from being the doyen of coopers in St. Helena, who called all winegrowers by their first names, and knew before anyone else when jobs were to be doled out, he was the town oracle on sporting events. As a consequence, Cleve was made much over.

"Picked them dogs out himself, he did," Port told everyone. "A born judge of pups. He's a side-kick of Giorgio Regola, too. And when that Hayes-Kanski mill comes off, he's going to it with Giorgio. No, we're not saying just now when's the date. Come along, Cleve. We're going to the shop."

In the shop Port reaped his jaw smooth at a bit of glass over the tap. He changed into his Sunday clothes and put on a tie, violet with pink dots. Meanwhile Cleve and the pups prowled through the shop, and found tools and curious woods to look at.

"We're going soon," Port said. He groped under the bench. "I got to bring along my present."

On the bench he set a small cask, and dusted it off. It was of perfect flowing shape: putty-green wood, with veinings, glazed with transparent fiddle varnish. The hoops had been pounded down red-hot. He had made it by hand of staves of old eucalyptus wood, the home divinely appointed for apricot brandy, which lent it the complexity and redolence of Certosa. In all California there were but five such kegs, and all had taken shape under his crafty hands. At his forge he heated irons and burned on the cask an A and an R.

"Alda Regola," he said. "By ordinary I stamp my name when I finish a cask or a vat. But not on fancy coopery. Those that know it—and I don't know more'n ten—will know where this came from."

Shouldering it, he set out with Cleve and the pups, and they went into the tamale parlor, which was just in front of the shop. Flores' establishment was really a tavern, but since there were many taverns he called it a tamale parlor, and his Mexican clients had made it instantly prosperous. Flores, though, was a Portuguese. He was vast-paunched, unshaven, with a hurricane voice and a gap in his snag teeth. He was a friend of Montino, a sherry blender by trade, still called in by the wineries; his aspect was piratical, his kindness unbelievable.

"Halloo, Port!" His greeting blasted through the din of the mob and the accordions. "Come right in! I got seats for you!"

He leaned over the bar in his red undershirt and lowered a paw at Cleve.

"Boy at Montino, eh? I know them pups."

"That's Mister Flores, Cleve," said Port as the two shook hands. "You got to watch out for him. He's a no-account hoodlum just one jump ahead of the Sheriff. You keep them pups behind the bar, Flores."

"Sure!" boomed Flores.

He filled glasses, unhooked an olla from the wall, a jar

with a spout, held it high, threw back his head, and directed a stream of wine into the gap between his teeth. Cleve looked on fascinated.

"Hector, he's over there," said Flores, drawing a hairy fist over his mouth, and pointing to a booth beyond the mob of dancers. "Mrs. Regola, too. Concha!" He bellowed, and the Indian girl came over. "You bring them dinner!"

"Listen," said Port.

The two men lowered their heads over the bar. They spoke mysteriously, with glances at the space under the bar mirror. It was cluttered with chunks of ore, volcanic tufa, asbestos and wood from the Petrified Forest, like agate or streaked ice; freak roots, lumps of ginseng, deer horns, and rusty horseshoes. Interspersed were bottles. Underneath, in the locked cabinet, were more bottles. Flores pawed among them and brought out a few, tenderly. Behind them was a bottle he lifted out with unusual care, as if it were an egg. He withdrew the cork. With eye set hard, as if aiming a rifle at a nail, he put the cork to his nose. Then his eye softened. The two men breathed over the bottle. It was an amber wine, with the delicate odor of violets grown on a crag of flint. They could not remember the summer when the grapes of a certain field yielded a wine that struck the purest note in the litany of the pre-phylloxera wines of the valley. The one had been elsewhere, the other had not left Lisbon. It was a phenomenon as transitory as a blink of August lightning, and it had not happened twice.

"That's it," said Port. "You'll bring it over."

Flores set the bottle among his rocks and laid a visiting-card over the mouth.

"She breathe here little while." He looked at the crowd

112

dancing in the blue-washed cave of his inn, jammed to-gether, merry and tumultuous. It would take force and the bulk of a rhino to carry the delicate lady through without a bump. "I carry her," he said.

The booth was hung with paper garlands, and Cleve sat in, wedged between Port and Alda. This was an island of especial jollity. Alda had a flower in her hair; Hector a green silk handkerchief and two cigars stuck in his breast pocket. Sometimes they danced, but not often; too many friends tacked in to felicitate them. More guests arrived, some by tally-ho, most of them, Swiss-Italian vineyardists, afoot. When things quieted a little, those in the booth pro-ceeded with the solider part of the dinner. Flores ushered in the bottle. He stood there as Port poured the wine into thin fresh glasses.

Hector looked at it. He was quick-scented, he caught the aroma before it filled the booth, then he bent his head over the glass.

"Where," he demanded, "where did you get this? It's not the—"

He rose, as if touched by a wire. But the others, and Cleve, their glasses upraised, were already on their feet. His eyes misted.

"The Regolberg!" he shouted.

"To the Regolas!" boomed Flores. "And Montino!" said Port.

It was a double toast, and one to be drunk slowly; then there was a babbling, then laughter and the accordionists, in Tyrolean garb, climbed upon tables and pumped oceans of music over their heads. Flores gave a lion's roar. The bottles and cutlery were lifted; tablecloths were ripped off: on the floor tumbled the paper plates with scraps of salad, crusts, fish-heads, other remnants—upon which the waiters swooped with brooms, to push over the floor, and leave it beautifully oiled from end to end. Then the real fun began; dancing that the men, coats off, had to put their hearts and backs into, clacking their hobnailed boots, swinging their ladies, most of them a healthy weight, in gavottes, quadrilles, and barn-measures. Cleve thought the music would never stop for good. All that kept him awake was the fascination of watching Port, who had one hoppitty step that would have kept him in one place if it hadn't been for the pressure and clattering of the other dancers who pushed him about.

About midnight Port led him into the coopery shop, and there on the cot, after listening a while to the brassy wailing of the accordions, he curled up and slept with the greyhounds.

7.

ON THE verge of their second harvesting, the Zinfandels were now four years old and the trellis work, as high as the pergola, was hidden by leafage and rambling cane. The grapes under their overlay of red dust were an opalescent blue. Everywhere in the tract, though the windbreaks of olive trees were dense, they were as mature as if all had ripened in unbroken sunshine. Cleve, with a basket on his shoulder, plodded through the soft, dry earth, gathering samples. Behind the wall came a pattering of hoofs.

"Where are you, Cleve?"

"Here. The gully side!"

Next moment the pony lolloped in, Jule on his back, hair flying.

"Lobo's asleep, as usual. Where are the greyhounds?"

"Hunting on their own hook." He listened. "In the next alley, and they'll be here in no time. Count thirty."

Jule counted thirty, gabbling so fast that she had to begin over again. The dogs had been trained so once they got started they went like clockwork, weaving in and out through the patch.

"Here they come," she shouted. "Flora! Coy!"

The dogs spun into the avenue. Flora paused, to thrust a muzzle into foliage and snuff quarry. A rabbit streaked out, twanged against a hidden wire, spun back, then tore off, the dogs in chase. Jule, drumming her heels, pelted after them. That was Cleve's chore, keeping the vineyard free of rabbits, but she helped him, and she rode fully as well. They both had ponies, twins, which Port had got for them at Soda Springs, and Cleve looked after them, saddling Jule's for her every morning, ready for them to set off to school together.

They were almost inseparable. Evenings, she was at the villa, or he was up at the Lane house, and they worked their lessons under the same lamp. Their tastes varied; she read more, he preferred drawing, and what he earned at hunting rabbits he spent in tints and brushes at Lum Yat's shop. He groomed her pony, and she relieved him at taking the greyhounds on their run through the field. He disliked hunting. Whenever there was a kill, with the beating of wings or the scream of a rabbit, he rode on without turning his head.

Lobo, the pampered watchman, no longer hunted. The greyhounds, who were adult now and no longer coddled, had to catch their dinner in mid-air, like birds.

This was the work Cleve preferred, gathering samples. It was still hot in late afternoon, the heat lifting in hoops and waves, the day steeped in the haze and mellowness of early September, the upland in shifting planes of gold, with purple wash in the hollows. He loved the odor of foliage and the sharp reek of grapes fallen and buzzed over by the wasps. As he picked he heard a rattle, like the chatter of a toy sewing-machine. Rattlesnakes were few this summer, and nobody at Montino, except the dogs, gave them much thought. They had always left him alone, even as a child, when he crawled into their green leafy caves to sleep in the heat of mid-day. They were used to him, per-

116

haps; he had always worn high leather boots when in the vineyard, and Wing had riveted a pair of bells to his suspenders. Rattlesnakes hated bells.

Cleve groped in the vines where the shade was thickest and plucked a small cluster. Its framework was a light straw color, and at the point, where a cluster is greenest, he chose a berry for tasting. It was sweet. He cut off the bunch with his knife, put on a tag, marked it, and moved on up to the winery, basket on his shoulder. Three days more, and the Zinfandels Alda had planted when she came to Montino would be ready for their first large harvest —the earliest vines of all to ripen this season.

Hector lounged in the doorway of the winery, arms folded, talking with Alda, who was in a chair under the shade of a mandrone, sewing. On an up-ended box in the sunlight sat Wing, in a coolie hat, half asleep, nursing a long pipe at his lips.

"Look at the blue mouth coming," said Alda. "How many grapes you tried, Cleve?"

"Oh, ten maybe, or twelve. But I spit them out quick."

"Four's plenty," Alda said, threading her needle. "You get all puckered up. You can't tell honey from vinegar after four bites."

"They look ripe to me," said Hector, lifting off the basket. It was a load. "Fellow's strong like a horse. Now we'll try 'em out."

He pushed the basket through the window, and went around to his laboratory. The grapes he mashed up, then emptied the pulp on a square of cheesecloth stretched over a pail, and pressed it gently.

"There you are."

Cleve poured the liquid into a tube and slid in the hydrometer. He droned the reading, picked up an end of pencil and made subtractions. Hector looked on, wiping his hands. He was slow at figures. He did all the rough work; Alda looked after the managing, and Cleve did the figuring for her in the laboratory.

"Nineteen," said Hector. "Was eighteen yesterday. Climbing. Hey, Wing!"

The Chinaman trod to the window and looked in.

"Nineteen by the mark," Hector said. "Ready to pick."

Science meant nothing to Wing; only the look and taste of things mattered. A week before he had looked at the grapes, and they seemed green. The twigs of the cluster he fingered at the window were yellow, the consequence of a sudden heat that had been as unpredictable as life itself. Heat with a night fog, he remembered. He plucked a grape, and though plump, its skin shirred. He looked into the vineyard, blew out a wisp of smoke, and nodded.

"We pick-um to-mollow."

"Guess we're the first to ripen on the slope," said Alda.

Jule dashed up on the pony, the greyhounds after her, their tongues lolling, and she flung herself off, breathless.

"Wasn't a rabbit anywhere. All scared out. You're coming up tonight, aren't you, Cleve? Isn't any school tomorrow, and you can stay late. Can't he, Hector?"

"Not terrible late," said Hector. "We're picking at sun-up, and he's got to have an early start. But you can both ride down to Lum Yat's, and tell him we need pickers."

"Aunt Marthe won't let me ride after dark."

"You can walk, then. Go along down with Wing."

"Fine! There's a moon, too," said Jule and she walked on with Alda, who had dinner to prepare.

Sometimes Jule dined at the villa, as if she were part of

the Montino family. Once a day, at least, she and Cleve played duets on the piano. The Regolas lived mostly in their large kitchen, which was kept warm at evening with an armful of twigs in the fireplace, and comfortable to study in, by the globular red lamp, Alda sewing as the boy and the girl read aloud, did sums or their history lessons. Less frequently, Cleve dined up at the Lanes'. Miss Lane approved of Cleve, thought him neat, reasonably intelligent, and was pleased, since they were neighbors, that the two got along well together. As for Alda and Hector, she saw less and less of them after their marriage, and had, indeed, called upon them only once.

The chimney at the villa lipped smoke. Stars prinked through the blue dusk. Cleve hung about at the winery, watching the flights of owls, and listening to the sparse talk of the men.

"All ready to be picked at one time," said Hector. "Aren't many small ones. They're running big. You could durn near pick any cluster blindfold, put it in a bottle of spirits, and it'd take something at the County Fair. Berries would look bigger'n crab apples. We're not going to, though. Alda's put aside that vine of Rish Babas for that."

The Rish Babas were undeniably huge. Alda had ringed their trunk and slipped off the narrowest possible strip of bark, the wound bridged over now, but not before the mounting sap, unable to flow back, had set the clusters handsomely.

Wing was thinking of something else, walking up and down in the dusk, hands clasped behind.

Cleve often found himself wondering how the Chinaman managed to dispense with all utterance in the course of a day, even when he was deep in the concerns of the vineyard. It was as if he thought the vines spoke all that one need hear or utter: with fluttering of leaves, lush, fog-damp, or paper-dry; with their looks, or the crackling of joints as the canes reached or strained for the trellis. And Wing, who had been at Montino for forty years, listened to these voices, and asked few questions of anyone. He plucked another grape from the basket at the window, and contemplated it, looking in the dusk with his coolie hat like an immense mushroom.

"Make-um good wine," he said.

"Good for what it is. But this side of fine."

Wing ate the grape, dust and all, and strolled on with Hector.

"Why you glow-um?"

"Money crop."

"Gamay, Chablis, good too."

"Zinfandel's the best we can do on that field," Hector said. If only he had that field across the fence! He turned to look at it in the twilight, and Wing followed his glance.

"That field," said Wing, "good fo' Pinot."

A pause, then Hector gave a low whistle, and grinned.

"So you knew that too, eh?"

"I know long time."

Wing turned for home, the brass bowl of his pipe glowing. Later, Hector and Cleve went to the house. Alda, in a starched apron, her hair done in braids, helped the dinner, which was beef in an earthen dish, salad in a wooden bowl, bread sticks, and claret. Hector ate in shirtsleeves, elbows propped on the oilcloth. They had drifted into a plain, solid, peasant-like way of living. When they dined out at all, it was at Flores' place, or with their Swiss-Italian friends.

"That was a queer thing happened to me when I was

out there with the Chinaman," said Hector, holding the cup in both hands. "We got talking about grapes, and I was thinking of Pinots. He didn't say anything. You never know what's going on in his head. Well, he turned and pointed across the fence, right into that stony pasture. And there was the whole hillside to pick from, too. It wasn't a field anybody'd pick out, unless he wanted to start a quarry, or he knew something."

"What was queer about that?"

"He said, 'Good for Pinots.'"

"You reckon you can buy that field some day?"

"Small chance. It'll run into money, if the Lanes ever did think of selling it. They never sold any land, not even in hard times. But I could grow Pinots there; very tall, on poles, so they'd shade over and protect the fruit from sunburn. I'd make a Burgundy."

"They'd grow well, you think?"

"They did once." Hector gave a laugh. "The Regolberg grew there."

"What did it look like?" asked Cleve.

"Draggled. Like a measly bunch of currants. A sparrow wouldn't look at it twice. Wasn't a grape you'd pick for looks"—he gave Alda a thump on the back—"like a woman, or a horse. But it was a Chardonnay White Pinot, kind of."

"Maybe there'll be another like it," said Alda.

"I don't know."

Cleve was copying a dragon from a label on a packet of fire-crackers. He drew on large sheets of paper—wrapping paper that Hector saved for him—drew with a bold line, and colored luridly with brushes dipped in black, red, and yellow tints. Wing and he were to build a huge kite that Wing was to fly against Lum Yat's, and they had got together a pile of bamboo splints and wires from old umbrella frames. Hector, rocking himself back and forth, arms folded, as was his way in his outpourings of slow talk with Alda, kept half an eye on him. He was proud of the boy's talent in drawing, fostered it in many ways, and even burned vine twigs to make charcoal for him.

"What Father did wasn't any more than we could do here, if we had a mind to," Alda was saying. She had fetched her sewing to the table. "You cross and cut and graft. Then you cut and graft and cross again. Patience. You go as far as you can, then a flash comes, and you try something you never thought of before. And you get something quite new, what you've been looking for."

"Like a royal flush," grinned Hector, "or falling in the creek and coming up with trouts in your boots."

Pulling out the drawer, he groped and took out a tin box. It was full of letters, congressmen's packets of seeds, bits of wood, bird skulls, herbs, and dance tickets. A notebook made of four envelopes held with a pin was covered with faded writing. He murmured, ran his eye through the notes, and read aloud:

"Rupestris St. Geo. 3BX Chardonnay, recross Oxhill Vitis B, = Pendle White."

He rubbed his chin. "That was the Regolberg strain. I dunno who wrote it down. Something must have been dropped out. Some X or other. But it didn't work with me, nor anyone else."

He pushed the tin back and closed the drawer. "Freaks like the Regolberg don't happen twice." He smiled. "When I was a little fellow, Lane was clearing that barley field uphill. His China plowboy found a rabbit limp by a madrone stump with its neck busted.

122

"That China boy, he wrapped himself up and camped near that stump every night for a month, damn near freezing, to wait for another rabbit to run head on and bust its fool neck."

"Did it?" asked Cleve.

"Not exactly. His luck had run out."

Jule was calling outside.

"Coming!" shouted Cleve, and pulled on his coat. "You want anything from the shops, Mother?"

"You bring me a dime's worth of yeast. And some smoking for Hector."

"Old Lumberjack Plug," said Hector. "Don't let them hold back the coupons on you. There's a dollar. You better hurry."

Cleve, with a candle lantern, joined the girl down the path; Wing followed them like a shadow. It was late, and when they arrived at the shop it was smoke-filled, for Lum Yat's was also a clubhouse for the few Chinese workmen remaining in the district. Wing spoke. Lum Yat, bowed over his accounts, lifted up a golden moon of a face hung with spectacles and etched with a sparse moustache. His answering was keen, sure, and voluble. Cleve heard the names of other vineyards. Some difficulty had cropped up. Other farms likewise were gathering, and help had been bespoken. Wing was peremptory, and even more voluble. With brush held poised above the inkpot, Lum Yat peered over his glasses and spoke at the workmen. Responses came through the smoke, and Wing nodded, satisfied.

"Boy want paint," said Wing, lapsing into English. "Paint fo' dlagon."

Lum Yat, without getting up, slid a dozen cans of paint over the counter. Cleve was surprised. It was car-

123

riage paint, all colors, and wouldn't drip off in rain. He picked five tins, bought the yeast and the tobacco, not forgetting the coupons, and the three trudged on homeward.

"You're using all that for the kite?" asked Jule. "Is it that big?"

"It's too big for Wing's shack. We're going to build it in the old stable, where the turkeys roost."

"I'm going to fly it, aren't I?"

"You'll have to grow some. It'll pull you up like the roc in the *Arabian Nights*. It's Wing's anyway. But you can ask him in March, at the kite-fly."

In the darkness by the gate, the three dogs merged with them, and when Cleve went into the house, continued up the path with Wing and Jule. Hector and Alda were still at the table.

"Look! Paints for the dragon. Wing bought them."

"He'll sure go broke," said Hector. "Did you get the help?"

"They'll be here. Other vineyards are picking, and Wing had to coax Lum Yat. We almost didn't get any help."

"We'd get it," laughed Hector. "Lum Yat used to be boss for the Lanes. He's hillside. Hillside men stick together. He just likes to be coaxed."

Cleve went upstairs with his paraphernalia. He moved about quietly, glueing the paper, which was stiff and cut in the form of scales. He laid the paint on thickly, in lozenges, with green and yellow borders. The thicker the paint, the stronger the dragon; and when it was all built, in three or four months, it would be armored with shellac and broken-up glass. The room was full of paint vapor. He opened the window, and the candles blew out. Somewhere, far out towards the winery, he thought he heard a bark. The vineyard was a blackness; he could see only the tops of the madrones swaying against the stars. Somebody was afoot. He heard the dogs moving on the trot, then hung over the sill. No stranger ever approached the house from the winery this time of night.

A match flared, and in the brief moment before it went out, he had the glimpse of a man lighting his pipe. After a rap at the door, Port went in. Though a frequent visitor at Montino, it was not often that he came at so late an hour. Cleve lifted the pipe-hole cover, and applied his ear, but the voices were at the end of the kitchen, and low.

"Never missed the first crushing day yet at Montino," Port was saying. "And I'll be up early. But we got to be pulling out at ten. You told Cleve?"

"He's asleep now. We'll tell him in the morning," Hector said.

"Isn't what I'd like him to go to, a match. And it's a long drive," Alda said urgently.

"I've been promising him," Port said, "and only now I got word there was to be this match. Comes at a bad time, what with the crushing and all. But I got to go to that match. I've been holding stakes for some fellows in the village. They don't even know the match is coming off. They won't, until it's over."

"I ought to have some time to think," Alda demurred.

"Pretty late to be thinking now," Hector said, his pipe gurgling. "He promised Cleve he could go. A day off in the picking won't hurt him. Do him good to go out with Port."

There was more such talk. His ear flat to the cover, Cleve gathered up what scraps he could. But they had lowered their voices. What match was it? Why were they so guarded? Soon Port left, and Cleve turned in. Could it—could it, he wondered—be the fighting mill, about which Giorgio had promised to tip Port off?

It was still dark when Alda came up with the lamp and woke him. He sat up, yawning, and reached for his clothes.

"You're going with Port at noon, on a trip," she said. "There's a match. He came up last night to see if you could go along."

"Port always said he'd take me some time."

"Don't know when you'll be back, so you'd better practice right now. Just go twice through the pages I'll lay out."

He went sleepily downstairs, into Giorgio's den, and propped himself at the piano. Two candles were burning in the holders over the keyboard; and he romped through the sheets of "Myosotis" spread on the. rack. The banging woke him completely. He felt he was playing better than usual. Or perhaps it was that the piano was in such perfect tune. Every three months the tuner came up from Napa City, worked on it an hour or two, and shook his head whenever Alda asked him about his fee. That matter was taken care of, he said. She had her own notion who kept the fees paid. He was the most expensive tuner thereabouts, as she very well knew, and so the piano was in admirable tone, better than Miss Lane's.

The discipline over, Cleve went into the kitchen, swallowed his hot milk, and dashed out into the vineyard. The purple air was lightening; ghosts appeared, in pigtails and slippers, and began to grope among the swatches of foliage. It puzzled Cleve how they could see at all; but

126

they did, their shears clicking, the clusters dropping fast into the lug-boxes.

"Here's your wagon," said Port, driving up Chess and Ring. "You take over now. It's after four already."

Cleve hadn't much to do except drive the loaded wagon to the press, and return for another load. The boxes grew wetter and more stained at each trip. At the press, Wing and two of the farmers from the colony—refugees from Anaheim—emptied the grapes into a steamer, then into the mill. Port, waddling about crab-wise, with a battered silk hat, to save his head from being dashed against the pipes, kept watch at the crusher. It was a ceremony with him to help with the first run of grapes at Montino.

"Cool," said Hector, feeling the pipes. "Nothing like an early start if you're working for the dry. Juice won't start working until noon."

Flores came up, with his wife and daughter. The women joined Alda, Concha, and Jule, who went into the field with their baskets. Hour after hour the sun god, loosening his spears, drove his chariot across the glazed and cloudless blue of the sky. The heat grew, as if fed from the bowl of the valley, seething with invisible flames. Not a bird hovered in the inert air; the doves mourned plaintively in the olive trees. The women called and talked from under their sun-bonnets. The greyhounds coursed in and out of the avenues, mechanically, like toys that had been wound up for the day, their feet stirring up clouds of reddish dust. At intervals the laborers yowled a song, like a lullaby of fatigued mothers, but their voices were cheerful, as if the heat woke a vigor in their bones. When thirsty, they unslung gourds and sloshed cold tea down their throats.

127

Port gave a signal when Cleve brought in a load an hour before noon. "We're going now," he said. They put on other hats and coats, and got into the sulky. He had Augustus, his pacer, all groomed, with knee pads, in the shafts, and unobserved they whisked off, going through the town's back streets, and once again on the main road they tore at racing speed. Port, when driving fast, had the mind-workings of a horse: he was silent, as if the business of covering ground were too serious an affair for the frivolity of talk.

Beyond Napa City, where they rested a while, they went slower, and Augustus was not heated when he moved into the region of the fog. Sniffing meadow grass and the salt of tidewater, the pacer neighed. Port looked at his watch, then at the Carquinez Straits, smooth and jet beyond the lumber piles, a glossy-black plane exhaling a gouache of thin mist. Dust and paper blew about in a boisterous and cool wind that would be sharper on the Straits. No vehicles were around, no passers-by.

"It's yonder," said he, pointing. "Over towards Suisun, far out."

"The wrestling?" asked Cleve.

"Hayes-Kanski fight. Barge out on midstream, I guess. And we're making it in time. Good thing I was in the shop when Giorgio's wire came. In Dutch talk it was: 'Hay and cattle on board off Vallejo. Take lumberyard buggy.' Had a job making it out, too. It's on the q.t., with police on the hunt. Ought to be a scrap worth getting pinched to look at."

Cleve looked at Port with respect. "You think we'll go to jail?"

"Not likely," chuckled Port. "At the worst we'd only have to swim a half mile."

A dozen wagonettes and rigs were tied up at the lumberyard wharf, the pacer was yoked to a post, and at the naphtha launch Port showed his telegram. The skipper let them aboard, among the twenty passengers sitting chilled and disconsolate, with collars turned up. They had been waiting for an hour. Some of them were drinking beer and eating sandwiches, others reading newspapers or arguing.

"Who d'you know at the Club?" asked the skipper.

"Peter Jackson," said Port, "and Giorgio Regola."

"The Senator?" murmured the skipper. Giorgio Regola was a name, but few people had seen him; he was almost as little known as God, and it was as if his power derived largely from his invisibility. The skipper was doubtful, but impressed.

"Can't take a chance on these telegrams," he said darkly. "Names are on the list all right, but I don't know if they belong to those that give them."

A journalist from Sacramento, muffled to the ears, his cigar fraying in the wind, looked over the choppy water and growled.

"Anybody give a damn who's who on the Styx? I'll vouch for these gentlemen! They're the Benicia Boy and the Marquis of Queensbury. Friends of my aunt. Looks like they're passengers now on Lotta's Fountain. Show us a bit of speed now, Mister Skipper Charon."

The engine sputtered, and the boat went out. It was an uncomfortable voyage, in swirling tide, the passengers swearing, the skipper growing more truculent. Cleve, for all his horrid anticipations of a jail cell, was relieved when the launch nosed into the barge anchored out in midstream. The passengers handed over their fares and scrambled up the drop ladder to the bulwark. On the deck was a square marked off by a fence of rope. The barge was thronged with spectators, about two hundred, half of them rough-looking, in bowler hats and sweaters, the other half in fur-lined coats.

"Tar Flat lads," said Port, knowingly. "Kanski's crowd. Quiet, too. It'll be a scrap all right!" He espied a cheroot waved at them from the other side of the boat. "Hullo, there's Giorgio!"

Giorgio came over to them from the nobs, and shook hands.

"Been looking for you two. Glad you made it. Good crowd for an undercover fight. Purse is for two thousand." He lowered his voice. "And Hayes—he's in form. Well, Port, what's new in the valley?"

The wind was boisterous, and holding to their hats the two elders moved to shelter behind the cabin. Cleve sat behind the companion ladder, on a box, with cap between his knees, looking out towards the shore a half mile away. The tide was running deep and black, and riffled with white. A door in the lower cabin, against which he sat, opened. A man in jersey emerged, stood a moment cautiously, then laid a pair of boxing gloves on the gunwale and tightened up his belt. It was careless of him, but he dislodged the gloves and they dropped overboard. In the wind they could have fallen with no more than a blob of sound. But Cleve heard a splash, as if they had been weighted with iron.

"Oh, damn that!" he muttered, between an oath and laugh, as another man came out. This was a fighter in trunks. "Dropped your gloves, Kanski!"

"Forget them, Gus," said the fighter, the muscles on his back shifting like anacondas.

Nobody else heard the colloquy, because of the squalling of the gulls and the hubbub as Hayes stepped into the ring. He was slighter than Kanski, less dark, with roached-up hair and the light foot of a dancer. That was the bank clerk. The other was the rolling-mill boss. The man in jersey stepped next inside the ropes and paced the ring, measuring it. Cleve went forward, with Port and Giorgio.

"Kanski's second," said Giorgio.

"Looks like a Tar Flatter to me," said Port.

"Right!"

Kanski got into the ring, with hands bare. There was confusion, talk was flurried in the wind, and the crowd surged nearer the ropes.

"The articles," Hayes was insisting gently, "call for six-ounce gloves. Here are mine. Where are Mr. Kanski's?"

He held up his gloves. His hand was crisscrossed with plaster, the skin green, as from a bruise.

"Broke it in training, he did," whispered Port to Cleve. "He'd be a fool to go in with bare maulies."

"Where are Mr. Kanski's?" asked Hayes again, speaking for himself and his second.

"Lost them," said the man in jersey, sheepishly. "They fell in the water."

"Then another pair must be produced," said Hayes, "or I shall be declared winner by default. That so, Mr. Referee?"

Murmurs and a sinister yell or two rose from the crowd on the starboard side of the barge. The referee looked over the crowd, thought in a tense silence, then frowned.

"About right, I guess." He turned to Kanski's second. "Kanski's got to wear gloves."

"They're down the river," muttered the second. "We've got no more."

Hayes was unperturbed. "I'm giving you two minutes to glove your man. Or else the purse will be forfeit to me."

Giorgio stepped to the ring, lifted a hand, then pulled off his lined, dogskin gloves. All eyes turned upon him as he held them out.

"Mr. Kanski will put these on and fight with them," he said.

The second looked at them. "They ain't legal."

"Nor is the fight," said Giorgio in a commanding voice. "It is a little affair between two gentleman. If Mr. Kanski does not box with these inside of two minutes, he will never box in California again. With no gentleman. Nor—with—anybody else!"

Cheers rose from both sides of the barge. The second jammed the gloves on his principal's hands, reluctantly, as if they were manacles. The fight began. Hayes whacked down on Kanski's skull, but instead of dying at once, to Cleve's surprise, he pranced off, grinning. But of the two, Hayes was the more agile. After two hours, they were still fighting, Hayes pounding with his left.

"He's busted the other hand now, too," whispered Port. "All up with me, I guess. St. Helena's kissed a hundred bones goodbye."

Cleve thought the fight would never end. On the edge of dark, with the wind blowing chillier, and the gulls squalling doom overhead, it looked distinctly all up with Hayes. His face was ribbed by the sewed welts of his foe's gloves, and his torso corrugated as if he had been smashed by a washboard. His eye sockets were wells of blood.

"Looks bad to me," said Port under his breath. "Too

132

muscled up. He's been killed for twenty-seven rounds."

The boxers sank into their chairs, Hayes staring up at the sky and the curlews.

"No," said Giorgio, puffing slow jets from his cheroot. "What counts is what you fight with after everything's lost. He's got that little more. And it's a lot."

The bell clanged again. Hayes stood rocking himself from foot to foot, hands dangling. He inhaled a sudden breath, as if electrified, drove in and smote. Under his feet, shod in gymnasium shoes, the barge rang drum-like. Kanski went down, rose, seemed to lift high, dropped like a side of beef.

The crowd yelled, but the wind blew away the sound. Men were climbing into the ring. Others in the thick of the mob were counting out gold coins; then there was a rush into the tug warped against the barge, and with Giorgio and Port lost somewhere, Cleve hung over the rail, looking into the gloom, awestruck. It had been a collision of giants—like St. John's Peak fighting with Mount St. Helena, and the earth had rocked under the fall.

"It's in him," Giorgio said. "He's the best we've had around here since Heenan. I wasn't surprised." He put his hand on Cleve's shoulder. "What did you think of it, Cleve?"

The tidewater thumped and boomed against the hull. The wind was blowing up. Cool air, and moist. Cleve was feeling better now, but he was still trembling.

"I thought it—I thought . . ." he began. "It was very . . ."

Giorgio smiled.

"I know. It's your first. It's only when you're older you'll know what you've seen. It won't be that you'll remember so much as you won't forget it. You're growing, growing. Montino's good for you. Out of the fog, out of the city. Montino looks well? Haven't been there since we chased that loco bird of Wing's."

"Mike," said Cleve. "We could only find his bell. He tried to fight a coyote, Wing thinks."

"Wouldn't be surprised. The old slope breeds scrappers."

Giorgio turned to watch the rest of the spectators, the last handful, embarking on the tug. Casually, he asked, "How are the Zinfandels doing? I read in the *Chronicle* this morning they're crushing in upper Napa. Dammit, I could just hear the juice splash, and feel the sun warm on my head. We've had it foggy in town, and mighty chilly for old bones."

He thrust his bare hands into his pockets; the dogskin gloves, ripped and bloodied, he had thrust upon Hayes for a memento. Someone called from the tug. The siren fulminated. Giorgio ignored it. He was stiffly erect, but with chin sunk into the fur of his collar.

"Senator!" came a yell as the siren died out. "You coming?"

Giorgio said, "I don't say I wouldn't like to see another crushing. One more vintage at Montino."

"We're heading out now," said Port. "The sulky's over at the wharf, and Augustus can pull three as well as two."

Giorgio stepped over to the rail, called down, waved, then returned to scramble down into the waiting launch. They landed, then drove to a hotel, where, after their commands were jotted down, three banquets were whisked them by the captain of waiters himself. Port's fingers as he gripped the glass, were as awkward as

134

thumbs; he was mute, except for clucks as he sipped the dry sherry.

"Food's rather decent here," said Giorgio. "They've got the wits to serve you on china, which keeps the heat in. Mare Island docks close by. Couple of admirals there, snarky old boys, who know how to eat, and they keep the joint up to scratch. Sometimes we get lobsters here, shipped west in ice. Big fellows, with forearms like pugilists. Off season now. Cleve, you want some shortcake? Good! We'll carry on with the Burgundy until then."

Giorgio poured into the three glasses, lifted his own, and scrutinized it through the shaggy frieze of his eyebrows. "Old Refosco. The To Kalon people handle it right. They bottle it at twenty-six months. Like—"

"Zinfandel?" said Port helpfully, after a pause.

"St. Helena claret."

He shot out his cuffs, and scribbled a message on the back of the menu. "Telegram to Montino," he said, giving it to the waiter as he paid the account.

They left, Cleve still marvelling. It had been a day of wonders. The fast ride to Vallejo, the defeat of the great Kanski on the barge, which would be a page in history. And here was Giorgio going home to Montino to see the grape-harvesting. If only he could keep awake and listen to Port and Giorgio talk about the fight. But he was frightfully sleepy. The seat was hard, the wind ruffled his face and hair, and the dinner had been too heavy. Augustus' hooves tocked like a metronome, and put him to sleep.

He had been up at four. In the season he was always up early. Even in the spring, especially in April and May, when frosts threatened. Hector slept with an electric barometer at his bedside, and when the signal rang, the household woke, dressed and hurried into the vineyard. Montino was higher up the slope than most farms, and far colder in winter. They lighted bundles of straw waiting in rows, Cleve running from one to the next with a candle, until the tracts were alive with flame, the air thick with protecting smoke.

Beyond Yountville he woke. The valley narrowed, the farms pressed down to the road in moonlight, each with its peculiar hills, trees and patches of wildwood.

"Edge Hill," said Giorgio. "Indian fighter from the Presidio came there before anyone. The old sword merchant was the first to grow foreign vines here, I guess, except Montino. There's Manzanita. Pellet, a Swiss. Sold all his wine young, and never put his name on it. He liked the quick turnover."

Giorgio sat between him and Port, bony and pallid, rug drawn up to his chest, cigar pointed at the sky; garrulous still, his voice husky as if the Carquinez fog had congested his throat.

"Inglenook," he said with a nod. "Niebaum the Finn built him a house and cellar and winery like a bunch of cathedrals. House like Scott's Abbotsford. For a Finn he was a good Scot. He sank a half million into the place and pulled out two. Showy, but his brandies live up to it. Don't know why it is, but I never knew a skipper who wasn't a good judge of brandy.

"He had books, too. He went in for wine books. He heard Colnaghi in Rome had the biggest stock of old wine books in the world. He wrote. But I cabled, to my agent." A laugh escaped Giorgio. "I got it, all of Colnaghi's stock. I won hands down, a royal flush. Cost me ten thousand, but it was a good year for Comet. Then I sold them to Niebaum, same price. He's good fellow.

"They made a splurge from the start, the big shots of the Russian fur trade and the Alaska outfit. And they came here in broughams. They liked the country. The top fellows bought a lot of scenery, with sunsets thrown in. Leland Stanford bought the Geysers. Bourne bought the Lakes of Killarney. I bought Montino. I've got the best sunset."

Giorgio murmured on, his voice vibrating like the purr of a cat as he unpacked his heart of memories, his mind raking through the past, talking with Port of floods, pests, vines, and of men who had come and gone in the region.

"What did you make on Hayes?" he asked suddenly.

"Forty. Two-to-one shot."

"And Wing?"

"He doesn't bet on prizefights. He prefers fan-tan down to Lum Yat's."

"Where the company's more select," said Giorgio, drily.

Augustus was fleeting now, head up, inspired at the thought of proximity to oats and bed.

"There it is," said Giorgio, seeing the villa moon-silvered among its sleeping trees. "Hasn't changed, the old villa. It's no parvenu. No Johnny-come-lately. It was here before the rest of them were dreamed of. And I didn't come in a brougham. We didn't even have a stage-coach. I came on horseback.

"That was why I liked it. It was wild, and full of bears. The soil didn't cut like cheese, either. It rattled wet on the shovel. We chopped down trees, broke open new soil, and began from scratch."

137

Giorgio indulged a romantic streak at times. He had pioneered, but not too hardily, for he had a genius for comfort. Others shot bears and plowed for him. He had also contrived a shrewd marriage, and being half of a banking firm, he saw to it that the rule against regarding wine as collateral was not, in the case of the infant Montino, too zealously enforced. Then he brought in the experts. He had about him only men cleverer than himself. Hybridizers like Pendle, oenologists like Bual.

"The young fellows have got it pretty soft now, Port. The pioneers were the right strain."

"Well, I don't know about the strain," grunted Port. "We never froze enough to be Abraham Lincolns. For a pioneer you slept pretty soft. Montino wasn't no log cabin."

"Oh, we pioneered all right! Chateau Julien at four-bits the bottle. French labels, French corks, French straw and nails. We even tried Chateau Mar-goose and Romanée Contée. Montino had to pay from the first. I let the other fellows worry and grow their best at no takers. And could they top my Regolberg?"

Cleve woke at the barking of Lobo and the greyhounds. Alda helped him down at the terrace, then with Hector brought Giorgio into the den, where a fire had been lighted. They had not got over the surprise of the telegram, though Alda came in briskly with a tray of refreshments, and Hector, huge and awkward, with Sunday coat tight over his shoulders, mustered up a cordiality that was patently short of ease.

"I had been planning all along to come," Giorgio said, erect before the grate, his white head shining in the glow from the candles on the piano.

"Had to see Montino once again. But I thought I'd

better wait until the Zinfandels were picking. At my age, a man doesn't gad about too much."

"The vineyard looks very beautiful," Alda said, pleased, "and you couldn't have chosen a nicer time to come. This is only the first day of the vintage."

In her heart she really wondered what was the compulsion that had sent him back to Montino; she hoped, for the sake of peace under the roof, it was only sentiment, which would be reason enough, and as she thought of that, she was suddenly touched. Time had not softened him. He talked to them with his old directness, eyes bright and quizzical, his lip curved in the same wry smile. The night ride had been severe on him, she felt; he looked spent and pale.

"Good-night," said Cleve, crawling on to bed.

"Grown," said Giorgio. "One would hardly know him for the same lad. Goes to school, I suppose. And learns something of vines? Piano, too? I've had it kept in tune."

Alda thanked him. He gave her a bow in response.

"I want to give Cleve a key to that escritoire. It's full of music that hasn't been looked at in years.

"Now, I remember you were growing some Rish Babas. They came off well at the County Fair?"

"Yes. Montino's done well with clusters. We hope to win again this summer. The judging is next week."

She had not referred to her complicity in earning these triumphs for Montino. He looked about him at the unchanged room, then through the window at the moonlit slope to the gully. He put his hands to the casement and stared out. To the Mission field that had for a long estranging space lain fallow had returned an old rich splendor. The Zinfandel in tall black rows, like companies of monks, trod on gray soil, looking up under the moon at the villa. A whippoorwill cried into the night. The odor of firs had blown into the room, reminding him that Montino was but a thumbnail of clearing in the forest that reached to Mayacamas. Giorgio breathed in the cool balsam-laden air.

"I'm very tired," he said. "I should like to wake before the sun goes behind the trees on that slope."

Jule came running up, and scrambled into the cart. "My turn to drive now. All morning I've been picking."

"That was work in the shade," said Cleve. "If you'd wanted to drive, you could have got up at four, like I did."

"Where were you yesterday? I couldn't find you. You didn't say you'd be away."

"No, it was a secret. There was a fight on a barge, and Port and I went, and Giorgio was there. We couldn't tell anybody because of the police. We might have got pinched, Port said."

"Why didn't you tell me?" she blazed out. "I could have gone with you!"

"Weren't any women on the barge. If a raid came, we'd have had to jump overboard and swim."

"I could have gone!" She grabbed the reins and gave a small, angry stamp. "Let me drive."

"There you are," he said. "But hold Ring tight now, or he'll canter and shake off the lug-boxes."

"Don't I know? Didn't I drive all yesterday, when you were away?" Jule, with her boy's face, her brusque insistence on her own rights, met with him on even terms. "Can't I drive as well as anyone?"

"Sort of." He jumped down, glad at the prospect of a dip in the gully. "You can keep driving until noon."

"Don't go too far away," she said. "There's going to be a dinner in the vat-house. For Giorgio. And Aunt Marthe is coming."

He walked on, over the hot dusty earth. The grey-hounds and Lobo were not afoot today; they had surrendered in the heat, to sleep it out on the veranda. The quail, trickling over the leaves and feeding on dropped berries, made holiday.

Only Giorgio, sitting far up in the pergola, saw him weave through the tracts of dark purple and sunlight to the basin, then the splash into the water. Tall, box-sided wagons on the far road were trailing amid dust to the wineries. Crickets twanged in the vine-shaded pergola; now and then a grape plopped on the hot tiles; wasps and enamelled blue flies poured up and down in the heady sunlight; behind him was the golden march of the hills towering over all. Giorgio was aware of a benign continuity of life. Something about the slope, when he first saw it, reminded him of an Alpine valley where he had lived as a child. Vineyards were the same everywhere, and so were the vignerons, bound to the earth and their plants by a feeling deep, subtle and reciprocal; their affections reaching out, the vine tendrils holding upon them; the rhythms and tensions of the seasons answering in the depths of their being. He found solace in the recollection of his early past, and the tie with it visible in the life on the fields of Montino below him. There were even harvest melodies: Flores singing at the wine-press, and the pickers, led by Wing, chanting the Watermelon Seed lullaby.

He fell into a doze, and bluejays screaming in a madrone woke him. Alda was coming up, in her apron. Handsome she looked in the sunlight, like a shock of wheat. Hector had not always been wrong; he had got him a wife worth having around. The daughter of Pendle of Oxhill, and he must have been proud of her. Giorgio felt a twinge of envy. Queer how his enmities were dropping off, like old bands of raffia crumbling on vines: he couldn't go around hitting people any more, because the people weren't there, they were just ghosts. He had changed, too. *Tempo é galantuomo,* his father used to say. Time was a gentleman and changed things.

"Luncheon's about ready at the winery, Giorgio. They're hollering for you. You can hear Flores from here."

"I heard it. Quite deafening! Who are those two fellows at the press with him? Never saw them before."

"They're colonists. They were from Anaheim. Hector got them here to work for a couple of days, to help us out." She smiled a moment, then added, "One of them said he'd heard of you, knew your name anyway." Giorgio put on his old mask and frowned, but she went on quietly. "It was a Regola, he said, that got them five thousand cuttings to plant, and some plows, when they had to come here and start all over again."

"A loan, girl!"

"It was a gift. They didn't find out it was until the other week."

"Hmm. I must have forgot to put it down. Memory's failing." He got up. "I'll walk down with you. There's something I want to say. That boy of yours, he's part of Montino now. Draws, doesn't he? I saw the big dragon he's painting for Wing—anyway, the head of it. Not bad, not bad! But he likes vines, too. That's what matters."

They left the pergola and went slowly down the path, pausing now and then as he talked quietly, and entered the winery. A table was spread between the vats. The vintagers sat about it, noisy and merry, sleeves rolled up, arms stained purple with juice. Wing and Concha helped the meat, frijoles, and tortillas. The air was tangy, reeking of must, heady with the carbonic acid from the vats. It went exhilaratingly to the head like the accordion music flooded in by the blind Mexican at the door.

"Listen, Cleve," said Jule. "Listen to this, here." She pressed her ear to the damp cooperage. The must was working, foaming, bubbling. "Sounds like a million bees."

"It's just livening up," he said. "You wait until tomorrow."

"Jule," called Miss Lane, "you sit right up. You'll get your hair all soppy."

"No harm," said Giorgio, tying on his bib. Everyone wore a bib, stamped with a big "M," and tied behind with a knot like rabbit's ears. "Only young wine. It washes off easy."

"Why didn't you bring Vic along?" she asked, reproachfully. "Jule was asking about him. She quite misses him. They'd gone to school together, you know."

"Vic? He's no farmer," Giorgio said, toying with his fork. "And besides, he's got his fiddle lessons."

Cleve was impressed. He had a vision of Vic with his pale face, eyes like blots of ink, drawing his bow gracefully in a parlor. Neither Vic nor his mother ever came to Montino any more; he had become a dream, and only Jule, who saw him in the city on holidays, ever spoke of him.

"He should have come to see the vintage," said Jule. "And the dragon Wing is making. It'll be ready when the big winds come in March. He's going to fly it for Montino, and Lum Yat will fly one for our place. It's as big as a real dragon. Did you ever see one?"

Giorgio struck a match for his cheroot, and it went out in a draught blowing through the cool, humid winery. He tore another splint from the match block, and guarded it with a shaking hand until the flame changed to blue. He had begun to feel again the chill that had oppressed him in the city; and, no doubt, he should not have ventured into that tule fog on the barge. He got his light, and shook out the match, a liveliness in his eyes.

"Dragons are scarce now," he said. "They fade out, like the gods, when people no more believe in them. But you may hear talk, and perhaps it wasn't so far wrong, that there was a dragon on Montino once. It meant well, though."

Jule laughed, and Cleve laughed.

"I heard of a man once," said Giorgio benevolently, "that did actually believe in dragons. A mandarin, he was. He had one embroidered on his gowns, painted on his cups and walls, and sat in a chair cut in the shape of one. He was plumb dragon-mad. Well, the dragon up in Heaven was so pleased at this that he came down, got to the man's house, stuck his head through the door, and pounded the ground with his tail, like an earthquake, he was so pleased. The man was scared out of his wits. He lit out the window, over the garden wall, and didn't dare come back for a year."

Talk and the shouting of healths grew louder. Hector pointed to a beam; Flores went up a ladder and brought down a half-gallon bottle, gray with dust and cobwebs. He drew the cork amid dead silence, slowly filled his glass, then, with most patent slyness, moved to the right.

"To the left!" yelled the vintagers, rising. They pelted him with their rolled-up bibs. "To the left! *Alla sinistra!* Clockwise for luck! To the left!"

Flores, ducking his head, wheeled about, grinning, and poured according to ritual. He waved to the head of the table. Giorgio lifted his glass.

"To Montino!"

The toast was drunk. Soon the party was over, and the floor cleared. The pump started up with a clatter of echoes; before the door, the Chinese, who had been squatting in the shade with their rice bowls and gourds, flitted back singly to the tract. Giorgio went out, his hand on Cleve's shoulder. The tray wagon, with Jule and Wing, bumped past, and Cleve wanted to join them, but felt chained to the old gentleman. They went up to the arbor. Giorgio was in sunlight again, his limbs and chest enfolded in the strong, revivifying warmth. The vineyard was swimming in haze: the sky a hot, quaking blue, the olive-trees silvery; the earth red, and red, too, the trunks of the madrones and the bridge across the gully, a rift full of sunlight, from which drifted the chant of the pickers. Giorgio looked over the landscape from the chair, his eyes crinkled.

"That was a lovely summer we drank. Eighteen-ninety. That vintage we had a week of dewy nights. Flores had a steady hand and he didn't jolt that crust in the bottle. It was from that little parcel of Refosco we grew down there, by those olives; and it was a wine

145

without a name, because it never went out of Montino; I'm glad we kept that last bottle for this day. After all, no matter what they tell you, the prettiest wine is only to drink."

Giorgio whistled silently. He bit off the end of a cheroot, and a chipmunk flashed down a trunk, sat looking at him with paws clasped, then scampered up again.

"We can do even better. I want you to stay here, Cleve, and grow it. You stick to the hillside, and don't you bother with the flat nor with the gullies. They'll go out in a flood.

"Nobody listens to me any more. No blame to them. I've made mistakes—more mistakes than anybody here, but only because I've lived longer than anybody else. I've learned something, too."

He talked so simply that Cleve began to wonder if he had ever known anyone so well. Giorgio fanned away smoke and murmured on, going back to the beginning of things, and the bears that romped where the villa was built.

"They say the mandrake cries when you tear it from the ground. And the vine, sometimes. But I didn't hear the Regolberg. I wished I did, and I've got to tell someone. That Chinaman did. He wouldn't lay a hand to the pulling; he stalked away, and didn't come back for three years. Hector missed him. He was a little boy then. We used to have good times, and picnics in the woods. There's always been somebody at Montino that loved the place. Always somebody that came when very small, and grew up with the vines.

"I want you to stay here and look after Montino.

"I want you to grow a wine. A better wine than Giorgio ever grew. I'm going to buy you a field. Hector

146

will plow it and Alda will plant it with Black Pinot cuttings. It's a very good field, and I've told her. But what else I told you is between you and me. Something for you to remember old Giorgio Regola by. He's like the dragon, he would love to be remembered."

More chipmunks came and went, unseen. The air was heavy with the slope odor of dust and balsam.

"A field?" said Cleve. He felt no elation. He saw himself rising before dawn to hammer down posts and hoe in a long, wet furrow.

"And a good one. High ground. But I must go home first. There's got to be a paper. You've got to have a paper to show for it."

The pergola was in deep shadow now. Giorgio rose, buttoned his coat, looking rather shrunken, and Cleve walked on with him to the villa.

8.

IN TWO days Giorgio was about, his fatigue gone. It never took the Regola breed long to mend. For a week he sunned himself on the step before the cave, or in the pergola, with the greyhounds heaped at his feet, or on the bench under the madrone. Now that the Zinfandel and the Gamay tract were cleaned out, he could see better from the large window in his den. It was a pair of French doors, screened and kept open.

Hector's wife had been looking after him. The parquet floor and the mahogany sample-lockers were rubbed and shining. His decanters were filled. On the table were blocks of matches, a humidor for his spikey cheroots, an opium bowl heaped with pomegranates. They gave him in the course of the day, these small things, an intense happiness. This afternoon he would leave Montino with regret, for his quarters in the city. The sun had warmed him to the marrow. He thought of the grumbling of old Bettina, the fog, the whanging of the cable-cars going up and down his hill like weights on a clock. But he had much to do; a bank meeting to attend, a dinner for some diplomat at the club, and then some work at his office in Montgomery Street, gas-heated, the walls stained with damp. More damp to get into his bones. He had that paper to draw up, for his lawyer to go over. Marthe—he had talked to her yesterday—was reluctant to sell the pasture, but she had agreed. He was sorry now that he had ever sold it to her father, but old Wildcat was property-hungry, he just ate up land.

Sitting in his chair he relaxed, with a binocular to his eyes. The pickers were now combing through the Malbecs below the old stable. At the side of the winery was a hill of pomace. The turkeys were out picking on it. A Chinaman trundled out a barrow-load of fresh pomace. He spat on his hands, drew a full breath, braced himself, darted up a plank runway to the top, and there emptied his load. With pigtail flying, he shot down, the turkeys escaping right and left. They were pretty drunk this afternoon. That hill, a boggy red-purple, humming with wasps and flies, Giorgio could almost smell on the breeze. It still had the right ferment, vinous not vinegarish, but in a day or two more it would turn.

Cleve was driving the cart, Jule riding with him, in butternut overalls. The gray horse plodded sleepily in the deep ochre dust, where the sun picked out bits of mica-like jewels. A rabbit semaphored directly into Giorgio's lens. It sat up under a hood of vine leaves, to stare unseeing at him, its eyes a luminous, soft brown. Giorgio watched actively in delicate and passive enjoyment, and felt himself one with the rabbit. He still had left the exquisite satisfaction of his senses. Then he espied Alda, down in the Malbec field, filling her basket, saw the twist of her lip and the moisture on her forehead.

"I had the Malbecs planted there," he thought. "Grand earth for them. It was all Grenache once. They made a grander profit."

Giorgio smiled wrily. They had profited him in

Eighty-two when the storage mob in the city engaged the old *"Stella,"* loaded her up with a jumble of wines—almost a hundred thousand gallons—and sent her overseas. The phylloxera, that Moloch the size of a pin head, had devoured the French vineyards and in brief time cost the people twice as much as the war with Bismarck. The *"Stella"* venture was a coup. The white wines had a finish, though some palates missed the breath of mold, *la pourriture noble*, never to be got in these resplendently sunny and dry airs of the valley. The reds, bottled under thirty chateau labels—including all his Grenache—were neither better nor worse than the wines grown in Algeria.

The venture had been a quiet one. But the *"Stella"* had smashed the bulk of the overseas trade. Next year only a thousand gallons, and those of Napa's best, went abroad. The outcry was hideous in the extreme. The Commissioners, and the hierarchs among the vignerons, like the Wetmores, De Turk, Wente and Charley Krug, were wroth. Giorgio knew what was coming. He sold off all but the heart of Montino, which, later, he trimmed still more, before deeding it over to Hector.

For himself he had weathered the storm without damage. His name was not on these red wines. He knew how to cry with the hounds. And besides, he had been enhaloed with the Regolberg.

Montino had already cleared him a million, and he wanted a flyer in the shipping trade. He had done far better by his acres than had the rancheros with their vast holdings. Those Spanish grandees (half-pay lieutenants at the Presidio, most of them, with a passion for cards) and Russian explorers had loped over this paradise of chaparral and wild oats, and regardless of the rights held in fee simple by the paisanos and their longhorned cattle, filed claim to everything in sight. Their sons gladly exiled themselves to the city. Excellent fellows, though. Good old Baronoff, amiable Valdepenas! He bought the slope from them, at a song for an acre. They came back, sometimes, to hunt deer, and to dine and empty a bottle with him in the pergola.

The curtain had long fallen on that epoch. It was pleasanter to forget the sad argosy of the *"Stella,"* and to think of the stubborn little farmers—Montino, too, was now a pocket farm—who were getting somewhere with their vines.

The farm ought to be larger. It would soon be larger by one field.

The Swiss clock whirred in the kitchen, and the cuckoo piped twice. Giorgio put down his binocular. Soon he would have to be leaving, and stop first at the Grange fair in the town. And Carola would be down from the Lane place any moment. It was just like Carola to come pelting over to the slope as soon as she heard he had not come straight home from the barge. She had been fidgety over his cold. And ever more fidgety, he was sure, over his being at Montino without her. They were to leave together as soon as they had looked at all that stuff at the fair—pumpkins, jars of spiced peaches, pens of Black Minorcas, and exhibits of grapes. He didn't know exactly why they went, but Carola approved of it, the Regolas being, after all, a county family, and they still kept up their membership at the Grange. That business over, they were to leave by train, Carola leaving him at Napa City to go on to Sonoma, for a visit with some of Bayne's cousins at a ranch.

He picked a cheroot, clapped on a Panama hat, and taking his dog-headed cane, went out to the vineyard.

His things were already in the wagonette on the terrace.

He found Alda; they went over to the pasture and rested their arms upon the fence. "I remember," he said, "how it grew, the—White Pendle—in rows straight that direction, so it got all the warmth and little shade. It didn't mind sunburn."

His face looked transparent, and a light was behind it. "I wish I had it to do all over again. Perhaps," he smiled, "I'll come and help you plant the cuttings. What do you have in mind for him?"

"The Regolberg," she said. "When it's found. Until then, the roots will be growing, ready for it."

Down in the field, as the last cartload went up, Wing shouted and waved his hands.

"Malbec all in!"

Cleve drove in with the load, helped out the boxes and gave a hand at the stemmer. On the floor of the cart was dust, and Flores gathered up a double handful. He cast it into the crusher with the grapes.

"Hair of the dog! *Buena fortuna!*"

The shouts went through the winery and the yard. The pickers left at once, going down the road towards Lum Yat's. Jule stood with Cleve under the madrone.

"We're going to the show tomorrow, aren't we?"

"Of course! Didn't I promise we'd go?"

"You didn't speak about it today."

"Well, I did yesterday. And I've got the tickets. They were hard to get, too. It's Pepper's Ghost, and music. Almost like an opera, Port said. He brought the tickets up for me. And we're invited to dinner at Flores'."

"Flores'?" she said, a little hesitatingly.

"He's having a dance and a late dinner. Port's taking us."

"Oh, but I couldn't. Aunt Marthe, she—she wouldn't think of my going. It's a tamale parlor. And common."

"Common?"

He was thunderstruck.

"She wouldn't like it."

"There's nothing common about Flores' place. Alda and Hector go there." A gust of loyalty stirred him. "And even Port."

Jule stood convinced, but helpless.

"I'll tell him we can't go," he said. "Alda and Hector are going down later, in time for the dance. So we'll drive down with them, and have dinner first at the house."

"Oh, I'll come," she said, and they walked up to the pergola. "There's Alda now, down by the pasture."

They waved, but Alda, talking with Giorgio, who pointed with his cane, did not see them.

"They must see a fox."

"No foxes in that pasture. Perhaps," he said in an unlikely voice, "they're going to build a new fence. There's some posts down."

Alda and Giorgio then walked slowly on to the villa and the terrace, to the waiting vehicle. Everyone in the vineyard had already bade him goodbye. Port came out of the winery, pipe in teeth, watched Marthe drive her wagonette down to the highway, then went in again.

"He looked peaked," he said to Flores. "Giorgio looked peaked. Did him no good to be on the barge with that cold. This morning he began telling me about his father. And when he was coming past here he dropped his cigar. Never knowed him to do that before." Port waggled his head.

The wagonette reached the Grange fair, Carola saying

very little on the journey, and they went into the display rooms.

"It's already three, Father, so we can't stay too long."

The place was thronged. They ran into Bascomb, and the editor of the town paper, and Doctor Beers. A chat here and there, a handshake, and they saw all the hens, the potted jams, displays of honeycomb, pears, and walnuts. Marthe paused at the refreshment stand to talk with Mrs. Beers. Giorgio sauntered on and came to the grapes. Bunches of them, on trays, and in tall glass jars of the kind one sees in drug store windows. And there, in the middle of them, was the Rish Baba. Suspended in fluid that magnified it, the cluster was like a hasheesh dream. The grapes were distended, marvellously huge and smooth, the stems a golden network of cords. A card lay against a jar. Giorgio put on his spectacles. It read:

"First Prize. Mrs. A. Regola. St. Helena."

"Wonderful! I knew she'd do it. Never saw such a cluster in the valley. Ought to go to the State Fair, or on tour, like a painting."

"Very nice," said Carola, indifferently. "Very nice, indeed—for her. The name of the farm has been overlooked. They were grown on Montino. But that, I'm sure, isn't at all important to her."

Giorgio replaced the spectacles in his pocket. "Nonsense," he said quietly. "Regola means Montino. And Montino means Regola. I wouldn't have believed it could grow a cluster like that. It's a credit to Montino."

"To her, if you go by the card," said Carola, annoyingly. "It's some kind of gardening trick. I'm sure Hector did the—"

"Hector? Not in a hundred years."

"It seems to me, Father, you're peculiarly interested in

154

her. You were down at that pasture a long time. I hear—indirectly—you've been wanting to buy it."

They strolled back to the potted jams, the refreshment stand, and Marthe, who was still there.

"You heard rightly. I'm buying it. Not for her, but for the boy. He's got to stay there. Montino's a good vineyard. I want it to be kept up."

Carolo flung her head up. Like a ship's figurehead covered with ice. "I see."

Giorgio looked at his watch. "Now for that train. We've got ten minutes to make it."

The vintage was over. A stillness lay on the vineyard that afternoon, a quiet like a bliss. What had been a dream had been achieved. The vines thrust into earth had flowed with sap, and the sap was turning into wine. Hector went to live in the winery, and Alda with him. She totted up accounts in the laboratory. The pickers had been paid on the nail. Old wine had been sold and the money paid out in wages even before the truckman had come for the barrels.

"Looks like we've come out even," said Alda.

"Knew we could make it," said Hector, hunched opposite her over the oilcloth. "The last two years were the hardest."

Also some bills had been paid off. Hector had made a trip to see the banker.

"That Zinfandel patch," said Hector, "will carry us until that"—he flicked a thumb in the direction of the pasture—"comes into bearing."

Hector, bare-armed, sat in his chair resting between spells of labor. The press, the stemmer, all the apparatus, he had taken apart and washed with boiling suds. He had also scrubbed the floor, to the last red stain, and screened off the windows and doors. The place smelled up like a laundry.

"You know what I'll give that pasture?" he said, scratching the ribs of the greyhounds under the table. "Lucerne. For cover."

"Ought to be good," said Alda. "It's nitrogen."

She gathered bills into a neat pile, bent her face to the ledger, and began to jot down entries. She was always calm and unhurried, and patient in details. In another old ledger she kept a diary of the vineyard for the season, like a ship's log, with notes on the wind and the birds.

"I was thinking," he remarked, "Carola'd ought to be with him instead of going on up to Sonoma."

"He did look frail. But he went light. He had only his Gladstone bag, and the parcel of cress."

The old Epicurean had been touched by the gift of the watercress. Alda had sent Wing to gather an armful of it far up the creek. Watercress grew tall and crisp up there, for the patch was within the fostering emanations of a lost apple orchard. Here in the gully, where mint flourished, it was dwarfy. She and Giorgio had gone up there for a walk to look at the trees, and then all the way down to the Santa Lucia firs. She was far closer to him, Hector knew, than anybody else on the slope, than anybody who had lived on Montino in ages.

"Cleve and Jule are coming to the tamale parlor after the show?" asked Hector.

"They're coming."

"All right with Marthe?"

"I asked her," Alda said, dipping her pen in ink. "She didn't mind. And they're having dinner up there."

Hector rose and knocked out his pipe.

"Where's he now?"

"Up in his room. He's got paper all over the walls, and he's painting the tail part of the dragon."

"When's the darn thing going to fly?"

Alda dabbed with a bit of blotting paper. "March, I guess. When the winds come. The head's already done, and the claws."

Hector scratched his head. "Well, if we're going down to Flores' tonight, we'd better go over those vats again." He moved to the door and cupped his hands. "Cleve!"

The greyhounds uncoiled and emerged at the shout. Cleve took his time about appearing.

"You get your pole," said Hector, taking up a notebook.

Cleve mounted to the walk along the brim of the vats. It was a wide plank, but he moved on it, balancing the pole, as if on a tight-rope. At each vat he stopped and punched down the chapeau, the thick raft of wineskins, pips, and stems, like spongy, gray lava. He smashed it into islands. The must swirled up, with bubbles of froth. Since the day was only fairly warm, the chapeaux were moist.

"If them caps dry and crack," Hector called up, "you'll get yourself vinegar."

"But they've got starter in them," opposed Cleve.

"Act as if there wasn't," said Hector. "And keep them caps wet. You can't learn too young being careful."

"We been punching twice a day."

"Got to keep them wet and aired," said Hector, lolling below. "Now what's the heats?"

Cleve stuck the thermometer into the vats, called down the readings, and Hector wrote them in the notebook. They made the round of all the vats. Now and then

Cleve lowered a tinful of must at the end of the pole. Hector flicked drops to his mouth. He looked at the color. It was an intense red. The sugar was going down steadily.

"Getting there," he said. "Now you can go."

Cleve got down, and ran up the hill, the greyhounds after him. Hector studied the readings at the table.

"It's working right. I've got to watch it close, though —mighty close for two days. And I got to haul away that pomace."

"Well, you can forget it for the night," said Alda. "You better give the horses a shine."

At eight, the four of them left the villa. They went down in the wagonette, in which they always rode to parties. It was moonlight, with a nip in the air.

Cleve had a pocketful of dollars. Alda wore a new shirt-waist and sailor hat, with a loose coat. Hector had on his best suit, with a bulge of cigars in the breast pocket. It was like going to another wedding. Their relaxations were simple. Flores' harvest dinner was the social event in the year's round. The small owners and their women, and the winery and vineyard people on the larger estates, which were owned by persons a long way off, no more dreamed of missing it than they would the Native Sons and Daughters Ball on Admission Day. Workers came, too, with their wives or girls in wagons with plank seats and somebody to play an accordion.

Stars powdered the velvet of the sky. A meteor caromed over the bulk of Mount St. Helena, and winked out. The horses, lightfooted after the slow hauling in the fields, kicked up powdery clouds, and the air was scented from tarweed in the ditches. Hector turned up a coat lapel to protect his blue Sunday tie.

"I should have put on a duster," he said. "But nobody does at night. Seem to think because they can't see it, there isn't as much dust as in daytime."

"It's only people from out of town that wear dusters," said Alda.

"They got to look fancy, I guess."

They drifted back to farm talk, for Alda talked of hardly anything else on these drives.

"Soon as you get that pomace hauled off to the vines and dried, I'll let those turkeys out. They've been cooped up a week."

"Better they were cooped up than drunk all over the place, and ill, like last year. They're hogs for pomace. It's beginning to sour, and that's all I'll do tomorrow, haul it away, or we'll have trouble."

They drew up before the theatre, which had an electric light above a billboard. "Professor J. H. Pepper's Celebrated Ghost, and Educational Varieties," said the poster. Cleve helped Jule out.

"Have a good time now," said Alda. "If that ghost scares you, you come right over to Flores'."

The theatre was packed, but the two groped to seats down front. The light was dim. A gentleman with a shirt-front and black beard gave a long talk that was hard to understand, for it had to do with manifestations and the secrets of the magicians of ancient Chaldea. The black curtain drew apart, revealing a cave lighted by two candles. The Ghost materialized on a table, sat up, moved in a sheet, fought a duel with an inferior ghost, flung its sword away, then lay back on its table and ebbed away to nothing.

Everyone liked it, everyone applauded. It had taken a rather long time, but the show was only half over. A pair

159

of dancers came on, then a Chinese juggler, who kept a cigar box, a lamp, a rabbit and five glass balls in the air, sent them running up his arm and into space again, and altogether was far cleverer than any Chinaman Cleve and Jule had ever known.

After that a curtain fell, a backdrop of elegance, with palms and a Hindu palace of marble. In front of it stood two men and two ladies in soft lights. Jule scanned the program.

" 'Renditions by Professor J. H. Pepper's World-Famous London Quartette,' " she read in a whisper.

"Sssh! They're beginning."

For singers come from afar off they seemed much at home, and they knew what songs were certain to be liked. They went feelingly through "I Dreamt I Dwelt in Marble Halls" and "The Boys of the Old Brigade." After that, "Mona, My Lost Love." Not even the Ghost had enraptured the house more. The basso, with a stout hand on his midriff, smiled and bowed as if to friends in the audience. Ushers trod forward and hoisted to the stage floral pieces bigger than themselves. The basso carried them to the ladies, who flung kisses right and left, whereat the house rose and applauded still harder.

Seats were slammed back like pistol shots. Half the audience pressed down front, the rest poured out, Cleve with them, and Jule, who walked backwards slowly, still entranced.

"It was marvellous. The singers too. Oughtn't we to shake hands with them?"

"I don't know," said Cleve. "They couldn't possibly know us, being from London and all that."

In the crowd outside stood a figure under a familiar square hat.

160

"There's Port," said Jule.

He moved along with them, nursing a pipe at his teeth. "Told Hector I'd look out for you. That was a show!"

"I liked it just as well as 'Trilby,'" Jule said. "The Ghost was wonderful."

"Spooks don't come no better than that. Natural as life. I saw it down to Fresno once. It was floating round the stage, and a fellow let go with a slingshot. Crack! Then down come a ton of busted glass. It was some kind of trick. And a magic lantern."

"Well, what if it *was* a trick?" said Jule. "What if it *is?*"

They were already at the tamale parlor, its entrance dark, a light at the side door, and went in through the kitchen to the room noisy with dancers and a string band. It was hung with lanterns. They squeezed into the booth where Hector and Alda were awaiting them. A waiter pounced up with beer and soda.

"Was a good show," affirmed Port. He knew his way around in music. In his younger days, when he could read notes straight off as well as anyone, he had pounded drum for the St. Helena band. "Sam Tarantino was the boy! Sam's quartette had 'em all backed off the boards."

"Sam?" asked Cleve, in a tone of chagrin.

"That's him," said Port, gratified. "The fat one. Sam's the winemaker over to the Greystone. Handy with the cymbals, too."

"Oh," said Cleve.

He was glad that in the uproar Jule, who was talking with Alda, heard nothing of this. Half the show had been a magic-lantern trick, and the other half had lost its grandeur. "Then they're not really from London."

"Don't know they could sing better no matter where

they came from," mused Port. "Sam's got the best funeral quartette Napa Valley ever had."

A waiter, backing with a tray, peered into the booths. Someone was being searched for. Following him came Wing, with a yellow envelope.

"Montino folks? Right? Here's a man—"

Wing gave the telegram straight to Alda. She tore it open. It was from Martinez. A small town the other side of Suisun Bay, on the way to Oakland.

"Giorgio's took ill," she said. "Dock Hotel. It's from the landlord, I guess. Doesn't say any more."

Hector read the words. His tongue clicked.

"Just half way home, too. Must be took bad if they had to send us a telegram."

The fermenting wine could be no more left alone than an infant, and there was the pomace to be hauled out before the next spurt of heat. Then his eyes strayed, his attention seized by a thought, and he looked frightened. His father had not been able to reach home. The field! Unless a paper had been drawn up, a deed or a receipt— that would be the end of the dream. From under her smooth, untroubled brow Alda looked at him steadily.

"I'll go there," she said.

The dinner came on. Hector waved to it.

"You just sit down. There won't be any trains going out until morning. And you can't hurry trains."

"I'm going right now," she said. "I'll go up to the house first, get some things, then drive straight on in the buckboard. The ferries run all night across the Carquinez."

"Sounds crazy mad," said Hector, "and it's late. I can't go with you. Somebody's got to stay home. If the wine sticks, we might as well pour it in the ditch. You think you ought to go?"

"I do."

"Buckboa'd outside," remarked Wing, as if it had just occurred to him. "And coats and blankets."

"I'm damned!" said Hector.

Wing looked at Alda and spoke with firmness.

"Coats and blankets I put in wagonette. You take wagonette with Cleve. You go Martinez now."

"I'm going with Alda," the boy said. "I know the road to the Straits."

They trooped into the foggy moonlight, the wagonette was at the post, and Hector saw that Chess and Ring, the freshest pair on Montino, were harnessed to it. The Chinaman had done some switching before coming in. As soon as the telegram had come to the house he must have surmised that something had befallen Giorgio. Telegrams came rarely to the villa.

Alda climbed in, then Cleve. They pulled on their overcoats, and he took the reins.

"If Giorgio can make it," Hector said, "you bring him back."

"I'll wire you if I can't. 'Bye!"

"Good luck!" shrilled Jule, and the horses bolted out.

He had never known Alda to be so silent. And the day before she had spoken so much about the field, what should be thrown on it for winter cover. Weeds for mulch, or pomace for nitrogen. Hector had debated on it until midnight, then dozed off in his chair.

Cleve wondered if she were not exhausted and asleep. When they came to a crossing with a lantern on a pole, he saw the glint of it in her half-closed eyes. Napa with its spraying of lights was left behind. The horses cantered into flatlands, the moon an oily blob seen through fog between rows of poplars. They passed packing sheds and desolate freight stations.

"Vallejo's straight on," he said. "Where you don't see anything at all. Where it's all dark."

Soon it was darker, with a shrouding of the moon, and the strong wind moist on their faces.

"The black fog," said Alda. "We're near the Carquinez."

The horses lunged on, with growing energy, as if animated by some element in the wind. They snorted. A tang pricked them in the nostrils accustomed only to the upland air.

"It's the salt," Alda said. "Makes them lively."

More stray lights, and they were at the edge of a village asleep and lapped in the reek of mud. Other wagonettes and high-laden farm carts hung with lanterns were moving down a road. Cleve followed them, then slowly over planks into a boat that was like a floating barn. Water plashed and lipped along its baseboards. A milkman whistled as he shunted cans into place in his wagon. He cursed when his horse lunged over to snatch a mouthful from a haycart.

"Th' old '*Amador*,'" said the woman. "We'll be over in no time."

The boat slid out with a tremor, gathered power, and on the wind lay the throbbing moan of the siren. Cleve groped out to the apron of the boat, hand over hand along the moist, salty rail, and stood under a lantern that glowed spectral and yellow in the fog. The boat wallowed in the trough of full tidewater, its cry, powerful but disconsolate, as of a creature pushed off to float in space, with no delusion that it would arrive anywhere; with no assurance that if it did, the voyage would not be futile. But with all the deep trouble upon it, it was a living thing that had outlived many despairs, and it plowed on, shouldering against the neap flood and the palpable darkness. Other creatures, equally lost, their destination forgotten, spoke in the night; with resignation, defiance, or cries that set up a vibration in his marrow.

"You see that, yonder?"

A deckhand in oilskins stood pointing at his side. Cleve discerned nothing, unless it was a hardly perceptible glow, a streak that attempted through the fog to be carmine. It was a horizon, and that was the East. Morning was not far off. They had been travelling a long while, and Chess and Ring had not been as fleet as Augustus.

"Yes, sir," he said. "It will be hot tomorrow."

"Not here. You're from the country. Aye, it'll be warm there, sure enough. But you see that, yonder? That black hull at the Narrows? That's where the big scrap was. Hayes and Kanski. That's the barge. That's something for anyone to remember, seeing that barge."

"I was there," said Cleve. "I was there, and saw it."

The deckhand smiled kindly. "You goin' down to the city?"

"Martinez. There's a hotel—Dock Hotel."

"It's late to be going to any hotel. Dock, Dock," he mused. "I did see the name once. Right off by the landing. Some of them places is clean as a whistle."

Pilings loomed ahead. The engines slowed, hull bracing itself with groans for the shock. A bump, then the apron dropped with a clanking of metal, and the vehicles pushed ashore. After a brief cruising Cleve found the hotel. A tumbledown joint, name painted on the window, and behind the counter a fat clerk in vest reading a newspaper. They went in.

"I'm Mrs. Regola," said Alda. "I got your telegram. The Senator is—ill?"

"Senator?" The clerk breathed heavily in surprise. "Wasn't anyone here knew he was a Senator. We sent you another telegram at one o'clock. After he died. Then the doctor looked at some letters. We sent a wire to a Mr. Bayne. He'll be here in the morning."

"Did the Senator leave a message? Word of any kind for us?"

"Not that I know of. He took ill on the boat. He came here—nearest place—and caved in. Heart gave out. You can go up, if you like." He unhooked a key from the board. "Room Four."

"You stay here, Cleve," she said, and went upstairs heavily.

She entered the room, switched on the light, and dropped onto a hard chair, resting her head on the bureau. The brass bed on which Giorgio lay covered was sunken. Strips of oilcloth patched holes worn in the carpet. The unclean, dreary shabbiness of the room, and the ignominy of the end sent a chill mantling about her heart. The end of so glittering a life, the ascent of the unquenchable spirit of the valley's first immortal, should have been framed with more dignity. Poor old Giorgio. He had always been fastidious, and he had never cared for loneliness.

She thought of Cleve waiting downstairs, she thought of Hector waiting at Montino, and she thought of the Regolberg field. Surely, Giorgio must have left a paper. She took off her gloves, went through the Gladstone bag

—he had borrowed Hector's—and found nothing. In the coat pockets were a few business letters and two gold pieces in a purse. Nothing that she was looking for. Not so much as an envelope with a memorandum scrawl about the field.

She drew on her gloves and stood by the bed. The immobility of the old fighter who had lived for struggle, and upon whom unwonted stillness had been thrust, moved her. They had loved the same vineyard, where the struggle was to be forever renewed, the battle never finally to be won. The reward was in the struggle itself, and in love of it, which like all love was not exempt from grief.

She turned. On the bureau were his Panama hat, his cheroots, and the parcel of watercress. She locked the door, and oppressed by homesickness and foreboding, groped down the hall.

The clerk met her at the foot of the stairs.

"I'm sorry for the trouble," she said. "And now, if you can give us some rooms for the night—"

The Clouding

The Clouding

9.

WINTER ran all its mild length, closing in a rain that for a fortnight dropped like needles, to break in the harrowed earth, and trickle deep into loam, to the gravel and the lowest capillaries of the vine roots. These filaments, once the sap quickened in April sun, would grope still lower into the moist subsoil. The first strong winds of March were blowing. The last shreds of fog had been blustered off the firs sheltered in the gully. In the yard wash was snapping on the line. The sky, Port reflected, as he sat on the veranda steps, had the translucency and hue of a pearl button.

"Wind's just right," he said.

Some bright leaves lifted to pause on the limbs of a bare pomegranate to close and open, then flit elsewhere. They were butterflies. "Real spring, too," he said, returning the pipe to his mouth. "They been plenty Chinamen showed up, Heck?"

"A crowd," said Hector, sitting flat on the veranda, honing his grafting knife. "Come from a long way off, too. A big kite-fly is something. Lum Yat's flying a triple box. They're all betting on it."

"Huh! No weight to boxes, and they're flighty. Takes

a dragon to hold up against a blow like this. I never backed anything here except dragons."

But kite-flying, though he had bet five dollars on the beast, was rather a frivolity, not to be taken seriously by anyone except boys and Chinamen.

"Greystone made you an offer on that Zinfandel yet? I was in the tamale parlor last night, and Bascomb came in with Sam Tarantino. And Sam wanted to know."

"He did?" said Hector, absently, swirling his blade on the hone.

"Said he'd heard they'd give you two-bits a gallon— and they wouldn't be stuck if they gave thirty."

"Maybe they wouldn't. It's worth thirty."

"Two-bits, and take it off your hands, is high for young bulk."

"I got plenty storage room. If I can wait, they can."

"Lyman's farm and Mr. Snowball, they haven't got poor Zinfandel, either." Port spoke into empty air. "And they ain't dickering."

Hector had, indeed, been offered thirty cents the gallon for his last batch of Zinfandel. Twenty would have been fair, two-bits ample, and thirty almost startling. The offer had gratified him, and when gratified he was silent. He had a notion of bottling the Zinfandel himself, under the Montino label, half of it going to the Poodle Dog and Cliff House in the city, and the rest to Manuel Silva, his Portuguese client who had a store in San Leandro, and a tavern famous for its wedding parties.

"Figure I can make it a dollar, bottled," he said, trying the blade on his thumb. "Bottle trade is fancier."

"Look up there!" called Alda from the yard. She dropped her clothes-basket and ran to the pergola. Jule and Cleve were on its roof. "The dragon's up!"

172

Port hurried out, Hector after him. The air was magically bright, the humid breeze steady. The dragon clambered up, lurching in spells, bumping up an invisible stairway. It was the sacred and invincible beast of Montino.

"Wing's flying from his yard," said Port. "He ought to be this side."

"He'll come. Takes a running start to get that thing going. And Lum Yat keeps to that other side. There's a mob for you! It's Sunday. And it's the ninth of the month. That's the best date for a kite-fly, they say. Win —or lose."

The dragon rose high above the sky-raking tops of the eucalyptus, and with a twang like the plucking of a violin string, the cord slashed through the foliage, and Wing, hat smashed over his eyes, and scooping handfuls of bark out of his collar, appeared this side of the trees. The yells that greeted him were like the voice of one animal. Next instant, a triple-box kite rose as high as the dragon.

"Eight foot long," said Port. "I saw it down to the shop."

Its cord flashed, being stiff with fish-glue and powdered glass. In a slash it could be as murderous as a razor.

"Lum Yat's out for blood," said Hector. "I've bet ten cartwheels he won't get it. That ought to square Cleve for not getting his paper," he murmured.

"I never got over Giorgio going that quick," said Port. "The kid lost his field by a hair."

"It wasn't the field so much as the paper. A paper would have his name on, and be something to show. But I'll get him that field yet, Port."

Wing's cord, being of catgut, was invisible. This made

173

his arm-wavings seem fantastic, as if he were a magician exhorting the beast to antics of levitation. The tug was powerful; his arms were pulled above his head, and he pranced about nimbly, as if he were a chessman getting jounced over squares. Cleve and Jule were on the roof of the pergola, watching the dragon in the sky. It caromed, it flashed with claws and barbs of tinsel, and mirrors jangled against its hollow sides.

The yells, fomented by Lum Yat's clerk to encourage wagering, were loud on both sides the great windbreak. The crowd had split, was drifting apart, everyone shouting up his favorite. The dragon began knocking the box all over the place. It was a fight close, vicious, and spectacular. The box flew with virtuosity. It lifted, it fell in diagonals, it smote the barbed head of its foe. As for the champion of Montino, it fought rampant, its cords singing in the air currents, its whistles screaming with fury. Neither had flightiness. Between the upward wind and the earth-pull, the fabrications were as things buoyed.

Lum Yat, behind the trees, was not to be discerned. One could see only the results of his maneuvers.

"Five to one he won't last an hour."

"I'd lay ten on that," said Port.

The kites duelled, they raced, they dodged, sideswiped, and recoiled. Their masters leaped and trotted back and forth, trimming to the wind. The blowing was not quite so steady. Before long the spectators were wetting their fingers and holding them to judge of the direction of the wind, which had abated below but was violent enough above the fronds, and also tricky. The box, as Lum Yat fed it handfuls of line, that tautened in the blink of an eyelid, and hauled in again, ducked and flounced with every change in the wind.

174

"Flighty," said Port, as Hector joined him. "And underweight, if you ask me."

"Look at the claws on the big fellow!" said Hector. "Sharpened nails. A regular porcupine. Lum Yat doesn't know the wind, and the box won't last a half hour. I should have doubled the bet."

The fight still kept up. Cumbrous and amiable, the dragon moved about now as if quite enjoying the air, asking no more than a comfortable wind to lean against, and regarding its foe with decreasing interest. The embodiment of cleverness, it would, when the moment came, gather all its forces for one lethal smash. It was powerful, the largest ever flown over the slope and the oldest turkeys, inured to kites, had, after one glance at its bulk and shadow, gone horror-stricken into covert.

Wing's face was moist from the exertion. He turned it in all directions to gauge the drift of the breeze, then looked at the stirring in the crown of a high eucalyptus. He was smiling; but he was a little annoyed, perhaps angry. The box had survived overlong. He flung out line, the dragon clambered fifty feet with a tinkling of mirrors, then hovered. The box was the dove below the hawk. He ran forward on slipper-toe, with that grace often shown by corpulent men in a quadrille; he swung his arms and pulled down in a curve. He was preparing for the coup-de-grace. Not in twenty years had the symbol of Montino failed to drive that last thrust into the heart.

"Now for the murder," said Port. "By the stopwatch!"

The cord was now hanging straight. Wing leaped for a higher purchase, then, lying back, half suspended, pranced forward stealthily, like a cat on piano keys. The dragon lumbered on, keeping pace with him. Hector stared up, tense with expectancy. No creature of paper and glue could withstand the rip of those claws. The box feinted. Only the lines engaged. One loud twang, as if a harp-string had snapped. Wing fell supine on the grass, bushels of cord clattering and coiling down about him. Hector watched the dragon, a stricken thing, trail its shadow over the villa, roll over and over in the pearl-gray sky, and drift into space, to death and oblivion. Port, staring at the derelict, removed his pipe.

"A goner. But it was the champ for twenty years."

Cleve dashed down to the corral, Jule following. They mounted their ponies and loped off in the direction of the forest. The spectators, either in high spirits or in resignation, trooped up to Wing's shack, for brandy and to settle the bets.

"Going back to the shop, now," Port said. "Well, that was a kite-fly. Wasn't the kind of luck I'd expected. Tough on the kid, losing his dragon like that."

"After losing his field," said Hector.

Port gave a sympathetic cluck, and went on. Hector stood under the madrone a long while, hands in pockets, then strolled to the cave and sat there among the barrels until the slope darkened; still deep in thought he moved on to the house.

"Had some work to do," he explained, as he and Alda drew up chairs to the table. "Where's Cleve?"

"Gone up to Jule's. For supper. Concha's fixing supper for them. Marthe's gone to the city. He went upstairs for a while after coming back. They couldn't find the dragon anywhere."

"Blown into the next county, I guess," said Hector.

He got through his dinner silently, pushed aside his

plate, and looked into the darkness of the vineyard. It had been his custom of late, sitting thus silently, withdrawn into himself. His heart had been set on the pasture, on breaking and setting it to vines for the boy. He had forgiven Giorgio. Touched, he had felt closer to his father than he had since childhood. He had forgiven him because of the intention of the gift. But the old antagonism had returned. To Giorgio's account now should be laid the sin of omission. Before Fate tripped him by the heels in that shabby hotel, he should have drawn up that paper he had promised Cleve. There was that inkpot on the table in his den, with a quill upright in a bowl of duckshot, and it would have cost him little effort to write out a draft, or a check, for the buying of the field. Everything he had—his town house, his library, stocks, all funds—he had left to the Baynes. Hector, not piqued in the least, but chagrined still at Cleve's loss, had talked a little with Bayne in the city, after the reading of the will. The Baynes had been left a half million dollars. And he and Alda had been left nothing. Giorgio must have felt he had done enough for those at Montino.

"Indeed, a field?" queried Bayne, quite pleasantly, as they sat together in the library.

"I think that if it had been his intention to buy a field, for investment or a gift, he would have acted promptly. Oh, quite promptly!" He smiled and pushed over a box of cigars. "That was always Giorgio's way. And I think, from your own experience, you will bear me out there."

Bayne was sorry, too, that with the wine market in the doldrums, it was hardly possible to consider the advance of a loan to buy a field. Deals of that sort were best done through the banks, and they were distrustful of small vineyard property as collateral.

177

"But don't think the door is closed," he said agreeably. "I know some banking fellows down on California Street, and I'll sound them out. You'll stay to dinner, won't you? Carola and I would like to have you stay."

Hector and Alda did not stay for dinner at the Baynes'. They dined, instead, at a Swiss restaurant near Fisherman's Wharf, rode out to the Beach afterwards, and in the morning caught the first boat out for Napa Channel and home. Neither of them had mentioned the Baynes after that.

"That kite-fly! I keep thinking about it," he said as Alda poured him fresh coffee.

"Yes. It was like something we knew being killed."

"Its shadow went over the villa and the farm. I didn't like that." His cup sloshed over as he stirred. "A sign. That never happened before on Montino. I don't hold much with superstitions. But there's been too many queer things happened here."

"One kite had to lose. It didn't really matter which."

"There's signs nobody wants to go against," he said. "In the moon, and the wind and the earth, and rains. They've all been omens. They're even in the almanacs."

"But not kites," she smiled. "Wing and Cleve are gathering paper and wire to build another."

A look of admiration passed into his face. She had no belief in omens. Even calamities and disappointments, however much they labored her, mattered nothing. She had the hill-folk stoicism. It reminded him of the great pines at Mayacamas, their outlines soft in the sunlight, breathing deeply of the incense of warm earth and balsam, rooted solidly in granite, impregnable to lightnings and tempests. That was a courage he understood. Fear he had

178

known as a child, but he had been long its own master on the farm, and he had outgrown fear. The twang of that cord had disturbed him, like an utterance of destiny. Again he felt the chill of that premonition that had touched him when he saw the shadow passing over the vines and the villa.

"I was over to the pasture this morning," he said. "You never saw such a tangle of old canes. That soil's good. They just keep on growing."

"Green shoots come up," she said. "And the cattle eat them."

"They might as well. If it wasn't for the pasturing the canes would be like heaps of telephone wire." Hector slowly spread out an old envelope and began to scratch figures. "Won't be any great job to clear out that field."

He tapped the envelope with a pencil.

"I was just thinking. You know, I think we can get that paper for Cleve."

"A paper?"

"For that field. I want to buy that pasture for him. And nothing's going to happen to that paper this time, either. I want to get him a deed, an ironbound deed—one of those trust papers that banks can make out. And the bank will keep it for him in the safe."

Her fingers stilled, then her hands fell on her lap. She smiled, blinking. It was on her face now that admiration shone. She had always hoped the ownership of the Regolberg field would return to Montino, and to Hector.

"I'd always been wishing it for you," she said.

"It's not for me. I've got fields. This is for Cleve. I want him to own something for himself while he's young. And grow up with it."

"You think we can buy it?"

"We can. Greystone can have the Zinfandel. And they can have the Gamay, too. I'd figured on bottling them and giving them glass age, and a label. Schmidt sent me a drawing for the label. The lithograph man. Printed the Regolberg labels. This one was to be Chateau Montino."

"You can do bottling and get more."

"No. I'm going to sell in bulk. Hillside bulk from Montino. *That* is trademark enough. We're just farmers, and I'd like us to keep on being just farmers. Sooner it goes to the winery, the sooner we'll get the field."

He rose. "I'll drive down to Greystone first thing in the morning. Late now, but I want to get that account book in the laboratory."

He patted her shoulder, and taking a lantern he went out.

To Hector the moving was an ordeal. Tarantino had sent up giants who could handle barrels as if they were eggs, but however gently they rolled each barrel into the low-slung truck, Hector groaned and cracked his fingers. No fussbudget of a nurse, carrying out an orphanage of infants, could have been jumpier or more irascible.

"God-a'mighty! You're not hauling cord wood!" he roared in the cave, or at the skids outside. "If you churn them so here, I hate to think how you'll churn them the other end!"

The driver grinned. He stowed tobacco in his cheek, and drew a sleeve across his mouth.

"Don't you worry none, Regola. There's a holy terror that end, too. We got 'em all now. Some job. Two days' hauling. You ridin' in with us?"

"I got some cleaning up to do. Where's Cleve?"

"He's gone ahead. Hour ago."

"Tell him and Sam I'll be there in a couple hours."

The horses strained; they moved with slow tread, hooves lifted high, going with all possible dignity and circumspection. They wanted only plumes to be funeral horses. Hector stood by the entrance, watching the truck creep slowly to the highway, then back into the cave.

It had been a profitable stroke for him. Port was right; the wine had been taken clean off his hands. It did not even have to be racked. The winery would do that, give it the last racking to prepare it for the mellowing through the summer. The entire stock had been cleaned out, to the last gallon of anything. He had never before seen the cave so bare. Nothing in it but timber frames and a few small vats. Overhead hung a trolley, with block-and-tackle. With this he hooked up timbers and jockeyed them into some order.

In the autumn it would be full again. Four years from now it would house the yield from the pasture field. That vintage he would turn over to Cleve, and he would help only with labor and advice. By then Cleve would be at the Experimental Farm, getting the hang of wine chemistry, and studying vines under Hilgard. The boy, he realized with humbleness and pride, was cleverer than himself. He had been taught much, he would learn more. Cleve was as his own son, bound to him by something more than an accident of the flesh, and that was the tougher link of spiritual kinship. He wanted to give Cleve all he had to give, and far more than he himself had received. He wanted to be more to Cleve than the imperious old Giorgio, estranged by his reputation and successes in another world, had ever been to the son left on the remnant of Montino. Giorgio had in the end come back to a tolerance for small people and little things, but it was on the ebb tide that he had drifted back. He found a closer bond with Cleve than with his son from whom he had been swept apart.

But that bond was something. It linked Cleve with the beginning of things on Montino, and it was heartening to feel that the farm would continue on and on, its line unbroken.

Alda stood at the entrance of the cave, looking in.

"You have been cleaning up! My, how queer the place looks. So empty."

She walked about, interested. "I never really did see it before. How huge it is! Almost like a mine."

He set the last beam on end in a corner. "Just like a mine. Only cleaner, and better lighted." He wiped his forehead. "Cooler, too, only I've been lugging around all that timber." He pointed to a room, a sort of wing, cut into the side of the tunnel. It had all the while been hidden behind a wall of barrels. "I'll clean that out next. Tomorrow."

They walked into it, Hector carrying a light at the end of a wire. The room was about ten feet square, with a vaulted roof, like a crypt, and it had a table and benches. On the dry limestone wall was a painting of jolly peasants at their harvesting, helped by Bacchus and his crew.

"A picture!" said Alda. "Can't we take it into the den?"

"It won't come off. It's painted right on. A kind of fresco."

"My, that is real pretty," she said, sitting on a bench to admire it. He held up the light. "A real vineyard, too. In Europe, somewhere."

"Somewhere in the Jura, where Giorgio lived. A real picture of the vineyard. Giorgio said he never saw Bacchus there. Nor anybody jolly harvesting in it, only three

182

old women in black, picking grapes like they were picking rhubarb. They all had plenty of clothes on, too.

"It showed, he used to say, 'the non-Bacchic character of the great vintages.'"

"He did?" asked Alda, head resting on her hands, elbows propped. "What did he mean by that?"

"I don't know. He was rather deep sometimes." Hector waved about the room. "Summers, when it was hot, he used to give luncheons here. It was very fine here, with glasses shining in lamplight. I used to look on from that corner. I saw Mr. Krug, and the Wetmores, and Governor Stanford, and Duke Liu and Ambrose Bierce, and the three Jacobs. I saw them all, and nobody could see me, any more than if I was a mouse.

"I want to fix up this crypt like it was before. Something for Cleve to be proud of. You couldn't scoop out a room like this nowadays, only for a mint of money."

He strode about, hands in pockets, whistling. He could see Cleve there, urbane yet simple, the hospitable master of the vineyard, his friends gathered about him, laughing, talking, drinking the wines of Montino. Friends from the college farm, with the same thoughts, and all to rise some day to eminence, in the valley or the world beyond.

"I'll leave you now," said Alda. "I've got some ironing to do."

Time to be going. A trickle of water seeped from the wall near the entrance. Hector washed hands and smoothed back his hair. Chess was already hitched to the buckboard by the corral and he drove out to the winery.

The clerk had a paper ready for him. "And we'll get the barrels up to you in a week or ten days."

Hector looked the receipt over. "Warehouse receipt, they'd call it?"

"Yes, but it's just a memo. The check was deposited to your account yesterday."

"Very well," said Hector, and left. Cleve was already in the buckboard. They drove to St. Helena and the bank, and the manager showed them into his office. He fished out a blank filled in duplicate.

"Mr. Cleveland Pendle, I think," said he, shaking hands with Cleve. "Glad to know you, sir."

"Here's the receipt," Hector said. "And the clerk says they've already sent in the check."

"Correct. And two thousand dollars of it has been credited, as we agreed, to Miss Lane's account, in a net sum."

"Is there anything more to do?"

"Nothing whatever." The manager tapped the papers with his spectacles case. "This is the original title deed, which we shall keep here for the security of the grantee, Mr. Pendle. And this one is a copy of the same, also duly attested and notarized, which the grantee will keep as prima-facie evidence of title to the field herein mentioned." He smiled amiably from behind his glasses. "And such, I believe, was the intention. As I said before, Mr. Regola, we are always glad to be of service to old and valued customers of the bank."

He folded the copy in legal shape and presented it to Cleve.

"That's your paper."

Cleve sat motionless. All that talk had been beyond him. But he gathered that he now owned a field—the field. His hope of owning it had vanished long ago. And now here was the paper, as if Giorgio, suddenly thinking of it in the fogs beyond the tomb, had thrust it towards him.

"Thank you," he said, in a stiff voice, as if addressing

nobody in the room. "I'm obliged to you for the paper."

All the way home he sat rigid, holding solemnly the windfall of the paper, the unexpected diploma, crackling in his hands, that proclaimed him full owner of a field. He showed it to Alda, who was on the back veranda, shelling peas.

"Now, that's nice," she said. She kissed his forehead. "That's mighty fine, Cleve."

Then he fled up the hill with the greyhounds. Jule was not home, she was again in the city with her aunt for the weekend, and he rushed into the shack to show it to Wing. Hector ambled up and down the veranda, hands tucked into his belt, chuckling.

"There was a lot of talk went clear over his head," he mused, shifting his pipe. "But I had the feeling he thought it was about the lost paper that Giorgio promised him. And he knew it would turn up some time."

"That's natural. He and Giorgio were pretty close."

Leaning against the veranda post, foot on the rail, Hector gave a nod. "I'd like him to think well of Giorgio. So it's all right. And I'm glad we could do it, give him that field. It's a thrifty start for him. It was late before I ever got anything."

"He's hill folk," said Alda. "They prosper if they've got a tree they own over their head. Next year he can help with its plowing."

"Until then, they can pasture on it. It'll be interest money. We'll have to get the right vines." He smoothed his neck. "It'll take some thinking out."

"Black Pinots," she said, going inside. "If you see Cleve, tell him I'd like him to do some practicing before it gets too dark."

Cleve emerged from the shack, but instead of descending the path, he went down along the file of eucalyptus with the Chinaman and the dogs to the vineyard. Hector stayed outside in the dusk. Owls bumped about the yard on silent wing. Soon it was too dark to see anything, but in the stillness he could hear the voices far out in the field.

Hector strolled through the yard to the path that led to the pergola where he would give the hail. Lobo trotted before him. A fine, cool evening, it was, and he looked up through the interweaving branches at the sky, with its glimmer of starlight. Fine tomorrow, also. The vineyard could do with a little more rain, another inch or so, not in one drop, of course, but intermittently for another five or six weeks. He noticed that the stars were not crusty and brilliant, but were more like summer stars. Even under Lobo's feet the leaves crackled, almost with the crackle of bark. He inhaled deeply, slowly, through his nostrils. The air was very dry and dust was about, floating like pollen. It was two weeks, perhaps three, since rain had fallen. No harm if none should fall within another two. It wouldn't make a particle of difference. Still, it had been an uncommonly arid spring, and tonight he would have another look into the rain book.

"Dinner'll be ready soon, Hector," Alda called from the veranda. "Is Cleve back yet?"

"I'll call him."

Mr. Wedge, the schoolmaster, rang his tuning fork. Cleve brought his hands down on the keyboard and the four voices, less ragged now, lifted in "Blessed is the Lamb." Again the tuning fork struck on the windowsill, where Mr. Wedge sat deep in a chair, with the shutters half drawn, murmured out, like a flurry in a beehive. Another hymn this time, "Hail to the Lord's Anointed,"

186

with volume and loudness, filled the book-lined study. Cleve slowed the tempo with firm, bellwether pacing on the keys.

"That'll just about do, I think," commended Mr. Wedge. "We ought to have a tryout in the assembly room tomorrow. And find out how it'll sound on that old chest of pipes. You think you can pump it, Cleve?"

"Oh, it's easy. I don't mind the organ, it's always best for hymns. Only, I prefer the piano for rehearsal."

"I can understand."

Easter was three days off. Twice a week, Cleve, Jule, and those in Mr. Wedge's class who were not flagrantly ungifted with song, came to the study at his home to rehearse for the Easter program at the church. Since the school had traditionally taken part in it, Mr. Wedge, whose taste in music was more secular, had to be the choragus. The piano he could play with competence. When Cleve was around, he just waved the lad to the piano, and listened. Nobody in the town could play a tenth as well. It would be hopeless to try. The boy hadn't imagination, nor the hands, but he had feeling and subliminal quirks. Discipline had hammered him into something, of course; but how on earth, living up there at that gloomy villa, with a vine-grubbing Swiss, no more than a plowman, and a placid farm-wife of a mother, good, ordinary people both, that had been done, and how he had managed to stow into his head, and let seep through those calloused hands, that arcana of music that nobody else in the valley was aware of, was quite beyond finding out.

There he was now, playing a fetching piece.

"What's that, Cleve?"

"Oh, just a little dance. I found it home. Some peasants, somewhere. In the Tyrol, I guess."

He played it as a toccata, rather showily as a boy might, but with something lumbering and sombre under its lightness.

"My, my," said Mr. Wedge, half rising to push open the shutter. There had been a dimming of sunshine. The girls were all chattering away. Miss Wedge, his sister, came in with a tray of chocolate and doughnuts. And everyone turned to the refreshments. Mr. Wedge leaned out and pushed the shutter back over the head of a basil plant. At the brushing it released a faint odor of clove. The purple of its stems and the green of the leaves and rosettes were unwontedly deep, for the lawn had been cast into shadow. Above the ridge an India-ink cloud was trailing. He hoped it was a portent of rain and a cessation of the unpropitious warmth. It was drifting towards the upper end of the valley.

A light fanned out, like a shaking of silver foil. Rain somewhere. But it would take more than just one cloud fittingly to round out the spring. He looked at the tanned hillside, and a black furrow lengthening behind the slow drag of a plow. Sunshine was full again.

"Thunder was it?" asked Cleve.

"Just summer lightning," said Mr. Wedge, lowering the shade a little. "The weather'll keep up. Better for the ice-cream shops than the hill farms."

The girls' talk fell into a lull. They were talked out on music, and besides the jelly doughnuts were fresh off the stove.

"I don't know much about farming, myself," he said, stirring his cup. "When I was a youngster I lived on a vineyard, over at Chiles Valley. We had one very dry spring, I remember. The wells were mighty low, and my grandfather had our five Chinamen deepen first one, then the other. Back-breaking work, with rocks to haul up. We hoped for rains, and nobody hoped harder than the China-men. They burned punk-sticks, they shot off firecrackers. The Rector prayed at church. I was wakened one night by 'Whah-wa-yee' on flutes, and a thumping on a gong. I went out into the orchard. There was a bit of light, like a glow-worm, circling the vineyard, then the music came nearer, with a sound of dragging. The Chinese shuffled by, musicians first, then one pulling on a rope, another pushing with a pole a box-sled. Inside squatted what I thought was a dwarf, in a coat too big for him and a hat over his eyes. It was a dog all dressed up, and not too happy over the hocus-pocus. Before the week was out, rain fell."

"Did that really bring it on?" asked Jule.

"The drought ended closer after the parade than after the Rector's prayers. So it may have been an incantation that worked."

In the pergola a vine limb, growing laterally, had pushed up three of the laths and a rafter, which were now at the breaking point. It needed trimming. Hector got out his taper saw, but finding it rusty and dull, took it to his vise in the laboratory, and filed it.

He worked directly before the window. The sky was temporarily clouded, but he could see well enough. At each stroke of the file, a tooth lost its rust and became a bright facet. Halfway in his task, lightning blinked over the ridge. He counted two seconds before he heard the thunder. It was not loud, but it rolled with incessant repe-tition of echoes. That proved it had struck near Castle Rocks, where even a rifle shot would echo four times.

Idly, he watched the downpour, two miles off. It was remarkably heavy, falling in slants. Evidently a cloudburst. Enough to wash away all life in that neck of the wood. He went on filing, then aware that Lobo, out near the madrone, was agitated. He snuffled in the air, tail between his legs, howled as if at some redoubtable and unseen intruder, then fled into the winery and cowered under the vats.

Hector threw down his file. Montino was again in full sunlight, as serene, golden and dusty as before. Not a leaf turned in the still atmosphere. He looked, not hopefully, to that retreating blackness on the horizon. At this time of year, and after such warmth and absence of wind, the high air currents would shoulder it over the ridge towards Sonoma. It looked scraggly. There had been a cloudburst. If the bottom of that celestial tank had dropped out just this side of the ridge, well—the slope would be in for something.

He rushed out, found a pruning pole, and ran to the basin. He jabbed and pried at the logs. The water lowered a foot, but that was not enough. He scrambled down, and holding to a root, for he could not swim, he dislodged a boulder. A white plume, like a feather, waved an instant above the lilacs at the bend. The run-off had already come to Montino. For the first mile it had been a projectile of compact water, roaring and white-snouted. Slower now, it was a flood overriding the banks. Hector turned. The spume dashed upon him, and he leaped. The torrent snatched him back.

Wing, aroused by the tumult, flung open his door and saw the crest of the flood smoke through the bridge. The water poured solidly through the farm, went in a cataract down the foot of the slope, and inundated the road until it drained into the meadow. It had tumbled down to the roadway with a sound like gunfire, and the drivers of a buggy and a grocery wagon drew up to wait until the water was only hub deep until they crossed over.

Wing hurried into the villa and called out. No answer: Mrs. Regola and Cleve were in St. Helena. Concha was up in the woods, gathering pine-nuts. He sped over to the winery, found only the whining Lobo, then walked up to the bridge. The basin and the alder trees, higher up, had disappeared. The gully was largely a dripping chasm. Gone were the sloping banks on which the vines had grown at their richest. Half the Zinfandel had vanished. He leaned over the bridge. He saw not the mirror that once reflected his image, but a snarl of branches, posts, rocks and wire, embedded in mud. A miserable business! The hurt to Montino was deep. To set things to rights would take him another lifetime. The thought of it wearied him to the bone.

A few of the roots were cast along the bed, but most of them had been jettisoned on the lower field, where the sediment lay wet and shining. They should be replanted. As he glanced about, he saw the dog leap into the gully. Fear chilled him as he walked down and peered over the edge. Face down, and half in water, lay a body with legs twisted, one hand still grasping a pole.

It was ten feet to the bottom, but he made the drop. No need to do more than lug and carry the body up to the bank.

Lobo remained on watch. How very tranquil Montino was! The air, bright with particles, and the trees were motionless. Naught stirred but the Chinaman, who went plodding up the roadway to the town. A dog whined, otherwise there was no sound. The mountains kept their silence. The villa, its windows golden in the light of late afternoon, guarding all, with eyes unblinking, waited.

10.

FROM the dining-room, the terrace, and the veranda, the young people began to drift into the parlor. Wing had taken up the carpet, given the floor a rubbing with bees'-wax, and himself attended to the door, for more guests were coming in from the town and the neighboring farms. Cleve, who had been pounding out duets on the old rose-wood piano with Mr. Wedge, took the bit in his teeth and broke away into a two-step.

"You could," said Mr. Wedge resignedly, feeling for a cigar, "have given us a schottische."

"I couldn't, not really. I'm rusty, and so's the piano." Cleve smiled. "Do stay here with me. You won't have to turn over any music. I'm not playing music."

His hands were of a darker tan, stained and clumsier. Mr. Wedge glanced at them. "You were talented once," he said brusquely, striking a match.

"I've grown out of being talented. Most people do. I don't even draw any more. And Vic doesn't fiddle. We gave up being precocious when we stepped into long trousers."

Mr. Wedge inhaled thoughtfully, and looked at his ash.

"You got a degree. What else did you bring home from college? What did you go in for?"

"Bugs, mostly."

"You're going too thumpety. Hold your wrists down."

The dancers swirled up and down the corridor. Vic danced mostly with Jule. He was over-tailored, and all legs, and his eyebrows met in a pale, shrewd face. He danced gracefully with Jule, and they were supposed to be engaged. That had seemed inevitable. They were both at the university, were much in each other's company there, and moved in the same crowd in the city. She was beautiful, no longer the hoyden, the girl on the next farm; she was slight, taller, with legs like swords. Cleve often admitted to himself she was rather wonderful. He also liked her reserve and the glints in her brown eyes. She often wrote him letters, and every five or six months he saw her when she came to spend a weekend with her Aunt Marthe. Vic he saw more rarely. Between Montino and the Baynes and the Lanes was a rift that only widened with the years, though hardly anyone outside was aware of the rift.

Wing came in with a tray and arranged glasses and bottles and olives on the buffet. This was Giorgio's old desk, which had been pushed to the wall and raised on legs. The den had undergone many changes. Year after year Alda had improved it, so that Cleve, coming home for the holidays or the long season in the vineyard, would be pleased. The folding doors were gone, the two-room suite turned into one. Alda had the villa under a long lease, and no matter what Carola said, she had her own way under its roof.

In the settlement of the property—Hector had left no will—the Baynes had taken the press, the oaken chairs, the gold drinking cups, the paintings (though none of the really good ones) and the heavy pieces from the bedrooms they had been accustomed to use.

193

All this had left gaps, but Port had filled them with things made of eucalyptus wood, and immeasurably finer. The piano, the Baynes didn't take. Bayne, looking at it, remarked that a junkman would thank you not to heave it into his cart. Cleve had been overjoyed at that. He and old Giorgio and Jule had romped in duets on this piano, and he had an affection for it.

"Pull down that waltz up there," said Mr. Wedge.

Cleve spread it on the rack. Flores came in with his guitar, talking and laughing in his booming voice. Also the Baynes' poodle, clipped in tufts, and bedecked with a ribbon. A good thing Port had kept away, or he would have been outraged.

"*Que diablo!*" roared Flores. "What you call that?"

"A refugee," said Cleve. "Another earthquake refugee. You give them some music now, Flores."

Flores left, stiffly in his best clothes, with a bottle and a glass, sat on a chair in the hallway, and as his tunes plunked out, the piano quieted. The dancing was perfunctory. It was a month after the earthquake, and few thought or talked of much else. From river warehouses in the city, oceans of Napa wine had poured into the gutters, and swept with them money from Napa pockets. Montino was unhurt. Cleve had trucked all its wine down to the Portuguese at San Leandro.

Carola, sitting with Marthe on the chaise longue, was holding forth on the earthquake, and talking remarkably well. Audiences were always respectful to Carola, and she exacted much of them. Marthe, of course, never tired of hearing Carola on anything. Alda moved about here and there, passing sugar and tea, lemon, and rice cakes.

As it happened, the Baynes had come off scatheless.

194

Their home on Nob Hill they had disposed of four months ago, and they were living near Palo Alto, not too far from the wineries at Santa Clara. Carola had escaped with no more than a broken sleep and a joggling at her window. But friends of hers, less fortunate, were burnt out, or their houses had to be blown up. Since their recitals were stirring, and of first-hand experience, Carola, who had heard them a dozen times, regarded herself qualified to speak with the authority of a survivor. She had the diction of a highly groomed club president; and untouched, her hearers wanted to move about. Jule (who had been staying with the Baynes a fortnight) and Vic, stifling a groan, managed to tiptoe unseen into the corridor.

"What I want is a drink," he said. "We'll go to the den. Where's Cleve?"

"In there. Talking with Bascomb. Our bug man."

Cleve paired off with Jule. Vic sat down with Bascomb and Mr. Wedge.

"When are you coming down our way, Bascomb? I want to show you a piece of vineyard, and a couple of real wineries."

"No doubt you can. But I'm not travelling much. My parish work keeps me pretty well tied down."

"We've picked up another couple hundred acres. It's in Grenache, mostly."

Vic talked with the schoolmaster. Bascomb, deep in an easy chair, was glad his colloquy with young Bayne had gone no further. For the Bayne family he had scant enthusiasm, though he wished the lad well, and hoped that the marriage—there probably would be a marriage— would be felicitous. It would mean that eventually the pair would settle in the villa, and have Montino for their

195

own. Carola owned the larger share of it now. Hector's error in dying intestate had certainly plunged Alda into a sad fix. Simple people, both of them. It hadn't even entered their heads that a will should have been made out.

But Alda had made up for it, partly. She had got a lawyer—a friend of Wedge's—and she remained on, as tenant-manager, a post bound up with a long-term lease of the villa itself. So she was still in possession of one wing of the fort, so to speak. Carola had been angered by that. In many little ways she made her displeasure visible, trying to dictate plantings, the sale of this young wine, the storage of that. She kept it up to just a year ago, when Cleve was still at the Davis experimental farm, finishing his course under Professor Bioletti.

"I'd like you to go over Montino," Carola said, coming into Bascomb's office at St. Helena. "Go over it very thoroughly and tell me what the trouble is. I am not at all satisfied with the way it's being run."

"You're not?"

He had no intention whatever of going up. Montino was doing remarkably well. Cleve came home often and put in heavy licks on the fields, and was always there for the vintage. And the farm had its own clients. Flores and Manuel Silva were its good friends, and it had all the trade with the Portuguese merchants and cherry and pigeon farmers at San Leandro and Hayward. Montino was a small farm but it was a crack farm. It kept up to snuff. If Cleve, working under Professor Bioletti, came across a new spray, or a vine of regional promise, there it was tried out. His hold on the farm was growing, as Carola, still hopeful of settling Vic on the property, was uncomfortably aware.

196

"It is part of my heritage," she said majestically, "and I want nothing to endanger it."

He tapped the desk thoughtfully a moment, then turned in his swivel chair and faced Carola. "There is a pressing danger. The farm is well tended, but the danger could be fatal. It would be a pity, Mrs. Bayne, if its farmer relaxed her vigil against that danger for a single instant."

Carola was impressed. She stirred. "And what is that?"

"Outside interference."

It was Carola who, after the dead pause, smiled first. The Regolas knew when to take their irons out of the fire. "I understand," she said, and they parted amicably. After that she let Alda go her own painstaking way, helped by Cleve. But her attempt on Montino gave her a taste of blood. A winery at Santa Clara came upon the market, and the Baynes bought it. It was a gainful start. Bayne sold off other interests, bought another winery, enlarged it, and took over the adjoining fields.

In Vic, thought Bascomb, they would find very little help.

Jule, at the piano, played a rippling dance tune, but nobody was dancing any more. It was a party that had run down, broken into groups that sat about talking. Mr. Wedge and Vic were discussing larvae, and Cleve drew his chair over to them. He was not listening to her playing.

After a long stay at college, and a journey to the Ozarks, where her mother, who had remarried, was living, she was happy to be on the slope again. It was home, and almost unchanged. One of the madrones by the villa had been uprooted by a wind. Frost had nipped the file of trees on the terrace, and Cleve had sawed them off. Lobo was gone; an outbreak of distemper had routed the grey-hound from this life. Beyond that, nothing had altered greatly. Except Cleve.

"What are you doing on that pasture field of yours, Cleve?" asked Vic.

That field was another delicate point. When Bayne learned that Hector had settled it upon his foster-son, and that the deed was inviolable, and nobody had a word to say how it should be worked, he broke out in monumental wrath. Hector had robbed the estate—actually robbed his next of kin—and it was his wife who had put him up to it. If he had wanted to make a gift of that field to anyone, he should have made it to his own nephew.

"Olives," said Cleve. "I'm running them for wind-breaks. And we've got down some vine roots. For the time being we're growing Rish Babas on them. There's nobody else growing them. And Alda's been getting the ladyfinger prize for them every year."

Those grapes had put Cleve through school and kept up the villa. Meanwhile, Alda was still working over her hybrids, to find the one wine grape fit to cultivate on the Regolberg field.

"Ladyfingers!"

Cleve laughed with him. One thing he liked about Vic was his lightheartedness, his gusto over everything not related to farming. He hadn't an ounce of interest in farms, and if he puttered about the winery it was only because he could not very well evade doing something. He had no fondness for the country, either. Montino he liked, but he could never see why his parents should be eternally fretting over it. That was a horrible example. They had let a farm become their corroding obsession. Bug-killing,

198

though, was a kind of sport. It was rather fun to match your wits with something out of a cocoon.

A plangent chord on the piano, that made the rosewood tremble; then Jule stole into a nursery air, made with variations to sound grown-up. It was a tune she and Cleve used to play years and years before, from a torn folder of music, "The Bird Suite." And this was the part about quail, the one they liked best. Quail were their favorite birds as children. She and Cleve knew all their nests. They crept into the green, sunlit caves of foliage to peer into the nests and watch the eggs. When the eggs chipped, broke, and the fledglings stepped shiveringly out into the world and looked up at them—the first human beings to see—the excitement was sometimes past all bearing. The way not to scream was to close one's lips tight, not breathe at all, and almost smother. The mother birds, of course, perched atop their heads, went frantic.

They were earth-children then. They practically lived in these caves, lying on their backs on brown earth, breathing in the smells, looking up through the vines at the clouds floating over the sky, like icebergs on blue water.

"Do you remember that, Cleve?" she asked.

The two men were going at it hard, discussing with Bascomb, but Cleve turned, gave ear a moment, then frowned in puzzlement.

"No."

She lingered over the close. "It was just an old tune," she said, drawing down the piano lid, as she rose to go into the parlor.

"If you ever run across Doctor Post, your entomologist down there," said Mr. Wedge, "don't ask him about the red spider. Butch will murder you."

"Is the old duffer back from Peru?" asked Vic. "I heard he went down to Peru, hunting big game."

"He came," said Bascomb, "and brought back two cannibal spiders. They're as scarce as Great Auks. Took him five years to nab a pair, after chasing over half the world. He saw himself hung with medals and written up in the encyclopedia. The Peruvians, themselves, wanted to give him a banquet, but no, he wanted to rush home, climb into a dress-suit and address the Entomological Society and knock them all dead.

"He got off the boat late in San Francisco, and turned into bed with the cannibals in a pillbox under his pillow. Then came the big shake.

"If there was one maniac loose next morning, it was old Butch, trying to dig his bed out of the ruins. It was gone, and so was the pillbox. The worst of it was that nobody believes he had found the Arachnida Dilatata. Scientists can be as jealous as mares. It was rough on old Butch. If he had come home a day earlier, or a day later, he could either run for governor, with grape votes, or else be next president of our bug society."

"Rough on us, too," said Vic. "We'll have to keep on messing with sprays."

Carola and Marthe entered, with Jule, and the few remaining couples. Most of the guests had already gone.

Carola, cup in hand, glanced about the room. She saw how it had changed. The room had been Giorgio's, and it should have been held sacred and kept locked. She was thankful she had taken away the paintings and the gold cups and the best pieces of furniture, where they would be safe. Alda had changed the place completely around. As if to work that Rish Baba field—not a penny from which went into the common holding, though it was

200

Montino funds that had bought it—were not outrage enough!

"The den has been quite altered," said Marthe.

"Quite altered!" agreed Carola.

Alda caught the tone, of course. But she was proud of the room, and fond of it. Queer how one could become so fond of a room! The rest of the house, which was gloomy, she had let stay; and this room where she and Cleve had lived, where Hector had read of evenings, had gradually altered with themselves, and become essentially home. She was thankful that the Baynes, going through the house for booty, had first just about gutted the suite.

"It took us rather a long while," she said. "It was so empty-looking. Port helped us fix it up, and we changed it over, little by little, into something for Cleve."

"Mighty fine cabinet work Port did," said Mr. Wedge, goggling at it through his dark-rimmed glasses. "Airy and strong. Eucalyptus wood takes a wonderful finish, but it's only a clever workman who can get the most out of it." His look had the innocence of an infant's, but this was deceptive. "There used to be stuff here like catafalques."

Carola brought her cup down to saucer with a click. Mr. Wedge had visited Montino once when Giorgio was alive. She recalled also, with indignation, that he had declared that if Senator Regola and his lawyer, General Bell Hackett, were elected school trustees, he would circulate a petition to have them flung out. Those were the very words—"flung out." All because of some absurd squabble over the funds the township had voted to build a road from the highway to Montino which, as everyone knew, was one of the show places of the valley.

Giorgio had been tactful in the affair. Rather than throw the town into disharmony he withdrew his name from the ticket. His running mate, General Hackett, who believed in good roads and plenty of them, and had voted for the one to Montino, was less tactful. He kept on running until Mr. Wedge, who had a caustic tongue, told the voters that the soldier-jurist instead of fighting in the Civil War had stayed home with the Guards, with the rank of Sergeant. Also that on disbanding he had, instead of turning in his horse, which was state property, removed with this "ill-fed nag"—Mr. Wedge stirred up much public feeling by emphasizing its bony and spectral condition—to St. Helena and started a livery stable.

"The Senator," said Carola sharply, drawing back her head, "spared no expense in designing Montino. It was, throughout, from the parlor to this den, his favorite room, where he entertained distinguished guests, furnished in the most elegant style of the period."

Jule held her breath. Alda looked elsewhere. The party was getting to be a strain. Mr. Wedge bowed to the reproof with an apologetic smile.

"Pardon," he said. "I am sure it was not the Senator but his period that was at fault."

Three or four more conversations were going on meanwhile, and only Bascomb and Cleve, firmly on Mr. Wedge's side, were paying much attention to this one. The room seemed warm and airless. Jule caught Cleve's eye, and he rose to join her in the corridor, but she walked on, he following, through the kitchen into the yard.

He caught up with her on the terrace. "Did you mind?" she asked. "I wanted to leave."

From the light before the windows they moved into shadow, then down the path to the basin. The Santa Lucia firs distilled their incense in the moist air, and the gully was resonant with frogs reciting under a full moon. Arms folded on the parapet of the bridge, they looked down into the runlet of water.

"Now it's quieter," he said, "and you can breathe."

"You didn't play the piano for me tonight."

"Didn't I? I've got out of music, I'm afraid. Ever since you went away I haven't done much else"—he waved over the slope—"but look after these. They belong to us as much as ever, even if Montino is less ours. And when I'm not here, I have to be out across the Straits with the wagon."

She knew that. And she knew that for the villa there was little gain beyond what it drew from the pasture field. She had heard Marthe and the Baynes talk of it, and especially Carola, who was eternally curious to know what was going on at Montino, and what Marthe saw and heard. And since the wine had to be sold favorably, if those in the villa were to keep up their end, Cleve roamed far with his truckload of wine, grapes, and olives.

"Aren't the banks sloping again?" she asked.

"You noticed it?" He broke a piece of redwood bark from the rail, and it dropped from his hand in crumbles. "It took very much grading. But Hector always liked vines growing on the banks, and after we had slopes again we put back the vines.

"The first year was bad. The Baynes took over their share, and there was hardly enough, after buying the pasture, to get so much as a keg of lime. We had Flores, and Port and Wing, and they helped us. But you were here then. I thought all the Zinfandels would wither because Hector was gone, and the cloudburst had washed out so much, and the farm was sad. But the grapes were wonderful. I told Mr. Wedge how strange it was. And he thought a while and wrote on the blackboard: 'And still the vine her ancient ruby yields.' "

She listened. She had not seen much of him since her return two days before, and he had said little when he came up to the house with Alda to invite them to the villa for the evening. If it had not been for Alda, who liked to have young life about the place, there might not have been a party at all.

"Oh, I never told you," he laughed. "You remember that knife you lost?"

"Yes. It was very precious."

Lum Yat had given it to her, in trade for an armful of old newspapers that he used to wrap meat in for his customers. It had had one blade, and a picture of Bryan on the celluloid handle. She must have been about six then, with pigtails. Its loss was her first heartbreak.

"I've got it for you. I found it when I was rebuilding the old nursery. Right under where Alda's bench is now. It wasn't very much rusted, either."

"I'm glad! It seems like an omen."

"I didn't think of that! Perhaps it is an omen to find something you've lost for a long time. You will soon find something else."

"Sympathetic magic," she said, smiling.

Perhaps it had drawn her, she mused, fondly. At least she had come back. She had been too long-lost in the world, away from the valley, the slope, the vines. It was on this slope that she had been the happiest, and been formed; the grape blood of it, the sunlight, the perfume of its earth, all absorbed into her being. The waving of the eucalyptus trees in the dusk, the greyhounds, the level eyes of young Cleve, stamped into her mind. The red

204

ochre dust had blown into her nostrils and pores. She had tasted its Regolberg. And she had heard young wine in vat; heard the awakening of new life, moving, turning upon itself, fretful, restless, with babblings of ancient secrets, vague and hidden desires and impulses; the vat sonorous as a conch, its vibration stirring in her bones. It stirred again in the spring, as if in sympathy with the sap rising in the vineyard whence itself had come. She saw the whiteness of Giorgio's head against the purple staves. The dragon on the hillside, its splendor wrecked. And on the bank, guarded by Lobo, the form that had been once the master of the slope. Birds were overhead, squalling, whirling in from the incense firs. The Rector and Mr. Wedge had come hurrying to Montino when Wing brought in the tidings. She remembered the blueness of the sky, the leaves a smudge of green fire on the roots. Spring had joined the vineyard in rebellion against winter. The birds and the scene must have returned to the Rector's mind when he spoke at church: "Wheresoever the body shall be, there shall the eagles also be gathered together. And the slain by the brook shall rise again, for its dew is the dew of life, and they shall see miracles."

The visible miracles were that Montino did not end with a smash then and there; that the eternal things went right on, like a clock wound up to run forever, that Alda tended the vines with abundant courage, and that the harvest was full.

"Alda's been up to her waist in cuttings at the nursery," said Cleve, "and one of these days, or next year, or ten years from now, she'll run into the hybrid.

"I can't think of anything," he went on, "that could make us happier on Montino."

The girl stirred again.

205

"No," she said quietly.

They walked up to the pergola, where Marthe was waiting.

"Good-night, Cleve," said Jule, holding out her hand. "I may not see you tomorrow. I'm going out driving with the Baynes."

"Good-night," he said. "Good-night, Miss Lane."

Up in his room he changed into old clothes, and talked a while with Alda, over a cup of tea in the kitchen. The party had been good, on the whole, she thought. Carola had recovered her humor, and Mr. Wedge, flushed with triumph (he was, after all, a guest in the den that had been Senator Regola's own), had mellowed, played an air or two on the piano, and become quite amiable.

"You saw Jule?" asked Alda. "She wanted so much to have a minute with you. She told me."

"I saw her. Down at the bridge." He rose and belted his coat. "I'm going now, and Port must be waiting. Goodbye, Mother."

On the hillside Jule saw the glim of the lantern as it moved past the olive trees to the barn. She had not wanted to come up. She was paying no heed at all to her aunt's chidings.

"After all, my dear, you were gone for hours. I'm not sure that Vic liked it very well. And we were in their old home. And Carola was practically the hostess."

"A little too much so."

"It was hardly the time for you to see so much of Cleve," Marthe insisted.

"Did I? He just about ignored me all evening. And what's wrong with Cleve? I'm still fond of him. Or didn't you know? You always said he was level-headed. That's more than you ever said of Vic."

"Jule, you can be exasperating."

"Sorry, Aunt Marthe."

"They're not to be compared. Who were his parents? Cleve is but a farm worker. Vic's a gentleman all through, a Regola of Montino."

"Like Hector," smiled Jule. "But I wasn't going to let Cleve ignore me."

Marthe drew a quick little breath. They entered the house in silence.

In the barn Cleve and Port worked by lantern-light. The large wagon, its wheels greased, was loaded with barrels of wine and kegs of dried olives. Port slid in a crateful of turkeys and an armful of blankets and canvas. The horses were already yoked, their harness brass shining.

"Past midnight," said Cleve, as they drove out, the horses exhaling steam. "The party kept up late, but we'll make good time. You had a sleep?"

"All afternoon," said Port, kicking off the brakes.

The horses went into a steady trot on the highway. Unless jobs came up, he always accompanied Cleve on these hauls to the town. If he had no sleep beforehand, he and Cleve slept by turns on the floor of the wagon.

"Who're the turks for?"

"Silva," said Cleve. "There's to be a big wedding. Maybe we'll stay over for it."

"Not unless there's some excitement."

"There'll be some. Manuel's parties are always good. And he's taking all five barrels."

"A lot of wine got spilled in the big shake. The price is up, I heard at the Greystone. The small vineyards are all getting it."

"If it was sky-high, nobody but Manuel gets these five barrels."

"Sure. He's all right, Manuel Silva is."

Port drove easily, reins on his lap, pipe glowing. He was blissful, like an nocturnal moth. A long drive was heavenly to him, in any weather, and this was a perfect night for the long run to Hayward. The moon was a blob in thin mist; the air bracing, and they were warmly wrapped up. The world was empty, not another vehicle in sight. As if they knew they were hauling Montino claret to a wedding, the noblest aim for which mortal horses could be born, the animals, fortified by oats and a day's rest, hammered out their bravura on the road.

"What kind of evening you had?" asked Port.

"Not bad. There was a dance in the early part. And Bascomb got talking sprays. Santa Clara's gone in for a new kind of dope to kill mites. Selocide. One cupful to a barrel of water, with a dash of sulfur."

Port was silent for a half mile. "Ought to kill any party, talk like that. But you had some good piano music."

"Bascomb's got him a motor car."

"He can have it. They say you got to put specs on to drive those things. I'll stick to horses.

"If I wasn't coopering—when I am coopering—I could drive all day and peddle wine. My old man grew some wine up to Silverado, and his best customer was himself, mostly. What he didn't drink up, I peddled. I could sell wine, but I couldn't never sell a dog or a horse, only trade 'em for another."

Port sang tunelessly.

"You keeping that place?" asked Cleve, absently.

"I've got it still. I never sold no land, either." Port chuckled. "Never had none but that little place. My old man raised a few pigs, too. He packed out in his rig for Calistoga one winter to sell a couple shoats to the butcher.

Then a storm came, roads went, and for five days the three of 'em just camped under a dry rock. My old man, he made coffee, and he played cards, and had a fine time, with the critters snuggled up to him close. When it cleared up, they all went straight back to home. He'd got to like their company too much to sell them out."

Then Port ran into a tune, but it got frayed and lost in the pounding of the hoofs. Cleve's mind groped for the thread of it, and wondered where he had heard it before. Suddenly he knew it was "The Bird Suite." The quail part, with the bob-white trilling, one-two, one-two-three, that kept running through his head! That was what Jule had played. He had forgotten, but she had remembered, and played it for him, for nobody else.

It flung him back into his childhood. He wanted to be alone, away from Port's voice, away from the hoof-beats. He did not want to hear "The Bird Suite" any more. He crawled over the barrels into the wagon-bed and wrapped himself up in the blankets. They were damp from wine, the boards jolted underneath him. It was towards morning before he fell asleep. An eternity after, he woke, because of the stillness. Someone peered in at him and a light flashed on.

"That's him, Manuel. The first wedding guest to come. And there's the wine. Five bar'ls."

II.

CLEVE hacked about the roots of an olive tree, cleared out a tangle of morning glory, then drove on through the Zinfandels. This second harrowing should take all the fight out of the weeds. A sweltering day, no wind astir, and in a cloud of dust he plodded over the field, hoe slung on his back bandolier-wise. The other tracts he had already tilled, beginning with the Gamays, and working down to these rows about the gully.

Wing clattered in a madrone, and feathers dropped to earth. A hawk had struck a bluejay. He did not look up. He was engrossed with the promise of the fields. The Zinfandels again would yield abundantly. He had pruned and pruned, but still there was no holding them back. If the crop were only half as large, the wine would be finer. Everyone else was pleased. Silva had liked those five barrels, and since his clients were getting weaned away from mere *consumo*, he had taken another load. Alda's share was yet the widow's portion. But the olives in his field—rooted from truncheons cut Spanish-style—a notion of Flores'—were doing fairly, and her Rish Babas were all taken by a shop in San Francisco. She was famed for them, and no longer sent a display jar of them to the fair, for they were *hors concours*. Now and again some other housewife got the prize for ladyfingers, but these were either Black Prince or Olivette.

And so the villa was kept up. Cleve went on a fishing trip to Lake County. Alda had a new dress made and a new hat. He took her and Jule to the opera house in town, where they saw "Lohengrin," put on with a broken-necked swan and an orchestra of piano, fiddle, and trumpet.

Last year had been prodigal in wonders. Mount St. Helena became a reservoir in clouds, its canyons and hollows packed with snow. It melted late. The mountain crackled white with cataracts, and suddenly was a dense green. Men old enough to remember when wild grapes were picked along Napa Creek could not recall so wet a spring. In the early growing season, rather more cool than warm, no vine leafed out untimely. In July the heats on the flat would have dazed a glassblower. Then fogs interposed, low-trailing fogs thick as sheep's wool, and not a berry suffered crack or burn. By harvest time the fogs vanished, and the grapes were picked dry, the Gamays with a heavy bloom, as if they had been dusted with pounce.

The heat and the fog, or some witchery in the microflora that was the bloom—these had worked a magic. The Gamay instead of being just sprightly and elfin, to be drunk young, had unexpected depth and breed. It was a full cousin to Moulin-à-Vent, and good for twenty-five years in bottle, perhaps thirty.

Port, helping Cleve at the first racking, was the first to learn of it. Then word spread over the valley, and farmers jogged over, even Duke Liu, who came all the way from Sonoma; and Flores came up, bringing his *venencia,* the dipper-tube he used only for ceremonial tastings. Port got bundles of eastern oak staves, seven feet long, like strong bows, and made a house for it, a butt that he put together in the cave.

The pressing, also, had been merry. Jule came from the East to help—staying with Carola and Vic at her aunt's —drove the tray-wagon, and was cup-bearer when Flores poured the Burgundy fetched down from the beam. She sat at Cleve's right hand, and he was in the chair at the head of the table, the post that had been first Giorgio's, then Hector's.

The last row was done, and the horse turned into the corral. Cleve washed in a shower outside the vat room, then walked on to the back veranda, barefooted, shirt outside, hair matted above his eyes. It was late afternoon, still hot, and Alda was rocking in the shade with her sewing.

"Jule was down," she said. "Came riding down with Vic and wanted you to come up to dinner. The Baynes are here only for a short stay. They're going home after the Grange sociable."

"You told her I'd come?"

"I said I'd tell you. You can?"

Cleve sat on the steps and combed back his hair. Alda wanted him to go. He would have liked to see Jule, but after a long day of it in the field he did not want to spend the evening sitting dressed up in the parlor. And he had already written a letter to the Baynes, saying that he could not go down to work at their place. Bayne had asked him twice. They seemed bent on luring him away from Montino.

"Well, it was Jule asked. I'll dress after a while."

Alda bit her thread, pleased. "I told her I thought you'd go, after you'd done all the harrowing."

They turned. Port was approaching.

"Cleve, you want to come out to Blanqui's? He's been trying to get a message to you all afternoon."

"What for?"

"He's all worked up over his Pinots. He thinks he's got the trouble. The phloxy. Bascomb's gone down to Lodi."

"Isn't there somebody else in the office that can go?" demurred Cleve.

"It's closed up for the day. And he says he wants either you or Bascomb."

"Well, it's late. And I was going to dress up for dinner uphill. But if it's Blanqui, and he's in trouble, I'll have to go."

"You could ride over in the morning," suggested Alda.

"I could. But if it's Blanqui—I wouldn't want to put off going." Cleve rose. "You better tell Wing I can't be up at the Lanes' tonight. You ready, Port?"

"My rig's over by the stable. We'll drive out right now."

Soon they were on the highway. Port drove his new white cob, half Arab, with a rolling canter that stretched into a gallop. Cleve sank back, eyes half closed in the haze, looking at the farms they passed.

"Healthy," he said.

"Yuh, but it's the small places—"

"So I hear."

Cleve was growing aware that influences as malign as they were unseen and erratic had been drifting about the valley, to fields where the auguries had seemed most bright. Phylloxera had smitten two little vineyards near the creek. The Anaheimers, as prone to misfortune as sparks are to fly upward, had been visited by the black measles. Some of their vines were old, and previous tenants had often let pools remain about them much of the winter, rotting the wood. Elsewhere there had been oidium, and on the flat a murrain of cutworms. Montino itself had warred against enemies. Leaf-hopper had got to the Rish Babas. Wing, uttering maledictions, had slapped them off with a horse-tail dipped in tobacco wash. Then red-mite came upon the Zinfandels, but this pest they had controlled when the grapes were only the size of buckshot. And now, this warm and serene August, there was nothing to combat but morning glory, and that was about all rooted up.

They turned up the hill. Through the pines they could see the tiny farm—five acres, a small, green house, a windmill, and a shed.

"There he is now, in the garden," said Port.

The old Swiss came to them from his rhubarb with a spade. His eyes were limpid with trouble, as if he had encountered a ghost.

"What's the matter, Blanqui? Don't say you've got the phloxy. You let me see."

"This way."

He led them through vines on a flat, then to vines on a sandy hill veined with water channels. It was a pocket handkerchief of a field. Going straight to a vine he laid a paw upon it.

"This little one."

The tips of it were yellowing, most of the leaves were dropped. Cleve dug with the spade, and with his fingers probed about the roots. Thin-skinned, foreign stock it was, easily vulnerable to nematodes and the assassin insect. On the rootlets, which were contorted, he felt nodules. He cut away with a knife, then peered at them with his magnifier. Very still he lay, flat on the ground, the soles of his bare feet turned upward, his face deep in the burrow. For a while he ceased breathing.

Port fished up a pipe-bowl. His eyebrows waggled as he struck a match and puffed. The old Swiss sat motionless, hands on his lap. The vines on the loam below were good, but these were his favorites, his delicate children, for which he lived. They grew on their own roots, bred at this height remote from the valley, far from any breath of contagion. Merciless to himself in toil, he had gouged out his hill patch from ground almost as intractable as granite. No vines had ever grown on it before. His hands were gnarled and massive, his frame tireless with the earth-renewed strength and the humble devotion of the peasant. From these grapes he made a small amount of an amber, rock-grown wine, six casks a year. It never varied in quality. His taste was exquisite, his judgment infallible. The great gifts are possible only to those fit to receive them. A very little of the wine he kept for himself.

Cleve stirred, peered again for a minute, then covered the roots, tamped down the earth, and sat up.

"Only black-knot," he said. "All right now. They had a bit of frostbite last winter."

Blanqui's eyes misted with relief, and he tugged slowly at his moustachios. In the flame of a match Cleve sterilized his knife blade.

"They'd be out of the freeze, of course, in that loam. It's more sheltered."

"*Non, non!*" Blanqui lifted a great hand. "They like it here, they don't nowhere grow so good. Them rocks, the sun heat them up all day, and my little Pinots they keep warm all night."

"One good way to look at rocks," said Cleve, rising.

Blanqui led them into an arbor of saplings roofed with creeper, and diffidently brought out a flask. The wine was a cool amber, austere, yet ethereal. It was a sanctuary wine.

215

Cleve knew he would remember it always, attaching it to this arbor and bright day, the hour and this scene, the two elders with hats on the ground, the half-bubble of glass lost in Blanqui's hand of gnarled oak. Had it been grown further away, it would have been turbid; lower on the slope, sharp and boisterous; on the flat, muskety.

Tall, green pines propped up the indigo sky. Over a laburnum bush in the garden hovered butterflies. Far off in the haze to the west was a cliff with a waterfall as white as a chalk-mark.

Outside of the valley no more than eight men knew where Blanqui grew his wine, and still fewer knew one of the secrets of its clarity. Cleve searched, and his eyes found it—an ivy-clad winery a half mile below, on the turn of the road. The true spores, as invisible as motes, journeyed here on currents, or on bees' wings, and brought the proper flora to Blanqui's vats. Wrong spores, and there were thousands adrift and waiting, would have been as calamitous as a hailstorm.

"Father Clare," said Blanqui, "he say to me, 'Étienne, you change roots on them vine and I don't let you come to my church no more—not to high mass.' Ha!"

He walked with them to the gate, and they drove off. Towards the town, Port gave a mute whistle.

"That Pinot Chardonnay, it goes to only six customers, they tell me. He don't want any more. He wouldn't grow another yard of it, not one plant."

"He's not so dumb as he looks."

"Not in farming. And he worked for Charley Krug right here. There's no trade that's all in a book. My old man learned me coopering, and he never could read more than his own name."

216

The white half-Arab, after galloping through the town, slowed on the long incline. It reached the crown of the hill at a walk. Montino wheeled into vision, its rows turning like spokes from an axle. The tracts were already in shadow, the leafage greener in the oblique light. Cleve looked at Alda's nursery, then at the hollow on the edge of the Rish Baba field. Between that dip and the sunset was a parade of olive trees, and he observed that even though the shadow was deeper, the leaves were a tone lighter.

"You changed your mind 'bout not going down to the Baynes'?" asked Port.

"No."

"It's a good chance for a young fellow. They got mighty big vineyards down there. They're all paying, too, more than here."

"After seeing Blanqui's, I can understand."

"Seems like a good offer," Port went on. "And maybe you can pick up something new. Everybody comes back here sometime. Like Mr. Wente and Father Clare."

"I'd rather work here." They were coming to the gate of the back road. "You'll stay for dinner?"

"No, I got to see a customer at the hotel. About a vat repair job."

"Then I'll walk the rest of the way."

He went up along the fence, out through the corral, and hoping that the lightness was on the Barbera patch, came to the hollow. No, it was on the Gamay. A clump of the precious Gamay, rocking in the wind, turned their pallid faces upon him. He charged into the hollow, ran halfway up, and flung himself upon the nearest vine. He rubbed the gray-white off a leaf, and beneath was a weblike stain. Oidium! Other leaves were tightly curled up, and he un-

217

wound them. Grubs of the leaf-roller were inside. He froze with dismay. A double calamity. The ravaging had been going on for a week, a fortnight. Vulturnus, the southwest wind, had picked up taints from the flat and wound trickily into the hollow where smitten vines could most easily be overlooked.

It would spread, of course. He computed the loss at a hundred vines. That was putting it high; there would be salvage, but the quality of the Gamay this year was gone. He walked on to the house, entered the kitchen and slumped into a chair.

Alda was laying the table against dinner. "I figured you'd be late getting home from Blanqui's, and wouldn't go up to the Lanes'."

"No, it's a long drive." He felt his unshaven chin. "And the way I look, it'd take me a week to spruce up."

"Blanqui had some trouble?"

"Only his eyesight. He was all of a tremble. He thought he had the phloxy on his vines, but it was only black-knot. I fixed it. Then he gave us some Chardonnay. Clear like a gong. What Pinots! And it wasn't so much them, either, as the making."

"A real farmer," Alda said, dishing the potatoes. "But mostly it's that he lives with his vines. No vineyard is good, Hector used to say, unless the farmer's been picking grapes from his own window for forty years."

Cleve then sat at table, bare feet hooked on the rung of the chair. Alda hummed a little harvest song.

> "*Health from the Father,*
> *And length of days,*
> *Vine give claret,*
> *That I may praise.*"

218

"White's good, too," said Cleve, buttering a crust. "Blanqui's is. I'll get me some cuttings from him."

"He got his first plants from Oxhill," said Alda. "The Pinot Chardonnays. They make a Montrachet, like a peacock's tail for show."

Cleve glanced through the window. A light gleamed above the trees. It was up at the Lanes'. He would have been glad to see Jule, he really wanted to see her, but she was entirely too much wrapped up with Vic.

"Jule was down again to ask," said Alda. "I told her you had to go to Blanqui's farm on business. Maybe you can go up after dinner."

"No." He had a sudden flicker of dislike for Carola, who had chosen this particular week to expand her graciousness over Montino and at the Grange. Alda would have to go to the Sociable, and take along a huge cake, crowned with a bunch of millinery grapes dipped in icing.

"They must have got my letter by this time. D'you know, it's all over town that I had those Bayne offers. Port spoke about it."

"Why didn't you bring him in for dinner?"

"Said he had to go to the hotel and consult about a vat job. You'd think it was a job for the government."

"Inglenook people, I guess. They're terrible finicky. Got their vats roped off so nobody can touch them."

Cleve pushed his plate away, and, as Hector had been used to do before him, tipped back, opened the drawer and took out pipe and tobacco. His brow contracted.

"Even if Carola wasn't there, I wouldn't go up tonight. When we were driving here I looked over into the hollow, and I saw something."

"In the hollow?"

"The Gamays."

"Bad?" she asked in a small voice, lowering her cup.

"I don't know how bad. But bad enough. Mildew. And the roller."

Alda's breath came slow. "A pity it had to happen now." And it was not Carola's visit she had in mind. "A pity."

They had counted on the Gamay. Harberg-Lowen, the imposing grocers, were to have taken all the wine of that patch, to put out in "kicked" bottles, under the new Montino label, black with green print. Alda's share of the money would pay off all the villa taxes, buy an olive press and a new shingle roof for the stable.

"Don't worry too much about that," he said. "It's not all gone. After all, the berries are set. A half is lost, maybe, or a third. It's the leaf-roller that did most of the mischief. I can knock it. Won't get any worse."

"After the five weeks it's had," she said calmly, "it's no more'n we should expect."

Cleve rose. "I'm going to fix up some sprays. Over at the stable."

He loaded up the wood-box with kindlings, then went out with lanterns. He put kegs into the wagon, filled them with chemical dusts, sulfur for the oidium, fluosilicate for the bugs, yoked up Chess, and drove on to the hollow. It was a windless night. The breeze, if it went at dusk, wouldn't return until morning. A full moon, too, and a bright powdering of stars. After pulling down the barrels, and taking Chess back, he strapped on a knapsack-sprayer, carried out a half dozen flares, lighted them, and began to spray chemical. He began at the far end, where the blights were heavier, pumping sulfur first. It whitened him like a miller. The machine rasped, like the scraping of burnt toast. The sulfur troubled him not at all, for he wore a respirator. Moths danced and hovered about the flares. Harmless moths, not the kind that spawned cutworm larvae.

At night everything looked perfect. Perhaps things weren't so bad as he thought. He dreaded to think what the dawn might show. Steadily he blew out dust. Owls swung ponderously, blunderingly between the rows, without ever bumping into anything. Once a raccoon, intent on its business, poked in, recoiled at sight of him, then trotted back into darkness.

Over at the villa, he could hear Alda singing a hymn, "David's Greater Son," as she sewed under the kitchen lamp. He knew she was thinking about the Gamay, and the burden upon him who had to save it. She thought more of the Gamay, which had been Hector's, than of the Rish Baba, which were hers, and had so often got her into the valley papers. "Fools' names and fools' faces, they ever are in public places," she said to him once, frowning as she threaded her needle at the lamp. She was glad to drop back into obscurity. Nevertheless, the Gamay was famous. Its wine lacked only the touch of fascination to be perfect. It had not the unearthly delicacy and the fairy-like fragrance of Blanqui's wine, but nobody knew Blanqui. He was a name on a cask, on six casks. How calmly he had inspected Blanqui's hurt vine, dispelled his fears and reassured him! And what a quaking had seized upon him when he thought of the blight on his own Gamay! But he felt easier now, for he was fighting. The vineyard was a perpetual battleground, the bush ever a creature to be guarded against thrusts, repulses, buffetings and all the powers of darkness.

Up at the Lanes' the four were sitting about the card table. In the fireplace, though the evening was balmy, a

221

handful of cones yielded incense and a slow flame. Jule had not wanted to drive to town, and the party was quietly sunk in whist, though nobody happened to be much in the mood for a game. Concha brought in a tray of biscuits, placing it on the table by the window, after drawing back the hanging. Marthe, cutting the deck, glanced through the window. It gave out over the hollow where the darkness was prinked with tiny glows as of matches.

"Must be Wing trapping down there. Gophers are pretty bad this time of the year."

"It can't be Wing," Vic said, dealing the cards. "I gave him a lift down the road only two hours ago."

Vic had raced to the village and back, burning up the highway, merely to fill the slack period after dinner. Jule, declining to go out at all, had curled up on the sofa with a dull book. She listened as she played, and heard the wheezing and clump of the duster.

"Spraying," she said.

The game played itself out. The sound of the machine was still audible. "Want to come for a walk, Vic?" she asked, throwing her hand down. "The flares are still burning. It must be Cleve."

"Sure, I'll come. It'll be a breath of air."

Carola waited until the door closed.

"She's been in nearly all day," she said. "Just what do you suppose the matter is? She couldn't be coaxed out. Why isn't she more interested in Vic?"

"Oh, I think she is interested."

"When she was staying with us, she went out with Vic only twice. A dance and a concert at Santa Clara. I really don't feel I should enquire into what her thoughts are. But I'm afraid she didn't enjoy herself as much as she should have done."

"You're imagining it, Carola. She just loved her stay down there."

"I'm not concerned for Vic, of course. He just about turned himself inside out to give her the proper attention. But we mustn't expect him always to come dashing up at the least snap of her fingers. Vic's terribly popular. I know he's fond of her. After all, they were brought up together, and they have so much in common. And that's a sensible basis for marriage. Jule really could be just a little more thoughtful."

"You think something's gone amiss?"

"I do," said Carola abruptly. "I don't believe she's interested. She's written several letters to Alda Pendle's boy. She's interested in nobody else. It's queer you didn't suspect that."

Marthe looked at her in cold wonder. She had more than suspected it. And here was Carola, sometimes the least bit too complacent, as a city matron might be towards a spinster in the country, and quite blindly wrapped up in her son, suddenly vaunting herself on her shrewdness. No marriage could have pleased Marthe more than an alliance between the Baynes, a reasonably old family, as lines went in California, and the Lanes, who had been established long before Giorgio Regola ever heard of the valley. It wasn't for Jule to hurl herself upon Vic's head. Vic's "popularity," indeed!

"The Pendles," Carola said briefly, "are just nobodies."

"I suppose," remarked Marthe, "that has just occurred to you."

She looked down into the night, and Carola watched the ormolu clock.

"How long has it been going on?" she asked. "Have they again been seeing much of each other?"

Marthe looked down upon the starlit vineyard. Cleve, she knew, meant far more to Jule than Vic did. The girl wrote to him, spoke often of him, and yet their meetings were rare. He seldom came to the house. He was aware, of course, that he was not approved, that Jule was a favorite of the Baynes, that she was to marry their son. It should be quite understandable to him and Alda why their ties with the household should not be closer. Nevertheless Marthe felt resentment. Her feelings, her pride ran deeper than logic. Cleve had not been overly attentive to Jule. Always there had been a man on the vineyard neglectful of someone on the hill. As she herself had been disregarded by Hector, so Jule was disregarded by the one who had stepped into his place. Strange, this pattern of relationship between the two farms. But not if she could help it would she let Jule be caught up in the same web. She hated Montino. She wanted Jule to marry Vic. And her pride forbade her letting so much as a suspicion drift through the other's head that another on the hill had been treated indifferently by someone on Montino.

"Jule," she said briefly, "has been brought up to look after herself. She's also of age, for a woman. So I haven't asked her."

Down in the hollow the duster thumped, and exhaled a wheezy last breath. Cleve went over to refill it at the keg. Voices and footfalls drew near. He peered through the aura of light into blackness.

"Hullo, Cleve!" shouted Vic. "We saw the flares and we came down. You're hunting gophers?"

"I'm hunting worse." They shook hands. "Sorry I couldn't get up tonight. Had to look at vines up on the ridge."

224

"You're spraying?" asked Jule. "You should have got us down. We'd have had a spraying bee."

Vic pulled off his coat. "Let me help. I'm a hellion with the sprayer."

"This is the only hurdy-gurdy we've got. Old one. Try it, if you like. But you'll get all sulfur."

Vic slung on the machine and left, buckling the strap. Jule sat on the ground.

"I hated to think of you not coming up," she said. "I'm glad we saw the flares. I was just waiting for a chance to come down."

"Don't think I didn't want to see you. I'd planned to go up there, and I was coming back from Blanqui's when I saw these vines. Right from the road. The light happened to strike them just so. It was oidium, for one thing—the mildew."

"I'm sorry about that."

"And leaf-roller for another."

"I'm just awfully sorry."

"Thanks. I'm getting my wits back now. I might be able to save a lot. But I'll have to wait until morning to see if I'm laboring under a delusion. A few hours, or a day or two, won't make a great difference. But if I fling on a truckload of sulfur and stuff, I feel I'm doing at least something."

He watched Vic, who was at a distance, pumping towards the end of the row. A flare cast Vic's shadow large upon the foliage of a wall of olive trees. A good fellow, Vic. He had offered at once to help, without stopping to ask what the trouble was. Vic didn't know much about vines. He didn't have to know anything. Merely to own grape property was enough for the Baynes, who were

225

wealthy enough to buy Montino fifty times over. They could give Vic and his wife everything they wanted.

"You're always so lost in your vines," said Jule. "Don't you ever have thoughts of anything else."

"You think I don't?"

"Sometimes I do. You're utterly lost in the vines, and Alda is lost in her hybrids—and I don't suppose anything else"—she smiled at him, her teeth shining in the light of the flares—"matters very much, does it?"

"There, that's done!" shouted Vic, coming over, pulling the strap over his head. "At least, the thing's empty."

"Dear Jule, if only I could tell you—" Cleve began.

"Yes?" she whispered.

Vic disengaged himself from the machine, and for a moment, as he stood before the flare, his figure cast a shadow upon them. He brushed off his clothes. "You goin' to call it a night, Cleve? Come on up to the house. We've got some cold beer. Got to wash that sulfur dust out of my throat."

"No," said Cleve. "I've a couple more rows. I'd just as soon have them all sulphured before I turn in."

"Some kind of pest is it, or are you dusting on general principles?"

"Pests. Worse luck. Mildew and the bugs that roll leaves up like tenpenny nails."

"You'd be happier with gophers, I fancy. Well, come on now, Jule. I'm so full of brimstone I'll blow up. Good-night, Cleve."

They were gone. Cleve refilled the machine. Tomorrow, he hoped, he might see Jule again. And perhaps he could tell her what he wanted to say. The two climbed the hill, Vic singing loudly to clear his throat. Cleve shifted the flares into the next avenue, still lower into the hollow, where the footing was steeper, and pumped on doggedly.

It was Jule who noticed the stillness in the parlor when they entered. There was not only stillness, but an air of tension. On the sofa sat Carola, heavy, correct and bodeful; in the chair by the window sat Marthe, rigid, hands clasped, and looking anything but patient. They must have had a flare-up, Jule felt. Carola had the Montino brand of temper, which was the devil's own and kept smouldering like a banked fire.

"Hullo, here we are!" Jule sang out breezily. "It's poky here, and you should have been out with us. Such a lovely night, and the air was good among the vines."

"Sulfury, though," said Vic. He rang the bell, and when Concha put her head in at the door, he asked her to fetch beer. "Cleve was dusting grapes. I gave him a hand."

"What was it in the hollow?" asked Carola. "Gophers?"

"Some kind of bug that rolls cigars. And a touch of mildew."

"On the Gamays!" said Carola. "Oidium and leaf-roller on the Gamays!"

"Do calm yourself, Mother!" implored Vic. "It'll be aw-ll right. He's been working on those vines for hours, smoking out those—"

A look from her withered him. He shrugged, then retired to a corner with his beer and a deck of cards until the storm frayed itself out. Carola stood before the window, looking out, outraged but majestic, her face ironbound, her jet beads trembling. They could hear the faint

227

thumping of the duster. The night was still, and in the hollow the flares were as steady as the light of glow-worms.

"It's inexcusable! There should be no pests this season. The only field they look after is the Rish Baba. Table grapes and olives—garden truck! No wonder Montino has run down." Carola looked at Marthe. "I'm going down in the morning to speak to them."

Jule saw it at once. Aunt Marthe had been setting Carola off against the two at the villa. Cleve worked no-where but in the vineyard. Her aunt's dislike of Montino and the villa folk carried her beyond all reason at times. She hadn't ever forgiven Hector, nor the Mayacamas girl he had married, nor Cleve.

"The Gamay wine will be ruined," said Carola. "Sheer negligence! I'm glad he didn't come down to our place. He would have ruined it."

"If—I—remember—" Jule intervened. She was sitting back in her chair, her long legs crossed, and the smile was only about her teeth. "The Baynes have been fighting phylloxera and vine disease there for the last year. Mon-tino's free of them. If you had nothing worse than those Gamay spots, you'd be lucky."

"Jule, Jule," cautioned Marthe.

"It was inexcusable to lose the Gamay," Carola went on.

"You're crying havoc before it's time," said Jule. "Be-fore you know anything's lost. The pests came on the wind, and nobody's to blame. It would be like blaming Cleve if the villa got hit by lightning."

"He should have watched out for them," said Carola. "It was sheer negligence."

"Sheer fiddlesticks!"

228

Marthe rose stiffly. "I might remind you, Jule, that it is Carola who is responsible for Montino."

"Nonsense!" Jule plumped out. "Carola's no farmer. The responsibility is Cleve's. Every one of us here knows that. As for the Rish Baba field, that's Wing's pet, and he runs it for them. But it's Cleve that runs the vineyard."

"And none too well, I should say," said Carola.

"Again fiddlesticks!" Jule got up, flicked away her ghost of a smile, and directed her gaze at Carola's frown. "And I might remind you that for the last year the Bayne firm has been trying to coax Cleve to work for them."

It was Marthe who looked uneasy. Perhaps if she had spoken fewer hints and criticized Alda and Cleve less, Carola Bayne would have come off with more dignity, perhaps unscathed. She did not dare look at Carola, she could only fix a glance of reproach on Jule, and feel thankful she herself had been untouched.

"You have been unjust to him," Jule continued. Her words had the chill fall of icicles. "Extremely unjust, both of you."

Carola's bosom expanded. For all her interior rage, she gave out only a little flustered breath. Vic gave a chuckle over his solitaire. The spitfire had given her a raking she wouldn't forget in a hurry. She had deserved it, too. Vic was a bit dull, even for a farmer, but quite a fine sort, really, and no one knew better than the Baynes, who rather did things on the cheap, that so prodigious a worker as Cleve, a "viti" man besides, would be a jewel in their winery and fields. It wasn't every qualified farm manager who could squint into test tubes, rustle up or grow the thirty-odd herbs for a vermouth, develop a strain of wine-yeast culture, and do a fair job of horse-doctoring. Only a few chaps had the knack of doing all that. Cleve was a handy one, too, at coping with pests. And the sooner they got him away from Montino, the better. Carola sent her eyes towards Marthe. She was still smarting, and both incredulous and annoyed. Why on earth should Marthe have let her expose herself to Jule's spear-thrusts, without the least chance of defense?

Marthe rose again, framed a "Well!", but said nothing, and rang for the Indian girl.

"Bring in some chocolate."

Jule sat at the piano, took off her rings, and played "Myosotis," airily, looking out of the window. The flares were still going. Vic, scooping up the cards, listened to the music. For all the lightness, she pulled tonality out of all the major chords.

"Vic, did you bring your fiddle?"

"No. I traded it for a motor-horn, old girl."

"Then we can't have duets."

"I prefer a single-hand game, myself."

The chocolate came, in an earthenware jar, and Concha, rolling the stem of a twirler between her palms, fluffed it up with cream. It was still screeching hot as she poured it into the cups.

"Nobody can quite make it like Concha," said Carola.

Tranquility had returned. Even the Montino temper had ebbed out. The heat of the chocolate, which had to be drunk in the minutest sips, and the task of balancing hot cups on one's knee, helped to distract thought from the quarrel.

"Aunt Marthe, shall I have that twirler for my dowry?" said Jule.

"The only one we have," said Marthe, briefly.

Her chocolate was renowned. Most of its quality derived from Concha's beating, Mexican style, with that redwood twirler.

"Port made it for us, on his lathe," said Jule pleasantly, to gloss the troubled waters.

"The cooper?" asked Vic. "I remember him."

"I used to visit his shop when I wore pigtails," said Jule. "There was a wild tomcat that just yowled at his window every time it heard the lathe whirling. Port's a dog man and he'd cuss and cuss, and he'd always open the window so it would stop yowling and come in. That kept up for years, and it was a joke with everyone, because he hated cats.

"Then the tomcat didn't show up any more. Port went all over town enquiring. When he found a truck had run over it, he was upset and went on a jag for a week. It was when he was sobering up he made that twirler for us. We sat on the bench and watched him, Cleve and I. That's going back a page," she laughed.

Marthe's spoon clicked. Except for the crackling of the pine-cones, the silence was thick and warm. The little ormolu clock rang midnight.

"I've got to be on the ridge at sun-up," said Vic. "To knock over some rabbits."

"It is rather late," said Carola, rising. "Good-night. Don't let anyone wake me up."

Their feet moved down the passage, up the stairs, and into rooms so distant that the closing of the doors was inaudible. Marthe sat ready, hands in her lap, and Jule did not keep her waiting.

"That's over now, utterly over."

"It was shocking!" said Marthe. "I never thought such a thing could happen under my roof. I must ask you to apologize to Carola tomorrow."

231

Jule laughed softly. "And undo all I've done? I've been looking for that chance a long time, Aunt Marthe. Believe me! It wasn't a hint either, it was a facer. I'm sorry you had to get it, too. But that'll make it easier for the both of you. You'd both been stamping roughshod on Cleve. And I didn't like it."

"Jule, it was monstrous!"

"Was it? I had to remind her I wasn't such a fool as she took me for. She knew that all she said about Montino was false. And she doesn't like Alda nor Cleve. And she knew I'm awfully fond of Cleve, fonder than of anybody else in the world."

"I was afraid of it. And nothing else matters? Your position, your bringing up, your future?"

"Nothing, dear Aunt," Jule breathed. "It's useless my trying to believe anything else matters."

"I'm sorry. We had plans for you. And I had hoped you'd have sense enough, and judgment enough, to marry Vic. It would have been an advantageous marriage. And if you wanted it deeply enough, I'm sure the Baynes would even have got Montino for you."

"It wouldn't be worth having without Cleve."

Marthe stared into the fire. "You could have shown more tact."

"Why didn't Carola? She was quite tough-hided! You'll never believe how much tact I did show. What I could have said!" Jule got up and put a hand on her aunt's shoulder. "Do think I've got at least a grain of sense. It wouldn't do to feel that all the Lanes are imbecile when young. Good-night, Aunt Marthe."

Jule carried the tray and the chocolate things into the kitchen, then she went down the hill. The moon hadn't shifted much overhead, the same stars were fixed in the velvety sky. Much had happened, but it had all happened in brief time. Wing's place was still dark; he was having a long night at cards. Under the black columns of the eucalyptus trees, the frogs were shouting. In the hollow the flares were gone, and in the moonlight the vines were like rows of white umbrellas. Someone came from the winery, latched the door, then came up. She waited under the madrone.

"Cleve."

He turned. "That you, Jule?"

"Didn't I surprise you?" she asked as he took her arm.

"No. Since you came back, it's seemed as if you were always very close by."

"I had to come down, had to talk with you. Oh, the frogs! What a din! Let's go over to the bridge."

"It's noisy there, too, at the water. But it'll be a walk. Let's walk."

They went down a path through a maze of olive trees, trellises and vines in clumps and rows; Jule first, in her long dinner dress, walking from the hips in her slow, easy stride. She knew every foot of the vineyard and the hidden openings in the trellises between avenue and avenue. The din was louder in the reeds under the bridge.

They rested their elbows on the sapling parapet and looked down the gully.

"I was going to take you and Vic riding up to Port's old place above Silverado," he said. "A picnic. Day after tomorrow, I thought."

He caught up a pebble and threw it into the water, blue-whited like ice in the moonlight. The tromboning muted the space of a sigh, then resumed majestically.

"That would be one way of seeing you for a while," he said. "For a whole afternoon."

"I'd have come riding with you anyway." She linked her arm in his. "I had to come down and see you tonight, Cleve. Something's happened. Carola went on a rampage. She said she was coming down to see Alda and—I suppose—give her a wigging over this Gamay trouble you've got."

"Oh, I say, I'd like to see her try that! Alda'd bring her over to see me, and I'd do what talking's needed. But she wouldn't have to come down. I'd just as soon go up there."

"You won't have to," said Jule with a short laugh. "And she won't come here, either. I told her off, Cleve. I took the Regola temper by the horns. And I told her exactly what I thought. I'd been planning for that ever since my pigtail days. So it's all up now between your little Jule and the Baynes."

"But—but Vic . . ."

"Oh, Vic can be sensible. He knows how I feel about it."

"What do you mean?" He locked her wrist in a tight grip. "I thought you two were tremendously in love, and all but married. And now—"

"Silly!" she breathed, smiling at him. "D'you think I'd have such a bust-up if I wanted to marry him? It's you I've been in love with all the time. I've never been in love with anybody else."

She smiled at him wet-eyed. Then, caught in his arms, she gave a laugh of pure happiness. He had held her often before, for he had loved since he didn't know when. But this was like holding another, a more real, a warmer, a more incredible Jule. He had once on a cold day seized in a vine a bird so beautiful that he half feared it, and instead of struggling it gave but a cry and a flutter, as if it had wanted to be caught up and warmed in his hands.

The myriad frogs tromboned their epithalamium. In the dry planking a cricket rasped at its wing-cases. A lamp for a moment shone in the Chinaman's window. The moon was gone, and between the mountain to the east and the sky a crack lightened. Then the two on the bridge stirred.

"Night's all smashed," said Jule, combing back her hair. "Time for me to be creeping home."

"When they're both gone, I'll come up for you," he said. "And take you away."

"I'll be ready."

They walked to the foot of the Lane slope; she sped up, and he turned into the villa. Over the vineyard was already a gray light.

He overslept, and it was almost eight o'clock before he was again in the thick of his work among the Gamays. At the first coughs of the duster—the vines were to get a snow of fluosilicate now—Wing came hurrying down in his slippers, queue flying.

"Mildew and roller," said Cleve. "I found out last night."

Wing gave a choked cry. "Lo-luh!" He grabbed agitatedly at a branch, unrolled a leaf here and there, and stamped heavily along the pitched bank, like a sailor in a gale. Halfway down the row his curses ran out. No reviling would have been adequate to express his anger at the injury to the vines—the Gamays he and the child Hector had planted for old devil Giorgio. He smote his forehead. The oidium was nothing. It had been caught in time, and these were the days of good sulfur. The leaf-roller was the wolf that had ravaged the lambs in the night. He relinquished a branch, then sat down, tied his queue in a hard, iron-gray ball, then shook earth out of his slippers.

Below, sitting on his heels, a cigarette pasted on his lip, was Cleve, squinting up at him.

"What d'you think of that, old-timer? Huh?"

"Too much lo-luh. Too fast. We lose plenty."

Cleve nodded. "Half, I guess. It looked so terrible last night I thought we'd lost it all. Not much mildew, but what there was didn't do any good."

"Alda, she see it?"

"She did. Before I got up. She figured a half's gone, too. Told me at breakfast." Cleve with eyes shut fast inhaled deeply from an inch of cigarette and flicked it into the air. "If it won't get better, it won't get any worse. A sufficiency of strong foliage remains to pull up the sap and keep the plants viable. Plenty leaf left, Wing. Gamays haven't gone to hell yet."

"I come down and make fire," said Wing, leaving.

He came back shortly under a wide hat, carrying a bucket and a roll of wire netting. The leaves not likely to unroll within a week, after another spraying, he picked off. He made a funnel of netting, poured in and fired the leaves. They roasted in dense smoke, and Cleve was driven, coughing, out of the hollow. He re-yoked Chess to the cultivator, and worked on toward the Pinot tract.

Wasps and midges hovered over the sweet-scented wake of torn morning glory and fennel. Turkeys followed, picking worms, headed by a bronze gobbler strutting like a beadle. Cleve moved drowsily in the heat, fatigued and still only half awake. The vines looked handsome this morning: Zinfandel on the one side, throwing out purple fires in the shadow; Palomino on the other, a cuirass of odorous gold, flecked with butterflies. The horse paused, muzzle in the dust, and Cleve rested a mo-

236

ment on the handles. The hollow was like a smoke-filled crater. Wing came up, fanning with his hat, his eyes cherry-red, and called out:

"Plenty shade on Gamay, Cleve. You take off leaf, and no sunburn."

Cleve nodded, and wiped his forehead. "Take off all you want."

He moved on to the Pinot tract. Alda's favorite vines were here. The midsummer chore of removing water-shoots she had done herself. This tract was her proving ground, along with the nursery where she groped for the thread that would lead on to the Regolberg. The cuttings she had grafted on were marked with knots of white cotton rag. Everywhere in the vineyard Cleve ran across them. Hundreds of knots. They reminded him of children with bandaged fingers. Here among the Pinots they were thicker. Scions grafted on other scions and stocks; on young roots and forty-year-old roots; hybrid upon hybrid, crossings upon crossings, related by descent, or laterally, like remote cousins, or not related at all. They were all down in her vine book. If that book were lost, she could recite the genealogies as one might recite the multiplication table.

Alda was coming into the tract now, and he watched her walk a row of vines, her hand touching this twig or that, lightly. It was only after she had passed it that he felt she had seen it intensely, in a flash, and had been merged with it. He envied her way with plants. She had innocence of eye. They were living things, and as she poured out her whole attention upon them, which she did in a split instant, an answering current from them met hers. She was immersed in things she had always loved because she had contemplated them deeply.

237

As she grew older, she seemed to be quieter, to be living in a self-forgetting attentiveness. He often wished,
because she played the piano so well, that she had not
relinquished it, to play only when Bascomb and the
schoolmaster came to the villa for an evening. It was as if
growing things, buds, the great madrones, a screen of
vine-leaves shaking out their foil, spoke to her with a
deeper note than music, with a language that her father
and Hector had understood. Leaves she could read in the
dark, as her fingers touched their mesh work of veinings
and lines. Cleve glanced up the slope, saw a figure coming down the path, then he waited until Alda entered the
nursery.

Carola was making her visit, after all. She came through
the yard, down the boardwalk, then on to the front door.
He was glad that Alda had gone on to the nursery, and
probably would be there for an hour or two. He entered
the house by the back, put on his coat and going to the
hallway he opened the door.

"How d'ye do, Cleve? I thought I'd have a talk with
you for a moment. I'll come in, yes."

He showed her into the den. She sat in Giorgio's old
chair, and looked out over the field, in the direction of
the service buildings and the hollow, over which the
smoke was thinning.

"You're having trouble here, I understand?"

She kept on her gloves. This would intimate a session,
and he saw himself on the carpet. Her authoritative manner, distant and crushing, was natural to her. There was
also something impersonal about it. She had identified
herself with what she referred to, in her letters, as "the
Bayne firm." And this she had put up as a supremacy, a
bogey before which all small persons should quail. Her

238

very faint smile was patronizing, and he had the suspicion that it was a trifle contemptuous. A little hard, too. She was still nettled after her brush last night. No, it had been a taking down. But it was still a smile, and she could afford to smile. The Bayne firm was the chief owner of the vineyard, and he was not even the manager. He was the workman.

"I saw the flares last night. And I hear that the Gamays have suffered mildew—and—the leaf-roller."

Her diction was over-manicured. If she were a vine, went his odd thought, he would cut her back to the ground, so she might start all over again. She was too rampant. Needed discipline.

"Yes," he said, at once.

Vic must have given her the names of the maladies. And that was probably all she knew of them. None of the Baynes knew much more of vines than that. He didn't think much of the Bayne outfit, though there was no harm in Vic, who made no pretence of knowing anything. Bayne had been having a rough time with the phylloxera and red spider. This year the nematodes would cost him another large piece of wine. Cleve hadn't seen their fields, but he felt, too, that their trouble this summer with black measles was due to just clumsy plowing. And Bayne left the white wines in cask too long before bottling.

"We shan't turn out as much Gamay as we did last year," he said. "I'm sorry about the accident. But what we do put up won't fall short of the mark. The first racking will tell. I hope the loss will be slight."

"You understand, I think, that Mr. Bayne had commitments for the Gamay wine." Her voice was crisp, eloquent of disapprobation. He knew she was just starting. If he couldn't cut her back, he would cut away the ground from under her. She would have to be squelched before she got up too much momentum. "We can't afford negligence here," she went on. "The Bayne firm will regard it as carelessness. Mr. Bayne had counted much on that Gamay. He will be very much vexed."

"I can understand," said Cleve. "Seeing how very— how rather unfortunate he has been with his property down there. All those maladies and," he added gently, "those accidents."

A pause. It was a pause that endured overlong. Cleve was glad Alda had been saved this unpleasantness.

"If you would," he resumed, "like to survey the Gamays for yourself, and see what—"

"No," said Carola abruptly. She rose. "I shouldn't. You'll tell Alda I called, will you?"

"I will. Thanks."

The leavetaking was perfunctory and she departed. He went back to his cultivator, awoke Ring, and drove on. Soon all the morning glory was ripped up, withered, gone. Like Carola. It would return, of course, but for a while there'd be peace.

Up at the road fork reports banged out. Through the firs he could see Vic's motor car, winding down to the highway. It was almost noon, the warmth mounting, and even Wing had succumbed to the languors of the day, lying under an olive tree, hat over his face. Cleve scuffed on to the villa, too drowsy to work further. There was little to do until the next spraying in the hollow, except to trap a gopher among the Rish Babas. He soused his head at the pump, and went into the kitchen, which was cool, for the stove was unlighted, and the shutters were drawn. Mostly they lived in the kitchen, which had improved. Water pipes had been run in, and wires for lighting. He found himself a crust of bread, some lukewarm coffee, and sat at the table, with a mail-order catalog propped on the oilcloth. He flicked through the pages, his head sank among the nickel-plated revolvers, and he dozed.

He thought he heard the door slam, but several minutes later, when he sat up, there was Jule opposite him, bright and fresh in a cool dress, sewing on a garden hat.

"Thought I'd come in for tea," she smiled. "Alda'll be here soon, after she's done some potting. She'll bring in some lettuces."

"I heard Vic's car. Thought the whole family had gone for a drive."

"They're having luncheon at the Geysers. I excused myself. I got up late, anyway."

Jule bit off a thread and appraised the bow on her hat.

"There, that looks like something! It ought to. It's my engagement hat."

"Carola was down. We had a little how-d'ye-do over the bugs. But she didn't stay long."

"I was in the garden with Vic. I told him. He understood perfectly. There's something awfully sensible about Vic. He doesn't take anything too seriously, not even himself. And I told him to breathe nothing about it until he hears from me."

"And Marthe?"

"She'll know after they're both gone. But I found Wing, woke him up, and told him. He wanted to go to Lum Yat's and bring things for an engagement dinner. I promised him he should, but he'd have to keep it secret for a while. That tickled him more than anything."

"We'll have to wait until the Baynes are gone."

"Carola's edgy. She's not even going to stay for the Grange Sociable."

"Not surprising," he laughed.

Alda came in with lettuce and sprigs of green basil, all wet from the pump. Jule put crockery on the black oil-cloth, and Cleve, lifting a board above the well, dragged up a bottle. When they were in their chairs, Alda made a salad in the old wooden bowl, fatiguing the leaves and herbs with oil, then with souring from a cruet. The bowl, shiny and dark, had been at Montino before she was born. Only she knew what was in the cruet, one of the few heirlooms she had brought from Oxhill.

"It's all in my head, and one day I'll put it down for you. Thieves' vinegar, Father called it. The Pendles always made it, back in Maine. Before that, they say, in England. Sweet tongue, hyssop, and basil—that's for the nose. Pot marjoram and bergamot for nose and taste. It's mighty aromatic. Thieves used to drink it for antidote when they went robbing in the Great Plague that was bad once in London. I don't know that the Pendles, being country people, ever robbed living or dead. But they thieved the formula, maybe." She laughed as she filled the plates. "They always set store by formulas—grapes or what."

"Oh, we had a visitor today," said Cleve. "Guess who?"

"Her?" said Alda, sending a glance up the hill. "She saw the flares?"

Cleve gave a brief and softened tale of the encounter. It might have been only a query, then an exchange of amenities. Alda clucked.

"Why didn't I know? I'd have invited her to the den.

There's some of that old Valente left that Giorgio was fond of."

"One happening a day's enough," Cleve returned, smiling. "There's something to tell you. We're getting married."

Alda put her fork down. "Well!" She patted Jule's hand. "I'm glad over it. Very glad."

"You know now," smiled Jule. "Nobody else does—here. Except Wing. I woke him up under a tree to tell him. He looked sort of dazed at first."

"People do," Alda said. "They do when it comes on them sudden the young are grown up."

"We made up our minds last night," Jule went on. "Didn't we—"

"I began hoping long ago," Cleve cut in. "When we used to go hunting with the greyhounds, the wind blowing through our hair, and you shouting—and always a little ahead. I was among the Zinfandels this morning, and two whirlwinds of dust went scudding between the vines. Then they turned the corner. Do greyhounds have ghosts?"

"Very little ghosts, I think," Jule said. "They must have left some, because they had great hearts."

There were many ghosts in Montino, she felt; and they clung to it with invisible fingers, as haze and aroma clung to the slope.

"So you're going to live here," said Alda. She got up. "It's been a while since I've gone all through the house. Come."

The week passed.

Since the foliage was thick, and the breeze came cool from the pines, the table was spread in the pergola. Cleve had put in the morning at the winery, going over the cooperage with Port. Flores, too, had come up, in his best suit, with a guitar.

It was a dinner that began with a gaiety that was subdued. Everybody was under Wing's thumb. They had to sit just here, or exactly there. All were seated where he wanted them; Cleve at the head, Jule at the foot, Port and Flores at their right hands; and Marthe and Alda together. Then he relaxed his tyranny. At the end of the pergola was a high-built barbecue, with axle bars laid across a fire of vine roots, and here he grilled turkeys, swabbing them with oil and syrup from a ginger pot.

"It'll be hard to realize they're married," said Marthe.

"At first," said Alda. "Then you get used to everything. But it isn't often there's been a bride at the villa."

"No, so we've got to make the utmost of it."

Marthe was relaxing into a generous mood. She had come stiffly correct, in black, already dressed for the drive to the rectory. (With everything except her prayer book, Cleve thought.) The marriage wasn't exactly what she had wanted for Jule. She had prayed for a match with Vic; and now she was praying there wouldn't be a breach with the Baynes, her closest friends of all. Though she would not have admitted a wavering, she had for so long identified herself with Jule that she was remotely pleased with the marriage. It corresponded with a deep, inner need; it was a justification, an alliance with Montino. Jule's happiness touched her with an emotion that made her indulgent. And no rigidity could fail to crumble in this sunlight, this merriness under the canopy of leaves. And Flores sang rumblingly as he plunked his guitar, teeth shining in a grin like a split pumpkin.

"Yo no digo esta can-cion,
Sinon a quien con migo va!"

That was the chorus everyone joined in, thwacking the table with knife-handles. Flores knew a hundred songs, though only two or three tunes, but made up for that by singing like a basso archangel. Wing, rolling a cigar, speared with barbecueing fork a yard long and helped the birds.

Toasts, toasts shouted out—compliments to Jule and Cleve and everyone. The hard-working Port came in for badinage. Flores boomed praise for his vats which, he averred, let in air through knot holes, and when they didn't hold wine, they made good chicken coops. The jests were traditional. They heightened the fun. It was all very gay and picnicky, and Jule, with her garden hat, was in the thick of it. She got along with simple people. Marthe warmed and felt content. The gaiety was full now. And she had always liked this view from the pergola, which she had known when the old Senator lived at Montino and all parties were fashionable.

"Isn't that a pretty bush," she said, looking into the field. "The one with the butterflies."

Alda turned. "That? Yes, it promises." Her eyes half closed as she watched it. "We had to coddle that one. It began from a cutting."

"They're all shapely. Loaded down, too—in their spare way. I never saw them look handsomer."

"Nobody sees the failures. I don't leave them in the ground. With that row, I had some trouble at first."

Alda pointed down the row. She recounted briefly the story of each bush in the file, burnished and silvery, lit by

245

the afternoon sun. Her fingers were nicked, they had the gunpowdery stain of bluestone, they were hardened but supple. She had, Marthe reflected, grown into her forties still handsomer, her face darker, her eyes quick with awareness when she looked upon growing things. Her nostrils flicked in the emanations from the heated earth and the grapes, like clusters of glass bubbles, dusky and smouldering.

"They came through, you see. I could see what they were moving to."

"The care," said Marthe.

"They only wanted a little help. Some were a temperament. Push them one way, and they go another. And some of them improved right fast, as if they'd got to believe in you."

"The grapes!" boomed Flores, hoisting his glass. "The bride and the grapes! The bride!"

"The bridegroom, too," interposed Marthe.

"Bridegroom!" roared Flores.

Then, having run out of toasts for the moment, he settled to strum his pet tune—with the right words this time—"La Paloma."

"She will be happy here," said Marthe to Alda.

"Aunt Marthe—listen!" Jule called out. "Here's a song."

Alda leaned back, smiling, only half listening. All this under the canopy of the pergola she had been hoping for since Cleve was small. It was a reward, like the flowering of a new vine. She leaned her head against the trunk entwined about a pillar, and she felt as much as heard the speaking of the foliage tremulous in the breeze. She was aware of a bliss, a rapt and still equanimity. The day was breathing with peace; the beauty of existence and a sense of continuity of life enfolded her like the perfumed dry air of the slope. Memories surged up, waves in the wash and surge and ebb of time. The struggles on Oxhill and Montino, the disasters, the floods and scourges, the days of grilling toil and the great and lesser vexations—she had endured them, and in the further enduring she would be untouched. Above was the sun, underfoot was the old earth instinct with life; there was always the dream, and upon her had been fastened the armor of fortitude and patience.

12.

THE gopher hole down at the Zinfandels was hardly wider than one's thumb, and only this very small gentleman in sunbonnet could have discovered it at all. With his own particular spade, that Wing had bought for him at the Bee Hive Notions, he enlarged it, almost the size of his tin bucket. The task had been made easier for him by the frantic help of a terrier, whose paws whirred at the opening like an eggbeater.

A voice quavered up at the nursery. Wing removed his bamboo pipe, closed his eyes, and listened reflectively. The call was for him. Who would be calling him this hot, drowsy afternoon, with Cleve and Jule away at town, and the vineyard asleep? Port and Blanqui were not coming here until five. He was comfortable here on the log, watching Gio dig, and good practice it was for him. They were the one pest this year, gophers.

"I go," said Wing. "Back in while."

"No, you stay here!" commanded Gio. "You got to help me."

Wing rose, paused irresolutely before the barelegged small tyrant, and knocked out his pipe. Gio stamped and roared. Such flouting of his wishes was unheard of. Wing had never openly disobeyed him before.

"Alda, she call," Wing tried to explain. "Call-um long

time. You stay here with Tam. Dig mo' hole. I bling down tlap."

"Bring a big trap," ordered Gio. "It's a gopher"—he stretched his arms—"that big."

"All 'ight."

The storm vanished, Gio and Tam returned to their digging. Wing trod in his slippers along the wall of foliage, keeping in the shade, and moved in dust and haze up to the nursery. Perhaps Alda wanted a hand to shift the callousing boxes outside, or cut away some of the vine over the glass-enclosed end, so that the sun might pour in more fully. These warm days she usually kept within the house, not coming into the nursery until late afternoon, to work about the hot-bed, or at her potting-bench, or in the tilled earth just outside the door, and on both sides of the walk, where coreopsis grew, and tall bushes of fennel and basil. They attracted butterflies, and in the dry, herb-scented air twanged bees and wasps, looping like gilded shot at the end of strings. Still, she was much in the nursery these months, working by herself, always keeping her hands busy, and more and more silent. A long way off a war was being fought. In the town had been parades. Wing had looked on from Lum Yat's shop, listening to the fifes and drums, seeing the men march by. The parades were over now. Young men had seeped out of the valley and the town was quieter. Lonelier, too, for Wing; all but a handful of his old friends had drifted to the city, there to spend their old age in the cool tranquility of the Six Companies House, where they had their cots, rice bowls, and pipes. Cleve could not go to war. He had a wife and his son Gio, going on six, Alda and Montino; and, help being scarce, he was three men in one.

Wing entered the nursery. He sat on a keg, and picked foxtail grass from his socks. Alda came in with a knife, and at the bench she whetted it on an oil hone.

"Gio all 'ight," he said. "He with Tam. In Zinfandel."

"He's safe. And time he had his sleep. You go bring me the ladder, Wing. Middle-sized one."

"You girdle?" He watched her sharpening the knife. "Late fo' girdle. Glapes all set."

She tested the blade, then turned.

"You know all the Rish Babas," she smiled. "I've been looking for a big, big cluster. Where would you find the biggest cluster on Montino?"

He sat with hands tucked into his sleeves, and thought. In the pasture the grapes were within a week or two of the ripening period, and all were moderately large. But coming to the nursery the other morning, and looking up at the roof, he had seen clusters veiled by leaves, and far greater than any in the field. It was a strong and large vine, this one grown by the nursery, the oldest on the farm, and rooted in deep gravelly sand. He had rather hoped he could keep the secret, but no vine on Montino could keep its secret from Alda.

He pointed to the roof. Then said, "I bling ladder."

"I'm going to thin the clusters," Alda said. "Just keep one, or two."

"Fo' Fair?"

"Yes."

Down at the stable he found the ladder, and marched up with it balanced on his head. Under its weight he ruminated. Not in years had Alda shown Montino's jar of Rish Baba at the Fair, to the confusion of all other rivals. Why should she trouble again? Word of her grape had gone far out of the valley, where nothing could be told of them that was not already known. It was the invincible, and so superior a grape did not have to ask for another ribbon in the town. Or perhaps she wanted to hear praise of it again. For many weeks now she had spent much time in the pasture, looking at the vines, even looking over the fence into the field beyond, where no vine had ever grown, and which was still in scrub and chaparral. He had seen her once or twice, also, standing for a long time with her attention fixed on the olive trees. Looking at them as he had long before seen her look hopefully at the Zinfandels.

He rested the ladder against the nursery wall for her, and she mounted it. One limb made the slatted roof all a bower. Her hand furrowed through the leaves, she examined clusters, then cut and cut, throwing them to the ground, all but two. About these she left a few leaves for shade, then she descended.

"They'll be very good, I think," she said. "They'll darken in the sun. They'll look fine in glass."

On the earth lay grapes, broken, a foot deep; wasps hovering over the sap. Alda, standing in their midst, with a hand on the trunk, looked up at the roof. Under scant leafage was the elected cluster. It would ripen alone, later than any in the pasture, but with greater promise of opulence, with thinner skin, and a hue that would offset the hint of coarseness inherent in unusual size.

"That one," she said, "isn't coming back. It's going away. Farther than I have ever gone from the valley."

He understood. "Fo' State Fair?"

"I got to have a big glass for it. Bigger than the ones at the Grange. Maybe the drugstore—"

"You come," said Wing.

They proceeded to the winery. Upstairs in the disused

lumber room, stuffed with old books, papers and boots and furniture, was an urn on a shelf. He brought it down. It was a blown-glass affair, larger than any at the drugstore; and had a stopper like a crown, and a base on which was "Montino" in gold letters. Giorgio had brought it here from Venice a half-century before.

"My, that's beautiful," said Alda. "That's for a branch and fruit. But how dusty it is. Wants cleaning."

Wing carried it to a bench downstairs, half filled it with suds, and poured in a tin of the birdshot that had belonged to Hector. Alda sat in the smaller vat room, watching him as he rocked and shook the urn patiently for a half hour. The room was cool. On a bench stood the cask that Port had given her for a wedding gift, and two plain casks—each housing a season's try of wine from her hybrids. These grew in a corner of the Rish Baba field, the fruit raised on crossings and re-crossings made in her nursery.

She still watched, cheek resting on her hand. In the indirect light the urn had the lustre of dark crystal, and on its shoulder flashed a highlight from the window.

"Plenty clean now," said Wing, giving it one last rub with a cloth. "Bottle go to house."

"No," said Alda, after a moment. "It will be safe here, and no dust will come in. Put it on that high shelf."

He obeyed.

"They'll be coming in soon, all of them," she said. "When you go to the house, open the transom in the den, and bring in the glasses. There's some smoked deer meat. Bring it in, thinly sliced. And a plate of crackers. Gio, where is he?"

Wing listened at the doorway.

"He sleep," he said, and went on.

252

It was very still in the vat room. No sound but the creak of a beetle in a pillar, and a faint stir of leaves in the madrone before the door. Alda, relaxed in her chair, gazed so intently at the glass urn that her mind slipped insensibly from the tranquil into the mesmerized state. She smiled with gratification. Something had been done today. Her pet vine had been thinned to its last cluster, but not without a pang in her breast. And a marvellous jar had come for it, out of empty air: a prize in itself, worthy of the Rish Baba, upon which crowds would look at the Fair. Giorgio had once spoken of her exhibiting the grapes outside of the valley. And she was doing so. For Montino. The world would read the letters in gold, and see the Rish Baba.

If anything happened to the vineyard—she dared not frame what even in unspoken words, and gave a shrug at the thought—there would be always the Rish Baba and the olives. They had thriven, the olives trees; grown slowly, for Abel thought there was no improving on the Spanish method of planting truncheons, not in the soil of these hillsides; but grown soundly, and grafted here and there with cuttings from older trees beyond Calistoga. So if the evil days came, and brought darkness upon the valley, there would always be bread—bread and oil, and the weighty table grapes, the symbol, if not the reality, of what men had lived for on the flat and this slope.

She walked on to the villa and her room in the lower wing that fronted the yard, and changed into her house dress. At these gatherings in the den always one or two more came than she expected, and Cleve might be bringing along someone with himself and Jule. Before the mirror she combed her pale-honey hair back in a Madonna parting, and fastened a cameo at her throat. She heard a tap.

"All right, Wing."

The door opened a crack, a hand slipped in with a tray holding an egg-shell cup of coffee and a biscuit and left it on the bureau. Then the door closed. Wing always came to manage these annual sittings. In grapes he judged by eye: his memory was an album full of images of grapes and leaves and twigs in color. She was pleased when last fall he remarked that the newest hybrid was the nearest yet to the Regolberg, though too wide in the leaf and not skimpy enough in the cluster. Ever since Gio had appeared at the villa, Wing was here all the time, going to the Lane house only to take up the morning cream. He had exchanged the cow for a twisty-horned Alderney that loved pomace and gave twice as much milk as the other. With Gio at his heels, and stake and rope, he was eternally in quest on the slope for tracts of richer grazing. It made little difference at the Lane house now, for Concha was living in, and the mistress was so often away in the city.

A vehicle pulled into the yard, and Alda, sipping the coffee—to clear her palate—looked out of the window. It was the sulky. Port came out of it, then Blanqui, then Mr. Wedge. That should make it a good séance. Who better than they knew the taste of the Regolberg?

Over at the stable Cleve was unhooking fat Ring and turning him into the corral with its shade of elderberries. A bark, and Jule, seeing Tam in the Zinfandels, strode thither, laughing, thumbs in her belt. So very much, went Alda's self-reflection, like herself when she first came to the slope. The vines, as Jule passed, would be aware of the resemblance. And Cleve was as another Hector. Alda rejoiced in samenesses. In the recurrence of pattern in

254

branch and leaf, she found a serene content, and in divergences of hue, line, or veining, the sharp delight of the moment. The younger pair, perhaps, were more headstrong and gay than she and Hector had been at their ages. Discipline and hard routine had been spared them, and if they had intensity of vision, they had at least seen more. And they were tolerant. For that she was thankful. That was not something to be acquired in youth. One was either born with tolerance, or it came upon one with age. As often as not, and she smiled at the thought, it never came at all. But she wouldn't have had her father different, nor Hector's father. Thorns were in the nature of the true, the perfect briars, and if she could not always rejoice in their perfection, especially when her thumb was stabbed, she could be indulgent, bind her thumb and turn for the while elsewhere.

When she looked at the new baby in Montino, Jule and Cleve asked her to think up a name for him. She was always good at names for kittens, puppies and vines.

"I wonder," she said, in a welling of happiness, into which entered all the outer loves of the slope and farm and villa, "how it'd do if we called him Giorgio?"

Jule laughed.

"Why shouldn't we? Hasn't a new tyrant come to Montino? I know what we'll do. We'll call him Gio for short."

There had been no trouble with Gio. After he had got over his teething, the whole vineyard was his cradle. His first steps were in a furrow among the Gamays, and he learned to walk hanging on to Wing's pigtail. The basin had been fenced off with chicken wire. Then Jule herself tore it down after Gio, naturally buoyant in water, had learned to swim like a turtle.

And Jule was always company when Cleve was away. Alda would never forget the night when they were sitting together in the kitchen, by the open window, looking over the vineyard in darkness and thunderstorm. Jule was telling her of a wet summer she had spent in the Ozarks with her mother, who had a large garden. It fascinated her to hear of gardens in a wet July. And the garden was full of gooseberries that flourished in the damp coolness. The names were entrancing. Early Sulphur, and Old Ironmonger, which was large, red, and hairy, and won prizes. Alda sipped tea, and listened. It was entrancing. No gooseberry nor a wet summer had ever happened in this valley. Then a zigzag of lightning jounced in the blackness over the stable. Rain clattered in a ripping of artillery.

"Oh, look!" said Jule. "The stable!"

They saw a dull, small flare. And Jule was gone instantly, through the window, right over the climbing geraniums. A swift vaulting. Anyone else would have gone through the door, after first grabbing a coat or umbrella. Alda did, and pulled on her coat first.

A bolt had ignited a pile of hay. After blanketing the heads of the animals, who had gone half mad, and turning them loose into the corral, they stamped out the fire. Nothing was much harmed except their boots.

It was Tam, watching at the gopher hole, who gave away Gio's hiding place. Jule groped inside, scooped him out of the cave, and when he woke had settled him on her shoulders. He yelled himself florid, howled and struggled to get back into his cave. Somewhere a bell tinkled.

"Let me go! I don't want to see anybody! We're catching a gopher!"

"Nice hunter, you are! Fast asleep. You come along now, and you can set a trap with Wing after supper."

That quelled him. He came up to the terrace, angelic. Cleve was waiting there for them.

"Look!" said Jule, shaking Gio's leg at him. "D'you hear that?" She shouted with incredulity, and yet her eyes danced in merriment. "And d'you see it? The bell!"

"I see it," said Cleve. The bell was fastened to Gio's high boot. "Copper rivets, too. Who did that?"

"It was Mike's bell, and Wing's saved it after all these years. Saved it for Gio."

"Lemme get down!" wailed Gio. "I got to catch my gopher."

"Sure," said Cleve. "But you come in first, and get a cake."

They went into the den. Gio quieted as soon as he got inside. The room, half darkened for coolness, was full of elders. Alda was sitting on the piano bench. Everyone was dressed for the visit; even Blanqui, who had put on a long, greenish tailcoat that gave him the look of a beetle. Atop the piano, between a photograph and a vase of pampas grass, were two bottles on which were glued written-over squares of paper. Wing filled glasses from the first bottle, which held the older wine.

It was sipped, and there was no interruption in the talk. The wine had not changed in bottle, save for a deepening of its green. Wing passed a plate of rice cakes, very dry and crumbly.

"I don't want any cakes," said Gio.

"He wouldn't," said Jule. "He ate himself sick on them this morning."

"I want some coconut," said Gio.

Wing went into his pocket and gave him some shreds of sugared coconut, mixed with bits of tobacco.

"No mo'," he said. "Lum Yat got no mo'. Only cakes."

Gio blew off the tobacco, ate half the coconut, and locked the rest in his damp fist for Tam. Inch by inch he retired, hovered unobtrusively in the doorway a moment, then fled.

"He was at the tasting, anyway," said Jule.

Wing opened the crucial bottle and sloshed wine into the glasses, with no more to-do than if it were water from the tap. And with no more to-do it was sipped.

"Dryer," said Jule, who was the youngest.

"Steely," said Cleve.

The bouquet was unwavering. It even seemed to increase in the glass. Port gave a nod and his customary grunt, then looked at Blanqui, who was the oldest, who had tasted more Regolberg than anyone in the den. Cleve held his breath. Alda had gone back to the hybrid she had grown four years ago, which had fullness, crossed into that, and come into something else. It had strangeness. And it also had struck him as would a face vanishing in a mist after it had looked at him with familiarity. He was nervous. It crossed his mind that Alda, too, was over-tense. She went to the window and without sound adjusted the slats of the French blind. But she made the room neither lighter nor darker. The least change would have disturbed Blanqui's silent interrogation in the corridor of his memory. The others, not touching their glasses, remained as still as chess players who had made their last move.

Cleve stared at Blanqui, and waited. The wine was already beyond the Chardonnay he had tasted with Port in the old farmer's bower up at the skyline. And when

Blanqui spoke, the verdict would be true. He had his vanity. But in greater measure he had wonder and rectitude. He raised his glass and tasted again, as if he were nibbling at the edge of a dream. Then he set down his glass, and without change in expression filled his pipe.

"That pretty near it?" asked Port, holding out a light.

"*Oui*," nodded the Swiss, bending his face to the match. "More near." He held up his gnarled hands and fanned them apart. "Li'l bit more full—li'l bit more stone taste, and rocks and flowers—and she pretty near there."

He sank back, holding his pipe, and exhaled with satisfaction.

"So I thought," smiled Alda. "But I wasn't quite sure. There's a little more grafting I want to do. Nurse it along to more sweet-acid. I think I know now."

"Well," said the schoolmaster, "I can't say anything. It's going too deep for me. But I know—I think I know—what you're groping for."

"I've a dozen vines ripening to what I had in mind," she said. "And perhaps—next year—"

"It's been a long journey for you," said Mr. Wedge.

"A long journey for Montino," she smiled. "I would like to bring it back—the farm and the pasture—to where he remembered Montino at its best, long before it was changed."

The visitors left at dusk, and Alda and Jule walked with them to the yard. After the sulky was gone, the two went on to the pergola to watch the silhouetting of the blue-gums against the redness of the sky. Wing glided in slippers down the path to join the boy and Cleve in the field. He was carrying his wooden gopher trap. He was still hatless. Alda turned to look at him. Something about him was amiss. In the den she had been unconsciously aware of it, but her surface intelligence had been engaged with the visitors, and she had dismissed it as nothing. Now she was sure of it.

"Do you see that, Jule? Isn't there something odd about Wing?"

Jule walked back to her, and looked down at the re-treating figure.

"Didn't you know? He's cut his pigtail off. Down at Lum Yat's nobody has a pigtail any more."

"But why?" asked Alda, puzzled. "Why?"

"Oh, they've gone forever. I thought everyone knew. Wing was the last to hold out, I guess. There's been some kind of revolution. Didn't you know there was a revolution?"

"Nonsense!" said Alda firmly. Then, "Well, what if there was. What's that got to do with pigtails? There's always been a pigtail at Montino!"

She took Jule's arm, and they walked on to the terrace.

"I don't like it. It's a change! I don't like to see anything changed here from what it was before. Not so much—as —one—pigtail." Then she laughed gently. "There have been too many changes, Jule. One foreshadows another." She gave a breath. "And what'll be next?"

They strolled as far as the gate, then turned to look at the carmine stain on the horizon. The earth, pale ochre, rolled up to it in a sweep, bearing the vines in rows of dark purple. The air swam with haze, bearing the scents, the California foothills aroma, of balsam, leaves and red-wood smoke, homelike, evocative of peace. Above the Zinfandels, with the master of the farm and his son sitting on the ground together watching him, the Chinaman lifted his hands as if in an invocation. He was unloosing

260

the cord of the gopher trap. The eucalyptus trees, frost-shorn, their swatches caught high, were like war chiefs with mantles lifted to their faces in mourning. Pigeons winged back and forth over the gully, dipping in the indigo-washed air, talking before they quieted down to roost in the firs at the basin. Then there was a stillness so heavenly that a rabbit sat on the road a full minute before it lobbed on to the wild fennel by the water.

Jule spoke. "You've just been listening, Alda. Taking it to heart. All those foolish rumors in the town. You know they can't be true."

"I've seen many things come to Montino, for good, for evil."

"But nothing like that!" the girl expostulated quietly. She pointed over the slope. "Look! Look at all these vines. You would think they had been here since time began. Since the first dawn. They have been living all the time since that dawn. Somewhere else. And these, they came into the valley to be ours, to make our vineyard. Nobody is coming here from—from the world, to crush it out."

"But this, too, is the world," said Alda.

"They can't pass such a law!" said Jule, desperately. "They can't! Why should anyone come here to the slope and kill all this?"

Alda put her arm about the girl's shoulder. Moved, she looked upon the vineyard and its loveliness in the dusk. The immensity of her pity for it flowed back to her in calmness and strength.

"There was never anything beautiful in the world, Jule, that men did not kill. I pray the slope will be spared."

Her lips hardly moved as she looked into the night, but so intense was her petition that it seemed to wing straight up to heaven. Prayer was only the frail body of the bird, but desire gave it driving pinions.

A light came on at the villa. Arm in arm they went silently up the pathway.

The Harvest

13.

JULE herself drove up to the State Fair and brought the medal home to Montino, and also the crystal urn, which Wing put away on its shelf after another polishing. Cleve lacked the time to leave the vineyard even for a day. A third of the pasture was in Rish Babas, that went out in boxes of cork dust, and earned a trifle beyond their growing, enough to keep up the rest of the field, where the Regolberg was flourishing.

The hybrid had been found. It had sprung from the oldest and largest root, in the middle of the field; and scions from this outburst of small-fruited canes had then been grafted upon all the stocks in the pasture, except those that grew the Rish Babas.

At the last tasting there had been little wonder and excitement, for belief in its coming had possessed them as securely as belief in tomorrow's sunrise. Flores, though, celebrated it with a dinner at his tamale parlor. The quantity of young Regolberg wine this time would be tenfold. Gio had been promised he could help in the picking. He had already outgrown his second pair of boots. He was, after all, going on eight; and since his arms were also strong enough to cope with a fair wind, he and Wing had begun gathering wire and paper to build a kite for March.

One night Port came in for supper. He came once a month from Silverado to the farm, where he stayed three or four days, except in early fall, when he remained to the end of the vintage.

"Alda," he said, crossing knife and fork on his plate, "I got to fix you some wood for that Regolberg. I got to fix you up a wood."

That phrase, bright with hope, he had been repeating for ten years. Now it meant something. If all the best Regolberg berries were picked from the best clusters, the pressing would indeed fill an entire cask.

"I'd sort of figured on taking one of the Gamay barrels," said Alda, beginning to click with her needles. "Burning a little sulphur inside, then giving it a scrub."

Port's eyes twinkled with promise. "Ain't good enough, those Gamay barrels. Even if I did make 'em myself. You got to have a new one. I'll build you up a oak slender in the cave. With buckle hoops. I got me a hundred foot of Baltic oak at the Trecasey sale. I packed it in."

"Now, that's mighty fine," said Alda. As she pulled at her yarn she turned her head to glance at Cleve, but he had looked elsewhere. "Nobody could ask for anything better than Baltic oak."

"Scarce, too," said Port. "You'd think it was all bought up for fiddles. But I got me plenty. It was a sale."

Trecasey's wasn't much of a farm, but it had cooperage and lumber oddments. The point was, it was selling out. As if its owner actually believed the dry law was going through.

For himself, Cleve was only rarely disturbed by the

thought. It was incredible, for one thing. As well believe in a massacre of the wine-growers as that their vines would be extirpated. The Baynes, however, were more than vaguely uneasy. He and Jule had dined with them at Sacramento, the day of the grape awards, themselves the hosts. The Baynes had bought another winery and a field, near Delano. They were up to the neck in paper and commitments.

Over cigars and cognac at the Senator, Bayne, who wanted to learn much, learned only that Montino had done more than rather well. A thousand a year clear on the Rish Babas and the olives, and that had kept up for five years, with a prospect of doing better. He did not learn that Montino had also banked half of its meager share of the wine earnings, but that he probably guessed. And he knew, too, that Jule had funds of her own from her father's bequest—five thousand, at least, he thought, perhaps six.

Bayne was singularly amiable, taking him by the arm as they poked about the grounds, talking almost with deference, asking him about Gio and Alda, what he thought of the wine future, and what his plans might be. Trying, in short, to draw him out and be utterly helpful.

Jule brought in a trayful of raisins to stone, and sat with Gio who was lost in a comic paper that Port had picked up for him at the hotel. She had a knack for making light and crumbly spice cakes, and she and Mrs. Snowball were going to make six in all, for the sociable in the Rectory garden.

"I'm working butternuts into my cakes," she said to Alda. "Port brought me down a whole sackful."

267

"Butternuts," said Port, "is the boss nut. There's about twenty of 'em around my cabin. Place is knee-deep in butternuts."

"You'd ought to grow some turkeys," said Alda, knitting. "They'll fatten up in no time."

Gio, marking his page with a finger, looked up. "Wing's got a pet turkey. My snake bell is on his neck. His name is Ting-An."

"Birds," mused Port, with a cob pipe to his stringy moustache, "is mighty hard to name. And a turk couldn't ask for a better name than that. We had one here once. Name of Mike. He was a terror when he was sober. But when he got lit up, he'd go around fightin' coyotes and just raisin' Cain generally. Hogs is better for company. I think I'll get me some little young hogs to fatten for the holidays."

"I'll bring some in for you," said Cleve. "Silva's got plenty. I'm going down to see him about help for the vintage."

Alda lowered her needles.

"There's somebody out front, Jule. Must be the fish man, and I don't know what he's got left this late."

It was already deep night. Gio, wearying of hog talk, had gone to his room to finish his comic paper in quiet. The windows were dark with a backing of fog. Jule rubbed the glass and looked out as a lantern flicked by.

"It isn't the cart. Somebody on foot."

A rap at the door, and Bascomb entered. He had the blown look of one fatigued. "Just came down over the ridge," he said. "From Chianti. So I thought I'd call in on the way home."

"Glad you did," said Alda. "You sit down. There's some dinner left. I'll hot it up."

268

Jule took his hat and coat, and he sat to the table. Cleve brought him a glass, and Port slid him a can of tobacco. He leaned back with his pipe to wait. It was a welcome. His face was wind-burned after sixty miles of it over the high mountain road; his eyes puffed, and half closed. The heady aspersion of the glass warmed him; soon he was rested, and with pipe in his fist he smoked in reflective little puffs, his eye cocked under a hedge of gray eyebrow. Cleve and Port hung on his comments. He had seen about forty vineyards. Up at Chianti, down as far as Duke Liu's and Lachryma Montis, then back through the clearings on the St. Helena ridge. He gave reports, one sentence to a farm, briefly and drily. Then his plate was brought him, and he leisurely ate dinner.

"You're early down, Port," he said, his cheek full. "Isn't vintage yet."

"I've got to make a Regolberg barrel. Baltic oak, and it'll take a week to swell it out. Dry as touchwood, but almighty tough."

"Tough—and scarce, if you ask me," affirmed Bascomb, stirring his cup. "The best we have is not a patch on that. But I did see a good stand of oaks near Sebastopol. It was the gall-wasps I saw first. *Cynips kollari.* Beautiful! I caught one with my net."

"I got my Baltic at the Trecasey sale."

Bascomb lowered his cup. "Trecasey? A sale?"

"Selling off a lot of stuff. 'Articles too numerous to mention'—the poster said. The oak was in them. The only thing I'd look at."

Bascomb was not listening. "Queer. A sale. Trecasey went too heavy on cattle five years ago, and a bank took over. It must have been hearing something."

"What?" asked Cleve.

"Nothing that spells good," said Bascomb.

"You think the storm's coming?"

"I'm not the clerk of the weather. But I don't think it'll be a storm."

"What then?" demanded Cleve, hunched forward, hands flat on the table. "Not a storm?"

Bascomb, ruminating in a cloud of smoke, legs crossed, looking towards the vineyard through the black window, shook his head.

"No. The end."

Alda stilled her knitting. Port chuckled. He was partial to arguments, he had been hearing talk of this sort for months, and nothing had ever come of it. He chuckled and refilled his glass.

"Isn't that nonsense, Bask?" Cleve went on. "It can't be such a fold-up as that! Even if we are nothing, and the valley's nothing—the State's backed us for sixty years. It can't let us down now. We've had a Hilgard, we've got a Bioletti. It took us a long time to work up to those fellows. And we've backed them, and the State. What's Sacramento going to say about us being outlawed?"

Bascomb removed his pipe.

"Does the tail wag the dog?" he asked.

Cleve banged the table, then stalked up and down the corridor to cool off. The session had been noisy. No use waking up Gio. He went upstairs to close the door of Gio's room, and looked in. The comic papers were spread on the floor. The light was still on. Gio was on the boards, his ear by the stove-pipe cover, fast asleep. He could sleep anywhere. He must have heard a lot of meaningless talk about storms. Hardly worth the trouble of listening at that cover. What difference did it make whether it rained or didn't rain? Cleve watched him a moment,

270

touched, with a pang at his heart. Little fellow would be growing up in another world. But that was all right. The young never really knew the world they were being transplanted from. They were merely being slipped, without knowing it, from one dream world to another. Cleve laid him on the bed, drew a blanket over him, then left, closing the door gently.

"He can't plan anything unless he knows," Alda was saying. "One way or another."

"Everybody in town wants to know," said Bascomb, shaking out his match. "I was just going to say, Cleve, that I wrote to the congressman. Had to go to the *Star* and find out who he was. Then I wrote him a letter. That was a week ago. He ought to know which way the straws are blowing. The answer should be here by Friday, at the latest. I'll hold it until then. You'll be coming in?"

"Sure," said Cleve. "I'll be on the way back from San Leandro, with Flores. We're bringing in some little Portygee hogs for Port."

"Going to fatten 'em up for the holidays," said Port. "Butternuts."

Bascomb put his hat on at the door, and turned.

"Try grapes," he said drily. "They'll be still cheaper. Good-night!"

Port chuckled.

"Gio asleep in bed?" asked Jule, looking up at Cleve.

"Now, yes. He was on the floor. Had his ear to the pipe-cover. I heard plenty there once, myself," he laughed. "At the grapevine."

Alda smiled at her knitting.

"You did. Everybody's the same. It's only the world, the valley, that changes."

Cleve backed the truck to the corral, dropped the tailboard, and helped out the four young hogs. They exhaled an odor of licorice, they had the eyes of gamins, and they plashed forthwith into very heaven—greenish muck, with rocks to scrape against, and clumps of elders with dangling leaves and berries. He barred the gate, left the truck there, and walked on towards the pergola. The vineyard was somnolent in the heat of late afternoon. The one sound was a recurrent "pa-tap." That was Port's mallet, echoing in the cave. He was making that cask, a small cask, to hold the fine Regolberg of the season. There was no need of it now, Alda's little wedding cask of eucalyptus timber would hold it all, and the Baltic cask would be a labor of love.

Cleve wiped his forehead, and walked glumly on to the madrone. Before the nursery the dogs were heaped up, asleep. The women should be there, for under that covering of Rish Baba limbs and stephanotis it was cool after mid-day. Alda was at her bench, cutting up raffia, and Jule in her camp chair, sewing, the light flecked on her heart-shaped face.

The welcome over, he sat on the bench, very still.

"I called in at Bascomb's," he said. "I read the letter. Blanqui was there, too. He was all crumpled up."

"It was that bad?" asked Alda, in a quiet, steady voice.

"Yes. I expected it. But it was only when I read the letter in black and white, that I really knew it was coming. Bascomb let me have it."

He gave her the letter, and she moved to the sunlight in the doorway and glanced at it. Jule resumed her stitching. Alda read the letter again, then her hands lowered, to fold across her white apron. The silence was prolonged. Somewhere a cricket twanged its dry note. A butterfly

272

left a stephanotis bloom and hovered in the doorway. For a while Alda gazed upon the dusty-green slope, then turned.

"A pity," she said, clearing another chair. "Does look like the end—just now. How were they taking it in the valley?"

"I didn't see many about today. Seemed as if everybody had gone in, and the valley had pulled into itself. We felt very sorry for old Blanqui, helping him into his cart. His hands were all shaky. He kept talking something about his plants, and how he had to get right home."

"Blanqui should make sacramental wine," said Alda. "He ought to see Father Clare and—"

"No. His wine isn't red."

Alda went back to the untangling of her raffia skein, Jule sewed on calmly, and Cleve sat on the bench, whistling softly. A thought moved him. He lifted his face, exalted.

"The vineyard is us!" he said. "I want to see Montino free. For us to look after it. It'll want looking after, now."

Alda turned in surprise.

"We can buy out the Baynes. They're caught, like everybody else. Only they're caught tighter. All those wineries they've got to keep paying for. They've got to keep on pumping even while the boat sinks. We'll buy out their share of Montino."

Jule gave up sewing. "I know Carola. I know what she won't do. She'll sell out everything else first. Everything!"

"Nobody's buying wineries," said Cleve. "Wouldn't take them for a gift, not with taxes to pay. And nobody's buying vineyards, either. Only people buying will be the spectators. They'll buy wine run-of-mill, and as cheap as they can. Next vintage they'll buy still cheaper. Young

and green wine that nobody could drink. And they'll
have only a month to go before it's contraband and will
sell like diamonds."

Alda cleared a chair and sat down.

"This vintage is our last," she said. "Montino never did
send out anything without its name burned on the cask.
We wouldn't even grow anything we'd be ashamed of."

Cleve was immersed in his own thoughts. On the back
of the envelope that the letter came in he scratched figures.

"Four thousand in the bank. Our share this season,
another thousand." He murmured, jotting notes. "The
olives and the Rish Babas—"

"Leave them out," said Jule, taking up her sewing
again. "I've still got six thousand in the bank. Never
touched that."

"What'll they ask for their share?" asked Alda.

"I did some thinking after Jule and I had that evening
with the Baynes in Sacramento," said Cleve. "He didn't
come right out and say anything. He was fishing a little.
He said he was only clearing six percent—I mean, he and
Carola—on his end of Montino. That ought to bring it up
to twelve thousand. But that was a year ago. We'll offer
him ten."

"Carola's stubborn," said Jule. "She'll think it unreason-
ably low."

"If she'd been reasonable they wouldn't have over-
reached. They can have ten if they want it. He'll have to
scrape all he can to get back to broking sea freightage to
get him out of deep water."

"If they ask more?" queried Alda.

"It'll leave us too little to go ahead with. A few hundreds. We'll be strapped, practically. Even if we do live
on olives and table grapes. There'll be lots of vineyards cut

274

over to table grapes—even if they're not Rish Babas—and the market'll be bogged down. And people are not up to olives yet. They'll never be up to olives."

"You write them," said Alda.

"Right now," said Cleve, and left.

In the den he wrote a letter, stamped the envelope, and set out for the truck to drive to the post office. From the sunlight he stepped into the chill of the tunnel. He would have to tell Port of what he had learned. Port was at his improvised work-table, with his tools and wooden vise.

"I was in at Bascomb's," said Cleve. "No use just telling you. But here's what the congressman said."

Port put on his glasses, rubbed hands on his apron, then unfolded the letter. His lips moved from word to word, slower and slower. His face suddenly went gray and pinched. He leaned on the vise and breathed hard. He indicated the vineyard with his chin.

"There's nothin'—nothin' to all that, any more."

"I'm afraid not," said Cleve.

Port slanted a stave on the table, squinted down it, planed off a long, curling chip, then ran a thumb down its squared edge.

"The hogs—I've brought them up. They're in the corral having a good time," Cleve went on.

Port turned, fitted the stave into the cask-head and hoops, and tapped with his mallet. He was still gray-faced.

"They'll do for company," he said. "You got to say for hogs they got plenty of sense. No harm in hogs."

The week brought ripening heat, dust upon the bloom, no solace to the valley, and from Bayne a cool, precise letter, tinged with incredulity. It should be perfectly clear, it said, that to anyone familiar with top-grade properties that twelve thousand was a token price merely. To Cleve that was not at all clear. But the letter, being long and expectant of a rejoinder, he carried to the bank. The banker —the one who had made out for him the paper to the Regolberg field—smoked out his cigar and listened to him.

"It's less than business, these times. You're taking on something. But you three are bent on owning all of Montino?"

"Yes."

"It's less than business," the banker repeated. His swivel-chair squeaked as he turned about to scrutinize Cleve a moment. "And in a way, it's infinitely more. Ten's ample, by certified check." The penholder hung over the ink. Then it dipped. "I'll make it out for you."

Montino after the harvesting belonged to the folk on Montino.

It was a good vintage, the last of all; and it was also Gio's first. He drove the tray-wagon for a spell, with Jule, and picked all through the Gamays with Wing, who was the only Chinaman in the vineyard. It was combed to the last cluster, except here and there in the Regolberg patch, where the less than perfect were left to drop off for the turkeys. The Portuguese went to pick on other farms in the valley. It was the season when everybody picked. It was the last harvest. When the valley was in darkness, the wineries were bursting with light. Half of them would press no more. Montino would not press, for next season their young wine would still be young must, fretting in the vats, under the shadow of the interdict and the axe.

Cleve scoured out the winery with boiling water and

276

soda, and scrubbed the apparatus and the walls. After that, not much else was as usual. No feast was held among the vats. Jule was arranging for a barbecue in the pergola, and Wing had first to get a parcel of things from the city, for Lum Yat was leaving and his store was already closed. The parcel came a week after the scouring, a tin of spice and a pair of ducks in oil.

Three of the Portuguese came back, and with horses and chains snagged out all the vines in the Zinfandel and Gamay patch. They plowed and harrowed the slope, and sowed it to barley. The stumps were piled up behind the stable and in the yard for firewood. Alda filled her nursery with Rish Baba canes, to root and to graft on the stock in the pasture.

"You've got slips from the Regolberg?" asked Jule in the nursery.

"No," said Alda. "It was a plant suitable for its time. We'll leave it to be remembered."

That night, when everyone else was abed, Jule and Cleve went into the pasture and dug in a ring about the largest Regolberg vine. The heat was gone from the earth, it was a soft September night, the valley a cool trough of starlit air. Cleve went deep and swathed the roots in burlap. They carried the vine to the yard, and planted it under Alda's window.

"It will be a surprise for her in the spring," she said as they went round by the terrace. "Coming out in flower. A talisman, a lone conspirator. They can't all be hunted out. They'll be alive here and there, like the old gods in hiding, who couldn't yet die because there were still a few who believed in them. 'And still the vine her ancient ruby yields.' How long, long ago it seems since we were children!"

It was a week of strong warmth. Port, his cask finished and the varnish dry, kept inside the winery, rapping the staves with his mallet, knocking at hoops and tightening buckles. It was in beautiful order now, all right for the year, all right forever. His candle guttered out in fat, he pressed the wick out with his finger, and emerged from under the scaffolds, blinking. On the cat-walk stook Cleve, and Gio who had the pole and was pushing down the chapeau of the must. For a while he gazed at the boy, very small and straight, his hair cottony in the dusky light, then he hobbled on to the pergola. Marthe was there, the women, Mr. Wedge, Bascomb, and Flores, sitting about. Wing had a fire of twigs crackling in the barbecue pit. He went to sit by Flores, who was in his Sunday blacks.

"That's the old strain down there, Flo," he said around his pipe. "The kid. I bin watchin' him. Way he poled down was as pretty as you'd want to see. It's in his bones. Born for somethin'. Sure's fate." He nodded at the razed slope untouched by green except of the olive trees and the firs at the basin. "He'll only have to wait until that's all vine again." He chuckled at the joke he made with himself. "That's more'n some of us can do, Flo."

Cleve, bringing a bottle of the Regolberg, came up from the winery with Gio. With his trident Wing speared meat from the grill, thrust it on plates, and Jule laid them on the leaf-garnished table. Flores, his velvet hat over one ear, a cigarette stuck on his lips, raked his guitar. The feast was no quieter than any the pergola had seen. Afternoon merged with evening in a twilight haze that was aromatic, pungent with the sweet acridity of burning greenwood. It was not from Wing's iron-barred pit. It was a dusky, autumn cloudiness to be breathed, and it gave a smoke tang to the wine.

"Bonfires everywhere," said Mr. Wedge. "Nobody's losing time in clearing for the plow. Wheat'll be early, Cleve."

Gio was gathering bones and holding them for the dogs to leap at.

"Come and sit by me, Gio," said Alda. She was at the head of the table, her face tinged by the light of the sun going down in hazy red splendor. "Here's a chair for you."

Towards Calistoga were a score of red points in the fields. More prinked out on the opposite hillside, like beacon signals. On the flat the great bonfires were roaring, the smoke lifting in plumes to spread out against the mote-laden sky. No wind was abroad, and all the way down the blue-filled wide hollow to Rutherford and across into the glens at Chiles and Atlas rose the poplar-straight smoke of a hundred pyres. The vineyards were in conflagration. Burning to make ashes for tomorrow. Would there be a phoenix in the ashes?

"Looks like all the world afire," said Port.

"Only our small part of it," said Jule. Her head was resting against Cleve's shoulder, their hands were interlocked. "Our valley."

Doves were homing at the firs. A rabbit was on the bridge, an exile hunting for a lost greenness. As he bounded towards the firs the dogs with belated cry streaked out, Gio running after them. The others remained still, looking at the flat. Port stirred, got up, made the round clockwise with the bottle of the Regolberg, and filled the glasses.

Flores touched the guitar strings, and played a tune, a very old harvest song. When it was done, Bascomb lifted his glass in the silence, and they rose.

California Fiction titles are selected for their literary merit and for their illumination of California history and culture.

Born in Wales, Idwal Jones (1890–1964) came with his family to upstate New York, where he worked in a steel mill, and then to California via the isthmus of Panama in 1911 to recover his health after having had tuberculosis. He worked as a journalist in the gold country, and in San Francisco he worked in the shipyards during World War I and later for the San Francisco *Examiner*, ultimately as drama critic. Jones married San Franciscan Olive Vere Smith in 1921. Publication of his first book—*The Splendid Shilling*, memoirs of his Welsh childhood and first years in California—in 1926 prompted him to take his wife and daughter to Europe for travel and leisure to write. Returning to the U.S. during the Depression, he worked as a columnist, feature writer, and book review editor on William Randolph Hearst's *New York American* until 1933, when he returned to California, settling in Laguna Beach. He worked as a publicity writer for Paramount Pictures and, from 1935 until the 60s, as a contributor to *Westways*, where he wrote the "minatures of Californiana" Lawrence Clark Powell calls "a treasury of history, legend, and lore" and six more books, including the short story collection *China Boy* (1936) and *Ark of Empire: San Francisco's Montgomery Block* (1951).